LOVE SPRINGS ETERNAL

THE WITCHES OF LOVING BOOK I

TIMBER PHILIPS

COPYRIGHT

Edited by Barbara J. Bailey

Book design by Maggie Kern at Ms.K Edits

Cover art by Dar Albert at Wicket Art Designs

Models - Ka'ron Harvis & Hayley Stavanger

Photographer - JW Photography

DEDICATION

To all the readers who wished for more diverse characters in romance. I hope I've done you proud.

PROLOGUE

*O*nce upon a time, there was a darkness over the town of Cooper's Port. A deep and seething hatred took root in men's minds after Jenny, a lone witch's heart, was broken. Long after her death, heartbreak and tragedy ruled the town and it became known as a breeding ground for misery, a place where love went to die.

The town fell into squalor and disrepair. During the early twentieth century, it became all but forgotten, until a new coven of witches arrived, determined to vanquish the darkness and put Jenny's soul to peaceful rest.

They worked a powerful spell, one that had a lasting effect through time, one that changed the face and name of Cooper's Port forever...

Welcome to the town of Loving, and the Matchmaker's Festival.

*M*iri...
I was done with love and especially done with the Matchmaking Festival. Tonight was the night. It happened every year, the residual power from that long-ago spell reverberating through time and space. *Unintended consequences...* I thought to myself, *Wild magic that had taken on a life of its own.*

Thankfully, we'd had years and years to come to understand it and the rules were simple. Men and women of age gathered inside the town's limits and at eight o'clock sharp, the spell took effect, and you fell in love – sometimes with whoever you were with, sometimes with whoever you just happened to be looking at, sometimes with someone simply nearby, drawn together as if by invisible strings.

Lonely souls came from all over the world to experience the true love the spell bestowed upon the revelers, but that true love only lasted for four hours at a time. At midnight, the spell ended and it was business as usual. The old adage 'If you're not with the one you love, love the one you're with,' never held truer – except magic had a funny way of doing things. *Again with those pesky unintended consequences.*

I don't know how many married couples came to the town looking for a quick fix, a way to rekindle things and repair their failing marriage, only for one or both of them to end up in someone else's bed for the night. Of course, with the sweet came the sour in those cases.

But sometimes – just sometimes - you found your soulmate in the bargain.

You see, if you happened to stay in love after the stroke of midnight, it meant that you had found your person, the one you were meant to be with for the rest of your life.

I had thought it had happened to me… but I guess he had other ideas. Seven months after I'd fallen so deeply, madly, and irreparably in love with Jackson Greene, he'd essentially ghosted on me.

It'd left me devastated, broken in ways I can't explain, and I didn't want to have another damn thing to do with the festival after that.

I'd locked myself away from this year's romp, alone in my big house, and I intended to keep it that way in the years to come, shuttering my windows, preparing a nice big cup of calming tea, and playing soft music to while away those four hours.

This witch wanted nothing to do with love, the town of Loving, or the matchmaking festival. I just wanted to lose myself in a book of herb lore and work my earth magic.

Just because I was bitter, didn't mean I didn't want to still help people. It just meant I was, well, bitter… burnt, hurt, and for the time being, unwilling to try again.

"Maybe someday, but not today," I murmured at my raven, Shade. He cocked his head to the side, blinking one beady brown eye at me and cawed softly. I smiled and held a bit of a treat through the bars of his huge brass birdcage. He plucked the offering from my fingers and I was all but forgotten for the time being.

I smiled, and moved through my big house, my grandmother's house and her mother's house before her.

We were one of the original families of Loving, before it even was Loving, when it was just plain old Cooper's Port. After the coven came to town and vanquished Jenny's curse, my great-grandfather had married one of the witches, and my grandmother had been born with the magic touch. My mother hadn't had any magic to her, but me? I'd had the talent, and my grandmother had nurtured it with every bit of love and encouragement that I showed any one of my seedlings.

I was a hedge-witch, a healer and an apothecary by birthright and training. I was so good at my craft for smaller ailments, I'd nearly put the doctor in town out of business. I didn't feel bad about it. I mean, he was close to retirement and even he came to me for treatment for his gout.

"Okay, Shade. Where did I put that –"

I stopped as a knock fell at my door and closed my eyes and sighed. I ran a bed and breakfast out of the house for a regular income and did pretty well. Usually I made a killing during the festival, but I was done with it and had closed this year.

It hurt too much.

I looked at the clock and chewed my bottom lip. It was seven-fifty-four, almost show time. I went to the door and opened it a crack, and said bluntly, "I'm sorry, we're closed."

I blinked in surprise when I found myself staring at a strong chest covered in a grey Louisiana State University sweatshirt.

"Oh, I'm sorry. I wasn't looking to stay, my car just quit on me out on the road and my phone's almost dead. I was looking to see if I could charge it."

His voice was pleasant to the ear, as rich and dark as he was. I looked up into his deep brown eyes, set in an equally dark face. His shoulder-length, pencil-thin dreadlocks were pulled halfway up, out of his face, except for a few escapees that hung almost artfully in front of his forehead.

"You, uh, you're the first person to answer their door," he said, when I'd stared a moment too long and hadn't said anything.

"Right, that's because they're all at the festival, in the heart of town."

"Festival?" he asked.

I blinked in surprise for a second time. How could he not know about the festival? It was literally the reason all the people who didn't already live here were here. The rest did live here full time, and didn't much have a say in the matter unless they found someplace else to be, like I was trying to do.

"The matchmaking festival," I said, frowning, trying to figure out if he were pulling my leg or not.

"Never heard of it," he said, and he was very convincing at looking like he was dead serious. Still, I couldn't be sure... "Is it cool if I borrow some juice so I can make a call? Or have you got a phone I can use?"

"Sure, there's an outlet right there," I said, pointing along the outside wall to where he would find it. "Help yourself," I said, quickly shutting and locking the door.

"Okay... thanks..." I heard, muffled through the wood. I closed my eyes and rested my forehead against the door, sighing. I hated sounding or feeling like I was being rude but it was almost time.

I jumped, nearly hitting the ceiling when he knocked on the door again. I checked the grandfather clock by the door: Seven fifty-eight. *Shit.*

I opened the door, and he looked apologetic. "Your outlet out here doesn't seem to be working. I don't have to come in, you know... If you could just plug it in for me and I can sit out here..."

"You're going to be out here a while," I said.

"Um, that's okay. It's a nice night and I can't exactly go anywhere else."

"It's just, the magic is about to start, and I want no part of it," I tried to explain.

He laughed a bit nervously and shifted his weight on his feet and said, "Magic?"

He really didn't know? How could he not know? Our town wouldn't even be on a map if it weren't for its magic.

"Um, the matchmaking festival," I started to explain again, repeating myself. I was flustered a bit, closed my eyes and shook my head. "You know what, never mind, just give it here and I'll plug it in for you."

I unlatched the heavy screen door and reached a hand through. He smiled at me and wound the cable between his hands and handed me the phone, cable, and the little brick to plug it all in with, around the door. I felt a tingling rush and closed my eyes, but I knew that wouldn't stop it. His hand brushed mine and I cursed, silently, to myself.

It wasn't his fault; it wasn't mine either... It just was what it was.

"What is that?" he asked, his voice strangled.

"It's eight o'clock," I murmured and opened my eyes. His face, while handsome, took on a completely different quality as I felt my already-broken heart break a little more, just before the sweep and rush of arousal swept through me. It was followed by the devastating crash of emotion that everyone came here for, some to experience at least once in their lifetimes – but I already had. I already had, and losing it had lain waste to my very soul. It had left me devastated, and I never wanted to feel that ever again.

A moment of what looked like fear flashed through the stranger's eyes and I opened the screen wider, my heart going out to him.

"It's okay, it's just a spell," I whispered.

"Are you doing this?" he asked.

"No," I answered simply and he reached for me, then struggled to drop his hand.

"It's okay, we won't be able to stop. I won't want you to stop."

"I don't understand," he said, and his breath quickened. He was trying so hard not to give in, to fight it.

"What's your name?" I asked softly, because if this were going to happen, I at least wanted to know his name.

"Kavion," he said. "Kavion Martin."

"Miriam Eilish," I said. "My friends call me Miri. You can, too."

"Now what, Miri?" he asked, drifting nearer.

I fitted myself against him as if drawn by strings, wanting him with all that I was in this moment, losing my ability to reason, to see this for what it was, nothing more than a spell.

"Kiss me," I whispered, but his mouth was already descending towards mine.

His full lips were soft, thick, and warm. He tasted green and earthy, and I felt drawn to him, my heart filling and overflowing with love for him. That was ridiculous, I didn't know anything about him, but that was the magic: ancient, white, and deep; nurturing and empowering; filling us up and spilling out in the best way that fit it, the purest expression of love between two people: sex.

"I don't understand why I feel this way," he whispered against my mouth, his hands the color of strong black coffee smoothing over my pale skin the color of milk.

"Shhh," I soothed. "Don't worry, don't fight it, just know that I feel it, too."

"Yeah," he said, "but do you want it? Because I'm not that guy." His voice sounding strained.

"I want it." I both lied and didn't. I knew that resistance was futile and wished to ease any potential burden he might carry. I knew that it wouldn't be long for myself, either, and had thought there was something almost cruel about knowing how it went. Knowing and not being able to put a stop to it... those damn unintended consequences again.

"Yeah?" he asked, snapping me out of my attempt to distract myself from the magic. My heart fractured even more at the way he said the single word. There was something almost… vulnerable to it.

"Mm-hm," I murmured, not to put too fine a point on it, and raised myself on tip-toe to kiss him, my hands smoothing over his chest, holding myself up using his shoulders. His own hands wandered unbidden, sliding down my body and coming to rest on my hips.

His kiss wasn't too intense and my heart splintered for my new lover, the magic growing stronger, influencing our emotions, sending him tumbling head first, in love with me. I felt grateful that he wasn't alone, that I was following suit, even if it were just for the next few hours. I didn't want to hurt him in any way. That wasn't me and never would be.

I'd been down this road before, several times in fact, from the time I was seventeen until now at twenty-nine. I just never thought I would feel this again. Not like this. Not this intensity. I didn't want to, not after having my heart broken, and especially not with a stranger. I worried about what that could mean but lost focus when he lifted me easily. I wrapped my legs around his lean hips and let him carry me into my house.

He deftly kicked the door shut behind me and whispered against my mouth, "Bedroom," fully entrenched in the spell now.

I buried my fingers in his hair, the texture rough like the green side of a kitchen sponge, slightly abrasive against my skin but not unpleasantly so. Simply unique, different from what I was used to. There just weren't many men of color in Loving, but this one I loved utterly.

"Third floor tower room," I whispered and he groaned.

"You've got to be fucking me."

"Anywhere you'd like," I said pointedly. "Doesn't have to be my room."

He laughed, striding to the staircase. He was fit, carrying me with little effort up the first flight of stairs before getting any kind of winded. He made it to the second landing, and I wriggled in his grasp. He set me down and my mouth tore from his, my hands fitting into his much larger ones, my fingers finding the spaces between his as I led us quickly the rest of the way to my bed.

He didn't even take a moment to look at the room, simply stopped inside the doorway and tugged gently on my hand. I turned and he reeled me in. I fit so nicely against the front of his body, his hands gentle on the sides of my neck, his thumbs cradling my jaw.

I stared up into his eyes and asked him softly, "Take down your hair?"

He reached up and pulled whatever was securing his dread-locks free, and they swung forward, nearly covering his face.

I reached out and gathered the hem of his sweatshirt in my hands and he raised his arms, bowing at the waist. I took it from him and dropped it to my bedroom floor.

It was tit for tat on the clothing, his sweatshirt, my sweater. His tee, my green pixie dress, the top a tank falling into an asymmetrical hemline, pattered to look like leaves.

He swept his basketball shorts, and the athletic leggings he wore under them, down his legs in one efficient movement and went to his knees in front of me, hooking his long fingers into the waistband of my fawn leggings, sweeping both them and the panties beneath down mine.

I put my hands on his generous shoulders and stepped out of them.

His fingertips trailed lightly up the inside of my calf, pausing at the inside of my knee, his eyes seeking permission as he looked up at me. I nodded and tipped my head back as his fingertips lightly brushed the outer lips of my sex, my breath rushing out in a heated sigh of surrender.

He massaged between my legs with those long, elegant fingers of his while his mouth played over the skin of my hip, teeth nipping lightly over my stomach, a finger slipping effortlessly up inside me. My hands gripped his head lightly, pressing his mouth to my skin, unable to get enough of his warmth, his touch, even as he stroked that long digit inside my body, stoking the fire of my passion, nearly bringing me to my own knees.

He relinquished his hold on me, his hand slipping from between my thighs as he stood. God, he was easily over six foot, his body lean and muscular, well defined in that way that whispered he wasn't afraid of hard work, and he was so warm. I couldn't resist cuddling against him, even though, through the magic, I knew he didn't like to touch. Of course, it was through the very same spell that I knew that he was willing to accept the closeness because he loved me. Both of us were trapped by the binding will of that coven from so long ago, their magic gone rogue, become wild, a light magic in the darkness of the world.

He pressed me tight to his body and walked me back toward the bed, his cock hard, long, and like a brand against my palm. I stroked him, slicking my palm over the head of his cock, his pre-cum acting as a decent lubricant as our mouths tangled and clashed and our passions rose.

"God, I don't understand what's happening," he whispered, voice tight. "All I know is that I've never felt about another female the way I feel about you right now. It's crazy. I don't even know you, but it's like I know everything about you at the same time."

"Shh," I murmured and crawled up onto the bed. He followed me, and I lay back, my hands guiding him over me, between my legs. He groaned and closed his eyes, his mouth finding mine once again, those full lips like silk, his tongue hot and velvet against my own.

I held him to me, my lover, my love, and there was no room for anything else. My heart ached fiercely with just how much I loved him and twisted with agony at the fact that this was only a beautiful dream, that in four hours' time, he would go back to being him and I would go back to being me, and the hurt would crush me all over again.

For now, though, there wasn't any room for anything bad.

Just the heat of his body against mine, his skin pebbling with gooseflesh as I trailed light fingertips up his ribs, along his arms, as I kissed the side of his neck, and he struggled with resisting going further, but I knew how much it hurt, how much it cost to resist the sweet agony that lay before him as our bodies united in the most intimate way possible.

I had been here before, but he hadn't, and so I tried to make this as easy as possible for him, this loving a perfect stranger so completely, so wholly, and so deeply.

"It's okay," I whispered against his neck. "I want it, I want this; I want you."

He slipped against me, his cock long and thick, not penetrating, not yet, but the feel of him against me, sliding up and down, pressed hot against my flesh, my pussy dripping wet for this stranger that I was totally in love with, God, it was amazing. I relaxed into the cloud of my bed and he stared down at me for a long moment, his lips parted, his breath rushed and labored as he bowed his forehead to mine and closed his eyes. He slipped inside me slowly, carefully, my hips rising to meet him, his face contorted into such beautiful agony as he fought not to do me too hard.

I knew that about him, more of the magic. That he liked things rough, harsh almost, that he tended to go hard and had a difficult time letting anyone know that underneath that stoic exterior was a man who had been hurt countless times, by countless women, a man who had his trust broken time and time again, who desperately wanted to love and to be loved in return.

Just as he probably knew that I liked things slow, sweet, a careful buildup before anything got too rough. Not that rough wasn't good, it absolutely was, but not tonight, not for the first time.

The fact that this man was so selfless touched a part of me and made this somehow... easier.

"Kavion," I gasped, his name unfamiliar on my tongue.

"Yeah?" he said, his voice rough as he eased himself in and out of me at a steady snail's pace.

"I love you," I whispered, knowing in my heart of hearts he needed to hear it with how much he felt it, and I could give him that. Magic or no, tonight it was the truth.

"I love you, too," he whispered and shuddered above me. "I don't know how, but I love you, too."

He drove into me a little harder than he had been and I gasped and clutched myself to him, biting my bottom lip as he bottomed out against my cervix, the sharp pain dulling into something sweet as he stilled himself and waited to make sure I was alright.

"You okay, Miri?"

"Don't stop," I gasped. "I'm okay, just don't stop."

He laid over the top of me and put a hand along the outside of one knee, raising it, getting deeper and I let myself fall, let myself be carried away by his embrace, let myself drown in the illusion of safety and drink in the peace being in his arms brought to me.

It was terribly confusing, heartrending in ways, but soothing and lovely, a terrible beauty, a sweet agony as we brought each other to climax over and over again.

I wound up on top and he gasped, his hands palming my breasts as I rode him carefully. He made eye contact with me and asked dreamily, "Is this a forever kind of thing?"

I smiled and knew it held an edge of sadness when I told him, "No, the spell ends at midnight."

He smiled then, and smoothed his hands down to my hips and asked, "Really?"

"Yes." I nodded and his smile grew.

I threw my head back and moaned slightly as he nudged that place inside of me, sending a shockwave of pleasure up my spine and through my body. When I looked at him again, he was smiling to the point it was contagious. I felt my own lips curl and I had to ask, "What is it?"

"Spell ends at midnight?"

"Yes, why?"

"Because it's two in the morning and I don't feel any different."

I felt my eyes widen and I faltered as all my panicked mind could come up with was, *Oh, snap.*

2

*K*avion...

She stared down at me, hands on my chest, knees buried in the bedding at my hips, pussy lips gripping my dick in a way that made me nuts and all I could think about was how much I fucking loved her, which was crazy. I didn't even know her! I mean, I barely even knew her name, which was honestly not entirely true. I'd been letting it echo through the chambers of my mind the entire time we'd been together tonight, ever since she'd first given it to me.

'Miriam Eilish, my friends call me Miri.'

Miri... it was a name as beautiful and unique as she was.

Her hair was long, to her waist, and the color of fire, and though I still didn't understand it, it was the same fire that had suddenly ignited on her doorstep, that burned me up from the inside out with this insane love for her. I ain't never felt this way about no female before, and I was, for sure, never going to feel this way about anyone again. This was one of those once-in-a-lifetime feels and it was scary as fuck, but I wasn't the kind to show those kinds of emotions – or any for that matter.

She had gone still on top of me and I throbbed inside her, wishing she would move again, in that sultry dance that had had me roasting over the coals of our passion just a minute before. Her eyes were wide and the pale blue of a high winter sky. That kind of blue was endless, boundless, and it suited her because she was bottom-of-the-ocean deep. I don't know how I knew that shit, but I did. She was for real, one hundred, and I was still trying to figure out all of this crazy business of how exactly I could love someone so deeply who I didn't even know.

"What's the matter?" I asked, softly, worried that I'd said something wrong, especially when she swallowed hard and it looked like she was barely holding back tears.

"Nothing. I, um..." She faltered and I raised an eyebrow and put my hands over hers, holding them lightly to my chest.

"Don't lie to me, please..."

"I just don't understand something. I mean, I really don't understand something at all, and I need to check with someone about it before I say anything else, I don't want to say anything in error or give you some bad information."

"For sure, it's cool... Um, I don't know if I should stay here, or if you want me to go –"

"No, don't go!" she cried, sudden and sharp, but looked like she was still reeling. I knew the feeling and it was fucked up, but she definitely knew more about what was going on than I did, so...

"You got anything for me, you know, about this magic shit that's supposed to be happening to us?"

She swallowed hard again and said, "I don't know all of it, I mean, I understand the basics – I've lived in this town all of my life – but I don't get why it's happening to me, especially now."

"How about you tell me what the deal is," I said, and she nodded slowly, her expression grave. She licked her lips and the motion was sexy as hell, even though she didn't mean for it to be. I lay back in the softness of her bed and waited her out.

"A long, long time ago, there was a witch named Jenny Northcutt. She was set to marry a man here in town. Loved him with all her heart, but he wasn't really interested in her. He betrayed her, broke her heart, and had her executed as a witch. Before she died, Jenny cursed the town."

I listened to her and nodded when she stopped for too long, staring at me to see if I was soaking it all in alright.

"Okay, then what happened?"

"For years, the bitterness and anger of Jenny's curse festered and grew. Anyone who moved here experienced untold misery. This was the place that love came to die. The problem got so bad, it took a full coven of witches to vanquish the curse, the power of the spell putting a new, almost-curse on the town, one that reverberates through time and affects us even today."

"Okay, explain," I said, and she bit her bottom lip.

"It's the festival. It sprang up around the curse-laying, which used the power of love, and, I think, some fertility magic to lay Jenny and her vengeful magic to rest. It's a love festival, and it happens every spring. For one night, beginning at eight o'clock, people fall in love."

"Like we did."

"Yes, but the spell is supposed to end at midnight."

"Okay, and then what?"

She shrugged and said, "And then it's over. People go back to their lives and it's like a wild night of drunk sex, only without the drunk and with the intense feelings associated with truly being in love."

"Okay, but it's two in the morning right now, and I don't feel any different."

"I know, and I don't either."

"Explain that, if you can, please?"

"That's part of the festival and the vestigial magic. If you happen to be in the town with the one you are meant to be with for the rest of your life, you stay in love after the spell has worn off."

"But you said that was impossible," I said.

"For me, it's supposed to be," she said, and looked genuinely upset and distressed.

"Okay," I said. "You want to talk about it?" I raised a hand and cupped her cheek, running a thumb along it. She closed her eyes and shook her head.

"Not yet, I want to consult some books, figure some things out. Something isn't right," she said. "We shouldn't still be in love."

"Why not?" I asked.

"I'd rather not say just yet."

"You're asking me to trust you a whole lot right now, you know that, right?"

"I know, and I know you don't know me, but I promise you, I'm a trustworthy person."

I searched her face and saw sincerity there, but I'd seen sincerity on a lot of females' faces before. Still, something about this woman was different. It was like she saw to my soul, but it wasn't just one-sided. I could feel it, see it in her eyes; hear the pleading in her voice. I nodded slowly.

"I believe you," I said.

She closed her eyes and sniffed, tears slipping out from beneath her lashes and I felt a surge of panic. *Shit, this wasn't good.* Last thing I needed was to come up here, all this way, and get accused by a woman of something I didn't do, and get locked up.

"What can I do?" I asked, and she pulled her leg over me and settled onto the bed beside me.

She sniffed again and wiped at her tears, clearly distressed and not wanting to talk about it for now. She murmured softly, "I know you're not keen on touch, but do you think you could...?"

I opened up my arms and she slid down and put her ear over my heart. I put my arms around her and said, "I gotta say, you're kind of freaking me out, home girl."

"I know, and I'm sorry."

I nodded softly. "You good to get some shut-eye?" I asked.

She nodded against my chest.

"There's nothing I can do until morning."

"Okay, I'll try to get my car figured out, then, and I guess, go from there."

"Just passing through?" she asked.

"Nah, but you've got your secrets and I've got mine. We're even for now on that, yeah?"

She swallowed hard and nodded, "Yeah, okay, even for now."

We lay still in her fancy-as-fuck bedroom with the old-as-fuck heavy canopy bed and high ceiling, and I stared at the square of ceiling surrounded by the rails and curtains on the bed, the deep forest-green sheer cloth layered with a lighter gold material fluttering around us, the windows open to the light spring breeze from outside. The unfamiliar smell of salt wafted through the room, salt and something else I didn't quite recognize, but was still trying to decide if it stank or if it wasn't so bad. An almost fishy smell, but not like dead fish. I didn't know what it was and I didn't want to ask.

Seemed like Miri had enough to think about, her body soft and pressed tight against mine, her fingers idly curling around one of my dreads.

All I could really think was *Man, Jack. I know you's white, brah, but could you have picked a whiter town to be in?*

I was surprised I'd made it this far in without being pulled over by no police. Now my car was out there, dead, and I still had no idea what'd happened to my adoptive brother.

I had a lot to think about myself, so I left Miri to her thoughts in pursuit of mine, and just tried to figure out what the fuck all of this meant. I mean, was the way I felt about her going to wear off? Because it was freaky as fuck and I didn't want it.

Liar... the back of my mind whispered and I ignored it.

Females traditionally brought me nothing but trouble and I wasn't here shopping around for pussy. I was trying to find my bro. That was it.

3

Miri...

I stepped into The Wick & Stone, our town's local little metaphysical bookstore and tea shop, the next morning far earlier than I would have liked. I had left Kavion sleeping in my bed, and my heart had ached at doing it, which frightened me.

"Hey, Miri," Gwen greeted me, and then stopped in her tracks, her empathy working overtime. She eyed me up and said, "What's wrong? Spill it."

I set my burden of a reusable grocery tote full of packets of my tea on her counter and she began to root through it as she listened, restocking the drawers and jars behind the counters with my more-popular blends.

The Wick & Stone had used to be the old town's drugstore, complete with soda fountain, and I took a seat across the tea counter at one of the beautifully-refurbished stools with a hefty sigh.

"Someone showed up last night on my doorstep, right before the festival started."

"It wasn't Bucky Daniels, was it?" she asked, her voice disapproving.

I shook my head. "No, that's a problem for another day. This was a newcomer, a stranger with car trouble…"

"And?" she prompted.

"And we were caught up in the curse."

"Spell," she corrected automatically, and I gave her a withering look.

"Oh," she said, then it dawned on her. "Oh!"

"Yeah."

"Oh, honey. I'm so sorry…"

I looked at the older witch and felt my eyes water, her immediate sympathy telling me what I'd suspected.

"He didn't walk out on me after all, did he?" I asked.

She shook her head and sighed, "I didn't want to be the one to tell you, and we couldn't know for sure, but if the spell worked with another last night it can only mean one thing."

"Jackson is dead." I covered my face with my hands and broke down. *All those months of hurting and being angry and thinking that he didn't love me and that he'd just gone.*

Gwen came around the counter and hugged me tight and I cried into the velvet burnout pattern of her black wrap and the cloud of her long, snowy white hair. The smell of lavender, rose, and verbena was comforting.

"That's not all," I moaned and she held me at arm's length. Her blue eyes, fanned with laugh lines despite how young the rest of her face appeared, held nothing but worry and concern.

"What, what is it?" she demanded.

"I'm still in love with him."

"Who? This new man?"

"Yes, his name is Kavion, and I'm still desperately in love with him, and I'm so confused."

She hugged me again and said, "I'll have to consult my books,

I've never heard of such a scenario. Not for as long as the spell has been thriving."

"I honestly don't know what to think, or what to do. I'm just feeling so much!" I cried.

"I know," she said and I knew she did know, it was her gift, after all, just as mine was with growing things and having a bit of the sight when it came to folks and their medical issues.

"Where is he now?" she asked.

"Back at my house; I left him sleeping."

She rolled her eyes and tugged me to my feet. "You need to talk to him! Find out more about each other."

"I know," I said. "I just needed to know about Jack…"

She sighed and nodded.

"I'm sorry, lovie."

"I need to know, to find out what happened to him."

She nodded and said, "Take care of the living first, my dear girl."

She was right. I was just such a wreck. I didn't do well with these sorts of things. Like, at all.

"I'll sort through all of this and PayPal you the money, alright?" she asked, and I nodded. I could trust Gwen implicitly, which is why she was the first person I'd run to. She walked me to the door.

"Blessed be," I murmured.

"Merrier part than meet," she whispered and kissed my forehead. "Blessed be unto you, too."

I stood out on the sidewalk and looked out toward the bay, breathing in the salt and the smell of beached seaweed before gathering enough of my wits to let my feet carry me back down the block to my car. I was both ravaged on the inside over Jack and excited beyond measure to see Kavion, and the clashing war of mixed emotions was becoming overwhelming. Especially when you threw the crushing guilt about the latter on top of it all.

And then, there was the urgent sense that pieces were missing.

My magical intuition was working, I could feel it, but I'd never had it work on anything that wasn't plant-related, or interpersonal if it wasn't medically related to the plants I was trying to use to heal someone. It was frustrating, the gaps just so, and I didn't like the feeling. The feeling like I wasn't in control, like something else had taken the reins of my destiny and I was bouncing along in a runaway carriage.

I got into my little old Kia Forte and engaged the clutch, putting the key into the ignition and turning it on. I paused, apprehensive for the first time ever about returning home, but I needed to. I needed to see Kavion, find out more about him; figure out how I could be in love with him so soon after losing Jackson. The guilt choked me, but I pushed down the tears.

One crisis at a time, Miri. Just one foot in front of the other.

All would become clear.

It made me wish I could call Blyn, but I knew better. She was busy with so many criminal cases, plus that wasn't how her magic, her gift, worked. She was a seer, but she had to have something to touch, and while I had things of Jackson's still, they wouldn't tell us anything. She would need an object of his from after he disappeared. That, or she would need to perform a greater working, and I didn't want to impose upon my friend like that.

I missed Ashlyn with a deep and sudden, fractured ache. Of course, Ashlyn wouldn't be able to tell me anything either. She could only scry the present and glimpse the future and Jackson didn't have either one anymore.

I felt as though I couldn't breathe, and pulled off to the side of the road... Tears sprang to my eyes, blurring my vision horribly, and I just needed to let it out, so I did. I screamed. Long, loud, and wordless into the echo chamber of my small car. Over and over again, hollowing myself out, pouring my rage and pain into the air, my heart breaking, my thoughts torn in two between sweet Jackson and gentle Kavion.

"Gods above and below, this is so fucked up," I whispered, hoarse from my emotional purge.

I put myself back together swiftly. Afraid I'd left Kavion for too long, that he'd be awake and I wouldn't be home and he would… What? Miss me?

I was certain he would, at the very least, have questions and want answers. He'd said as much the night before.

I jumped when a knock fell at my driver's side window, letting out a little shriek and putting my hands to my chest as if it would slow my beating heart. I shuddered at the uniform on the other side of the glass and cranked down my window.

"Mornin', Miri, you doin' alright, now?"

I felt the tension in my shoulders ease when I realized it was only Mack, Matthew Mackenzie, one of Loving's deputies.

"I'm okay, Mack. Just… just got some unsettling news, is all."

"Oh, yeah? How, unsettling? Police business unsettling?" He looked hopeful.

"Oh, I'd let you know if it was," I told him with a smile.

Actually, I likely wouldn't, because it would only send Bucky Daniels to my door. He was also one of Loving's police officers.

Mack frowned and said, "You sure you're alright?"

I nodded. "I'll be okay. I just need to get back to the house. I have a guest."

His frown deepened and it was almost comical on him. He was a big man, with a bit of a gut but he was so baby-faced he was relegated into the category of cute or adorable, the same exact way you would find a puppy cute, or a real baby adorable. He pulled off his Smokey-the-Bear hat and wiped the back of his hand across his forehead.

It wasn't hot at all, being only the first blush of spring, but for some reason, he appeared to be sweating. It was my turn to frown as I let my gift unfurl in the center of my chest, sending creeping vines of energy his way. I felt my face crush down in sympathy and put my hand over his where it rested on my car's window sill.

"Come see me later, Mack. I'll make you up some tea to ease your flu symptoms."

"Aw, shit," he mumbled. "For real, Miri?"

"I'm afraid so, but I'll fix you right up, I promise."

"You're a doll," he said. "You sure you're alright?"

I nodded. "I promise."

"Good, because if I mentioned I saw you out here, you know Bucky'd be up my ass."

"I know, Mack." I made a face.

"You know, he means well," he said, hopeful.

I didn't want to crush him, but if he only knew…

"It's just not there," I told him, shying from the truth, which was I had every reason to loathe Bucky.

Mack nodded and said, "I know, I'm sorry."

I couldn't figure out what he was sorry about. For me, for Bucky, or for himself. Bucky could be a real pain in the ass, so likely it was a combination of all three.

"Might want to let dispatch know you're sick. Get ahead of it," I suggested.

He nodded. "Be by for that tea as soon as I can turn in my cruiser."

"Sounds good. I'll have it waiting."

"Drive careful." He smiled and patted the sill of my car window and put his hat back over his blonde hair with just a kiss of strawberry to it. I sighed, watching him traipse back to his patrol car. I hadn't even seen it roll up behind me.

Small town… everybody knew everyone else and their business.

I pulled back onto Tucker Avenue. and ranged out towards the near edge of town and my grandmother's big, old mansion.

I'd lost a lot in the last five or six years. It started with my gran, then one of my childhood friends, Oaklyn, who also happened to be a part of our little circle, passed away. The one thing that sucked about being a witch was that we were also, sadly, human with all of the vulnerabilities that entailed.

Oaklyn had been diagnosed at seventeen with bone cancer. A big piece of her hip had to be removed, and she'd been given an artificial joint. She'd done everything she was supposed to, chemo and radiation, and she'd gone into remission. But, the cancer had come back with a vengeance and by the time we had known anything was wrong, it was too late for her. She'd passed the year after my grandmother, and our little group of four girls had scattered to the four winds.

I had never been able to figure out why I hadn't known the cancer had come back, that it had spread, and I felt so awful about that. Worse still that I just knew that Blyn and Ashlyn blamed me somehow. I felt it in my bones that they thought that I'd known and just hadn't said anything, but I hadn't. I hadn't known, and I didn't know why. There was a rift between us as a result, a deep and painful chasm that I didn't know how to bridge.

I'd stayed here, but Blyn had gone to the city and Ash had, too. There wasn't much in the way of solid work here in Loving, and it'd felt like the world had gone on without me in some ways. That I'd been left behind.

I pulled into the driveway of the grand old Victorian-era mansion that was now mine, with its lush surrounding gardens and the greenhouse out back. I was surprised to find a newish Dodge Challenger in the drive ahead of me, parked in front of the four-car, double-bayed garage. I slipped my car into the space next to it and pulled the parking brake.

Kavion stood up from beneath the hood and looked over at me, his expression a bit stormy, clouded with confusion. I turned off the engine to my white Kia and opened the door.

"What's wrong with it?" I asked, and he frowned harder.

"That's just it. I got in her and started her right up this morning. There's nothing wrong that I can see."

"You're joking," I said and shut my door. I came around to the passenger side of my car and leaned back against it. He shook his head, sending his dreadlocks swinging and I lightly chewed the inside of my cheek.

"No, for real, I can't explain it," he said and came around, leaning his butt against the driver's side fender of the taupe, metal-flake paint job of the expensive muscle car. He faced me, looking down at me from his six-foot-plus height, and I met his gaze evenly. His face went from frowning to concern in the blink of an eye and he reached out and grazed my cheek lightly with the back of his knuckles in a gentle caress.

"Why you been crying?" he asked, softly.

"I went to see a friend of mine," I said evenly. "Another witch, my mentor, actually."

"And?"

I let out a long, slow breath and said, "The, um…" I cleared my throat, which was choking up and tried to figure out a way to phrase this that wasn't going to leave me a puddle of embarrassing goo all over again, only this time, with witnesses.

"Take your time, love," he murmured, and had the grace to look embarrassed himself for the slip of the endearment.

"No, hey, it's fine," I reassured him. "I still love you, too. It's, um, it's not going to wear off."

"I'm of a mixed mind about that," he said and it was clipped.

I smiled bravely and said, "Yeah, me too, just probably for different reasons." I let out an explosive breath.

"You want to go inside and talk about this?" he asked softly and I nodded.

"Yeah, that would probably be best. I'm expecting one of Loving's finest over soon."

He froze and I rolled my eyes. "Not because of you. He's got the flu; I told him to come get some tea. That I'd have it ready for him."

"Oh."

"I'm a witch, you know… like a real one. Gift and everything." I shifted uncomfortably.

"I kind of figured that," he said with a chuckle as we crossed the gravel driveway, the small stones crunching beneath my boots and his athletic shoes.

"What gave me away?" I asked, with a hint of a smile.

"Well, if it wasn't the books, it might have been the raven."

"Shade?" I asked amused. "What did he do now?"

"I heard a cat meowing, was looking all over the damn place for it. Never knew those birds could do that."

I laughed.

"Ravens are smarter than some parrots," I said.

"So," he held open the screen door to my back door for me, "is he like your familiar or whatever?"

"Or something," I said and winked and he laughed.

"Ah-ho-ho, she's got jokes!"

"She's got jokes," I agreed and sighed. We entered my kitchen and I went immediately to one of my cupboards and brought down two cups.

"Tell me what's got you upset," he said, sliding into a seat at my breakfast nook. I took the kettle from the stove and took it to the sink to fill it.

"There was someone before you, someone I loved dearly," I said. "He died. That's, um..." I let out a shuddering breath. "That's how I guess, um, that the curse or spell worked for us. Why I'm able to love you."

"I'm sorry," he murmured. "That really sucks."

"Mm, I'm having some very mixed emotions about it right now, and I," I laughed uneasily, "I'm not really good at the whole, um, feeling this strongly about a stranger. At least when I fell in love with him, we'd known each other for a few weeks prior to the festival. I mean, he'd been around town. We'd met in passing, had a few conversations. It wasn't like, with us and –"

"Bam! Hollah at 'cha from your doorstep," he said, smiling and giving me a bit of jazz hands.

I laughed and nodded, saying, "Exactly."

"I honestly don't know where to go from here," he said.

I shook my head.

"Me, either."

"Guess it's pretty new for the both of us, even though you've done it before." He sighed and I nodded slowly. A slow and sexy grin painted his generous lips and he raised his eyebrows. "I guess that means we got at least one thing going for us," he said.

I tipped my head and hugged myself and asked, "What's that?"

"We already got something in common."

I smiled slowly and said, "You're right."

"I'd like to find out what else we've got," he said.

"Well, you're new in town. Have you got someplace to stay yet?"

He shook his head no, and I went out on a limb and said, "Welcome to the Eilish House Bed & Breakfast, Mr. Martin. Would you like to stay with me? There are vacancies available."

He smiled slowly, and though it was an overt flirt, he was perfectly shy about it when he said, "Depends, is one of those vacancies the third floor tower room?"

The tea kettle started to simmer lightly, the sound of it changing as I pushed off the counter. I went over to where he sat and stood near him. His expression changed, becoming more serious as I dropped my hands to my sides. He brought one of his up, carefully taking one of my free hands, the other one, he placed on my hip as he stared up into my eyes.

"I'm sure that something could be arranged," I whispered.

"I mean," he swallowed hard and let his eyes wander down my body, and I could swear, if he were as fair as me, he would be as red as a beet. "It's not like I'm suggesting it because I just want to smash," he said, and my eyebrow went up at the unfamiliar term. "I just want to be close to you and that's um, well, that's really weird for me."

I nodded carefully and let my hands graze up his arms and rest on the rounded caps of his shoulders. He met my eyes and said, "I just really want to know you, you know?"

"I know," I whispered. "I get it, I really do it's just –" The kettle blew, letting out a shrill whistle, interrupting me, making me jump and keeping me from baring my insecurities. I went to deal with it and he let me go, watching me move throughout my kitchen as I fixed us two cups of my own blend of immuni-tea.

"What's this?" he asked as I rejoined him and set the teacup and saucer in front of him. I set mine in front of the seat opposite of his and sat down.

"Immunity tea, it's got a special blend of herbs and spices to bolster the immune system. Mack is coming by and has the flu, remember?"

He smiled at me and said, "I've never really believed in all the holistic mumbo-jumbo," but to his credit, he took a sip, blowing on the hot liquid first.

I added a touch of raw honey to mine.

"My whole life is that holistic mumbo-jumbo," I said, with a slight smile.

"Tell me about it." His voice was soft, enticing, the timbre of it sending a shiver down my spine in all of the best ways.

"About what?" I asked.

"Your life," he said, covering my hand with his. I stared at them, our hands, his dark skin against mine, which was much, much lighter. It was a startling, but pleasing, contrast, lovely to look at, like a piece of artwork hanging in some gallery in one of those big cities I had no desire to ever really see. Except it wasn't there, it was here, in my kitchen, and I was so in love with this man that there weren't any words.

The crunch of gravel outside stayed my voice and I sighed. "That might be Mack, or a guest," I murmured and he nodded.

"We've got time, love."

I smiled slightly at him and he slid his hand back from mine just as a knock fell on my kitchen door. I went to it and opened it up. Mack was looking worse than even just a little while before. I made a sympathetic face and said, "Come on in, Mack. I'll grab your tea from my workroom."

"Thanks, Miri."

He stepped into the kitchen and I opened the door across from the back door and clipped down the stairs into my basement.

4

*K*avion...

Miri retreated down the stairs to her basement and left me with the big guy in her kitchen. I took a drink of the tea she'd brought me as we eyed each other up. He was in his uniform, but his gun belt was absent. That didn't mean shit to a nigga like me, though. He was probably packin' a backup. I would have been, if I were in his line of work.

Problem for me was, I didn't know what I wanted to be when I grew up. I'd just gotten out of the military a short time back, and like most dudes, didn't really have a plan for what came after.

I'd come here looking for my best friend, that was it, then whatever shit went down the night before got me all fucked up, because all of a sudden I was madly in love with this woman I didn't even know. Like, shit be crazy, and I had no idea which way was down or up.

One thing I did know, one thing that never changed, was you had to wait and be patient, get a dude's measure before you started poppin' off with jokes and whatnot.

Cops were people, too, and as complicated as what-all that

entailed. So I waited calmly to see if this guy was going to pop off at me, start some shit, or if he was gonna be cool.

"Welcome to Loving," he said carefully. "I ain't seen you around before, so I'm guessing you're new?"

I nodded and said, "Fo' sure, nice to meet you too, my man. I'm Kavion."

"Folks call me Mack, I'd shake your hand but…"

"Ah, nah, I get it," I said, laughing.

"Miri'll get me fixed right up," he said with confidence.

"Yeah, she good at that?" I asked, and he nodded.

He eyed me up and asked, "So, you just in for the festival?"

I shook my head, "Didn't even know about it until it hit while I was on Miri's doorstep."

"She wasn't planning on attending the festival this year."

"She said something about that."

"She had the B&B closed down."

"I noticed," I said, nodding, rolling my lips together.

"So, what brought you here?"

"Car trouble, actually."

"That's your Challenger out there?"

"It is."

"Awfully new, ain't it?"

"Yep."

"How many miles you got on it?"

"Haven't had much time to drive it, around eighteen k or so," I answered, well aware he was fishing.

"So, what's wrong with it?"

"Nothing, now. Went out and started it right up this morning. I can't explain it, it just died on me last night coming up the road. Acted like the alternator quit."

We heard Miri on the stairs and the conversation ceased. When she appeared, a paper bag neatly packaged and folded between her hands, she looked from Mack to me and back again.

"Sorry, I was low, and so I wanted to mix some more up for

you," she said, handing him the bag. "Hot water, steep for two to three minutes. Add lemon and honey, and get better soon, okay?"

"Yes, ma'am, I surely do appreciate it."

"Okay, Mack. I'm sure we'll see you later." She smiled up at him and he gave a nod and went for the back door, his eyes lingering on me as he slipped through it and out onto the back part of the mansion's wrap-around porch. He went down the broad steps and disappeared behind the red door she shut in his wake. She turned to me and leaned back against it, wincing.

"Did he grill you? I totally bet he grilled you, didn't he?"

"He was fishin', but he didn't get much. Why's he so curious?" I asked.

"It's not him," she said with another sigh, and this time she just looked tired.

"Something I can do to help?" I asked.

"No." She shook her head. "No, not at all."

I let it go, and she drifted back over to the table and slipped back into her seat across from me. I put my hand out, palm up, on the table between us and she hesitated only a moment before resting her palm in mine.

"This is weird, huh?" I asked her after a few moments of silence.

"Very," she admitted softly. "In some ways, at least for me, it's heartbreaking, but redemptive, but also more heartbreaking on top of that."

She covered her face with her free hand and struggled for a bit to keep her composure and even though I didn't know her, I knew things about her. Like how she craved contact, how she loved to be touched. That she was just as beautiful on the inside as she was the outside. I don't know how I knew these things, but I did. I just knew, and sometimes in life, you learned to just go with the flow and not question things like that.

So here I was, just tryin' to go with the flow.

"You got a lot going on, huh?"

She nodded, and she was having such a hard time, I could see it in her eyes. It was like she was desperate to talk, to speak her mind, but at the same time she just didn't know if she could trust me. That was cool. I understood. Like, seriously, I was the first guy to be able to relate to love not always equaling trust. No one could do you dirty like family, and they were supposed to be the ones to love you the most, right?

These thoughts and more drifted through my mind as I watched her drink her tea. She sipped at the liquid in her cup, her hand in mine, her blue eyes far away as she looked out the bay window the breakfast nook sat in. I was cool with silence, without speaking.

At least for now.

I wanted to ask about my buddy Jack, but I didn't think she would know him. Somebody in this town did, though, and if I had to go through all two-thousand-and-sixty-eight people listed on the sign at the town limits, I would.

"If you didn't come for the festival, why did you come?" she asked, her voice holding a bit of a dreamy sing-song quality.

I gave a shrug and she shook, like she'd just gotten a chill and asked, "What?"

"I didn't say nothing," I said, and she cocked her head and nodded but didn't press her question, so I asked one of my own.

"You're a witch, right?"

She nodded and asked almost timidly, "Is that a problem?"

"Depends," I said with a self-deprecating grin. "Is it a problem I'm black?"

She blinked and her hand tightened around mine where she held it, "No."

"Then I don't care what religion you practice," I said.

She smiled a bit ruefully and shook her head.

"It's not about religion with me, I really am a witch. Not just a practitioner, but by birthright."

"So, like, what can you do?" I asked.

She smiled and said, "Not a lot, honestly. I mean, my powers aren't super impressive. They're very earthbound. I grow things, have a rather special affinity for animals and people. Like, I have an intuition when something's wrong and sometimes, with the right herbs and spices, I can correct some of the lesser maladies."

"What can't you fix?" I asked and grinned.

Her expression became very sad and she returned her gaze out the window when she said, "Cancer."

"Shit, I'm sorry –"

"Oh, no, you didn't know. It, um, was one of my circle mates. She died a few years ago. I should have known it had come back, but I didn't and... Well..." She stared hard in silence out the window and finally returned those clear blue eyes to mine. "I thought that was what we were supposed to be doing," she said softly.

I nodded, picking up what she was putting down and said, "Getting to know each other? We are."

"So tell me something about yourself," she said.

"Uh, I don't know. I mean, I'm twenty-six, went into the army at seventeen and did my four years. Re-upped for four more. When I got out, I went to work out on an oil rig. I'm a Louisiana boy. Geaux Tigers!"

She laughed and I smiled; she had a good laugh. Light and clear, the kind I don't think I'd ever get tired of hearing.

"What about you?" I ventured. I hated talking about myself and I really just wanted to know more about her.

"Um, I was born and raised in Loving. I had three of some of the best friends any girl could ask for growing up. All of them witches, like me. We're all descendants of the original coven who put the spell in place here."

"I mean, how does the spell even work?" I asked, a little freaked-out about what some of the teenagers around here might be doing, and kids! Weren't there any kids in or around this town? Like, for real.

She smiled at me and said, "I told you, it's pretty simple. People near one another at the stroke of the clock at eight o'clock at night fall in love. At midnight the spell ends, and if you've been matched with the one you're meant to be with," she gave a little shrug, "you stay in love."

"But like, what about kids, though?"

She laughed, "Oh, you want to know about the finer details, I see. They sleep through it. Anyone under the age of consent does. We're not sure how the magic knows, but throughout the years, anyone under the age of what is deemed to be acceptable to be having any kind of sex, they simply fall asleep and are out cold for the four hours the festival runs."

"Wow, like, you guys ever…?"

"Oh, yeah, girls mostly. Some have even made it into bars and the like. Never any locals, they all come from out of town. The locals set up cots in back rooms and basements, just in case, because the spell begins and they typically drop like a sack of potatoes."

"That's crazy!"

She laughed a little and nodded.

"The magic knows," she said, and she finished off her tea.

"You look tired," I said, and she nodded.

"We were up half the night and I did get up early."

"You expecting anyone?" I asked. "You know, like to stay?"

She shook her head. "Not until tomorrow."

"Want to lay down for a bit? Maybe take a nap?"

She nodded slowly, "I think I would like that, but I would like to talk more, too."

"Of course," I said. "We've got plenty of time."

Her smile was sad and her nod faint as she stood and I wanted to know why, but I felt like it was still forbidden territory. Things felt so fragile and still so surreal, but I knew this was as real as it got. I guess that was magic, huh?

She picked up my empty teacup and saucer to take them to the sink and I caught it as she glanced down into my cup. She froze mid-step and frowned slightly, her mouth opening as if she were about to say something before she closed it. Cocking her head, she looked down into her own cup and, reassured by whatever she saw there, she finished her short journey to the kitchen sink.

"What was that about?" I asked, and she gave me an enigmatic little smile, standing near me and holding out her hand.

I took it and got to my feet and she said, "Nothing, it was nothing."

"Hey," I murmured slightly, hanging back a bit. "Not sure lying to each other is going to be the best way to start things out, do you?"

"No, I suppose not. You've been lied to enough, haven't you?" she asked and I felt a frisson of shock go up the inside of my spine, through my chest.

"Yeah," I nodded. "By a lot of people."

She arched a brow and said, "People?"

I laughed uneasily and tossed my head back to get my dreads out of my eyes.

"Females. I been lied to by a lot of females."

"Well, Kavion, I have never lied to you, and I don't plan to. However, I haven't told you everything, either."

"Isn't that the same thing?" I asked.

"I suppose it is," she murmured. "Come lay down with me, let's get cozy, and talk. I mean really talk."

I nodded. Having her close in my arms sounded pretty good.

*M*iri...

I'd accidentally read his tea leaves, and the messages therein had been mixed. 'Past' was fraught with pain and danger, hurt of the emotional kind, with a distinctly female tilt to the sediment in his cup. 'Present' swirled with ambiguity and made me want to know even more what he was doing here in Loving. 'The Future' concerned me, I couldn't see anything there, which made my heart seize in my chest. It either meant there was no future to be had or that there were just too many possibilities for even the fates to discern at this time.

I checked my cup, just in case, ignoring the clear sorrow of the past and the cloud of uncertainty that was the present and casting an eye to my future, which took two forks, the high one of happiness and clarity, the low of lost love and an unbearable heartache. I didn't know precisely what to make of it, but I really would have liked to go with option 'A' rather than any more hurt than I'd already survived.

I could see that option 'A' started with truth and honesty, hence why I had started down that path. As frightening as the outcome could be, the alternative… well, no one wanted the alternative.

We went up to my room and I put my bed between us as I changed from my jeans and light flannel shirt to a pair of sleep shorts, divesting myself of my bra but keeping my cotton camisole on. I was having a hard time taking my eyes off of Kavion, though, as he efficiently stripped down to his tight boxer shorts.

He gave me a cocky smile as he caught me looking, and I raised one of my ginger eyebrows at him. He laughed, and I pulled back the corner of my blankets and sheets and got into my bed, saying, "You keep that up, you can sleep on the floor."

"Pshaw!" He grinned and got into the bed beside me and we just naturally gravitated into each other's arms, holding one another close.

I closed my eyes, my ear over his heart and let the ticking echo of it sooth me, like putting a shell to your ear and letting the sound of the ocean sweep you far away even though you were standing still.

"Why you try to shut the whole world out last night?" he asked.

"I told you," I murmured. "The last man I loved, he's died, and I just…"

I shuddered, the pain welling up fresh and hot, spilling over the bridge of my nose in a scorching line before I could stop it.

"Oh, hey, I'm sorry. I didn't mean to make you cry."

"It's okay," I said. "I just, I met him at the festival last year and that's how we fell in love and when the magic ended…"

"You were still in love, like with me?" he asked.

I sobbed, unable to speak, and nodded.

"Is that how you knew that he died? Because you stayed in love with me?"

"I had to guess," I said, wiping my eyes. "I went to speak with my mentor this morning and she confirmed it, but it's so strange. I mean, it's never happened before that we know of, but if you're meant to be with someone forever… how else can you be meant to be with another, unless they're gone?"

"Shit, I'm sorry." He became uncharacteristically quiet, deep in thought.

"It's okay," I said. "It's just when I say 'it's me, not you', I really mean it, and as you can probably guess, I'm not trying to friend-zone you."

He laughed and hugged me a little tighter and sighed.

"What was your first guy's name?" he asked.

"Jack. Um, Jackson Greene, why?" I asked.

He held me tighter and sighed again, and it was a heavy thing.

"Don't freak out, okay?"

I stiffened and said gently, "Kind of hard not to, when you preface whatever you're going to say with something like that."

"I know, but-" He laughed but it was short, an uneasy sound.

"But what? Just rip whatever Band-Aid it is off for me, please?" I knew I sounded weary, because I was. My heart was aching, the shattered pieces grinding against each other painfully.

"Jack's my brother, I'm here looking for him. He disappeared and his family is worried sick."

I pushed up off of him and looked down at him, confused for several reasons. For one, Jack was white; for two, they didn't share the same last name Just… what?

"You're serious," I said finally, after searching his face.

"I am," he nodded.

"Jack's been gone for months," I murmured. "How are you only here now?"

"I was still deployed when he first went missing. When I got back and I would text him, I would get these texts back…"

I reeled, blinking stupidly, and echoed, "Texts?"

"Hold up, you were here. Why don't you catch me up, please?"

I sat up in my bed beside his hip and the pleading in his soulful brown eyes did me in. I took a step on faith and swallowed hard before beginning my tale.

"Jack came to Loving on some sort of wildlife mission. Something about a final thesis on the Seaside Blue Cap Woodpecker. He was observing them. Would go out early, come back late, notebooks full of notes and drawings.

"He was staying here, at my B&B, had booked the whole month. We were both in town, at the same bar, and the clock struck eight and the magic happened..."

I rolled my eyes and laughed, bowing my head and shaking it slightly.

"We couldn't get back here fast enough. What came next was the happiest five months of my life. He was going out to observe the woodpecker one morning, the skies still dark, and he was... I don't know... acting strange. He didn't kiss me goodbye, he took a bag like he would be out camping for a day or two, and he seemed distracted."

"That's not like him," Kavion said, chewing his bottom lip thoughtfully.

"I got some texts from him later the next morning. Texts saying that he didn't really feel for me what I did for him, that he was done with his research, and that he was heading home. The texts told me not to contact him, thanks for the free place to stay, and to, basically, 'have a nice life.' I was devastated."

"Okay, now that's like me; that's really not like him. Damn."

"Thanks for the warning," I said softly.

"The way I feel about you? I could never do that to you, love. I may not understand what's going on, but I'd seriously rather rip my own arm off and beat myself with it than do something like that to you... and that's the thing. Jack would have been the same way. Except he's – " He stopped, his face going slack, his expression clouding and closing down. "Except he was a freaking boy scout. He would have been honest with you from the very beginning."

"Nothing fit," I said honestly. "I waited and waited for him to turn up, to tell me someone else had gotten a hold of his phone, that it was all a cruel joke, but days turned into weeks and weeks into months…" I trailed off, my throat closing up.

By the time the festival came around again for this year, I'd made sure that I'd have no guests. I'd locked myself away and swore I would never let myself love anyone else the way I loved Jack. The fates had other plans, though, and maybe those plans were to rip the veil from off my eyes.

I was terribly unsettled. Feeling a whole host of emotions, chief among them disappointment in myself for not seeing that Jack was a good and decent man, for not believing in him enough to know something wasn't right, for automatically believing the worst of him, which wasn't even there.

"I'm so sorry," I whispered as Kavion sat up and pulled me into his arms. "I thought the very worst of him, didn't I?"

"It's okay, you had no way of knowing. You didn't even know him a year, but I'm telling you, I knew that guy my whole life and he loved you and if he loved someone or something he would die before he hurt them or let it go."

"Why are you just now here?" I asked again, sniffing.

He looked guilty and sighed.

"I'm not very good at keeping in touch. First, I was deployed, no communications with back home. Then when I got home, I shot him a text and he was texting back and it sounded like him. We planned to meetup in a couple months after I got out and he didn't show. I got on with the oil rigs and went out there and we're gone for a month at a time, or more, depending. I was used to it, and he was all like, 'Sorry bro, I missed my flight.'"

"I didn't think nothing of it, because shit happens, then I get back from the rig and he says he can't come down and I thought that was weird 'cause it was around the holidays. So I called our mom and she was a mess, said she'd lost my number and had been waiting to hear from me – that Jack was missing. I was like 'Naw! I'm talking with him!' and she said he was supposed to be home with the woman he'd met over the last holiday but he'd never come."

I felt my shoulders drop and he sighed.

"Our mom said that she'd called the police up here, but they wouldn't help her. Said Jack was a grown man and probably went off on his own to do his own thing and would be back when he was done or needed money or both."

That enraged me, but I wasn't really surprised. She'd probably spoken with our chief. A lazy man, uninterested in outsiders or any of their doings unless it affected our town negatively. Or rather, I should say, our image. He'd become far too comfortable in his position and really, his only competition was Bucky, who wasn't really any competition at all. He was too young to run for election and be taken seriously. Not for much longer, though. A few more years and he might have a chance.

"I'm so sorry. Loving loves outsiders for their tourist money around the festival. The tourists themselves? Not so much."

I had thought, with as long as he'd stayed and as pleasant as he was, that Jack would have been accepted as one of our own, but clearly not, by our police force.

"You okay?" he asked me and I shook my head.

"No. No, I'm really not. I'm shaken, I'm numb… I don't know what to think or feel."

"C'mere," he whispered and pulled me into his arms. I closed my eyes and let myself feel for the moment, let the overwhelming rogue wave of emotion crash over my head and soak me, let it drag me out to sea. I held onto Kavion as if he were the only rock strong enough to hold me up out of the emotional soup trying to sweep me away, and he held me back, patiently, lovingly, and kindly.

"I want to trust you," I whispered. "I want to believe you… but I'm scared."

He cleared his throat and looked uncomfortable when he said, "I don't do feelings very good. I mean, talking about them… my own… but I feel you. I mean, I feel the same. Trust don't come easy to someone like me."

"How come?" I asked softly and he gave a one-shouldered shrug.

"My mom's a crackhead; don't have a clue who my dad is; have something like six half-brothers and sisters that I know of. Oldest brother is in jail, youngest is doin' alright for himself, but we was in and out of foster care all our lives. I met Jack when I was in ninth grade. Shit wasn't goin' so well at home and he stuck with me, you know? Pretty soon, I started living at his place and that's just kind of how things went. His folks took me in. I got lucky. Graduated high school and went right into the military. Got around the age eighteen enlistment just barely. Been deployed twice, got a honorable discharge, but didn't quite make it eight years."

"How come?" I asked softly.

"I re-upped the first time, got moved around, and probably eight months before I was going to get out, I got into it pretty hard with one of my superiors." He made air quotes with his fingers around 'superiors' and I couldn't help but smile.

"They gave me the option to get out early with an honorable, and I took it. Rattled around trying to find some work for about a week and my cousin got me on with the oil rigs. Had to go like right away, and so I did that. Tried getting a hold of Jack to meet up, and you know the rest…"

I bit my bottom lip and felt my shoulders droop. He reached out and put a hand on my shoulder, warm and comforting, smoothing the pad of his thumb over my skin.

"It's been a hard five or six years for me," I murmured.

I told him about my grandmother and about Oaklyn. About Blyn and Ash, how they'd both moved and how I felt boring and stuck. I opened up and felt an almost-comfort doing it. Like Jack was still here with us both, and I had to believe he had a hand in it, that he was still here.

Oaklyn would have been the one to ask. She had an affinity for the dead. Could see them in the fire, talk to them. Probably because she was walking the line between the living and the dead for so long without even knowing it.

"Where do you want to go from here?" I asked finally, after what felt like hours of talking. He held me a bit tighter into his side and I brought my leg up over his, grateful to be tucked against his warm, hard body.

"I guess I need to find some work somewhere in town. Listen around, see if I can pick anything up about my boy."

"Something awful must have happened, but awful doesn't necessarily equate to nefarious," I said.

"No, you're right," he said after being silent for too long. "But somebody sent those texts, love. Somebody who wasn't Jack. Somebody that had a hold of his phone."

"Oh… right… I'm sorry, I'm just not thinking. My mind feels empty. Like I'm hollow."

He sighed and brushed a hand over my hair, twisting his head on his neck to press those full, soft lips to my hairline.

"I don't think it's a coincidence I found myself on your doorstep," he said suddenly, just as I had begun to drift.

"I don't think so either," I murmured while I thought to myself, *What I wouldn't give to see him just one more time.*

"Get some rest, I promise to be right here with you when you wake up."

"I love you," I whispered, even though it terrified me to love anyone again.

"I love you, too. Hard. And that scares me," he said.

"Me, too."

"Guess we're in this together, huh?"

"Yep."

"Well, we'll figure it out, one way or another." He sounded determined and I liked that.

I liked that a lot.

6

*K*avion...

I had to take things easy with trying to figure out what happened to my brother. I had to be cold, cynical, logical... and I had to say my plans changed in a big way with the addition of Miri. Knowing that she was Jackson's girl, knowing that he was dead, which I'd suspected for a while now, made me want to take care of her more, not less. That was weird, because I realized pretty quick, taking care of her meant taking care of myself. Like, for real. I couldn't let anything happen to me. I couldn't let what happened to her and Jack happen to her for a second time.

She was wrecked so hard over my brother. Everything was so complicated and twisted and I was like, *damn*. I thought I had it tough but the junk Miri had to deal with, man, she was goin' through it.

"Hey."

I jumped and turned around, she was standing with a basket overflowing with greenery against the open mouth of her garage door. The light from outside was behind her, casting her face in shadow. I squinted and stepped away from the saw, the blade spinning down.

"Sorry, didn't mean to startle you while you were operating dangerous machinery."

I chuckled and picked up the length of board I needed to finish, repairing the busted one in her back step.

"It's cool, it's cool," I said, and grinned. She was beautiful no matter what she wore and today it was her usual jeans with a pair of muddy rain boots, a purple neoprene North Face jacket hugging her curves up top.

"What are you doing?" she asked.

"Ahhh, you got a busted board in your back step. I got nosy and found the shop back here open. I don't like sitting still if I can help it."

"You don't have to fix anything around here," she said, surprised.

"Nah, I don't have to. I want to."

She smiled and bowed her head, lowering her basket in her hands and said, "Jack was like that, too."

"Yeah," I agreed. "Any idea what could have happened to him?"

"None," she murmured.

"Any kind of magic you could work to put us onto something?"

"I try to use magic as a last resort, not the first go-to," she said.

"I guess I don't understand how it all works."

"When you're done, I'll be happy to explain as much as I can," she said softly.

"I'd like that." *I'd like nothing more than to learn everything about her.*

"When you're done, come on down to the basement."

I smirked, I couldn't help it. I was a smart-ass by nature and while I suppressed the comment that came to mind, she rolled her eyes anyway and said, "Go ahead, I've heard it all."

"Nah, it's cool," I said trying not to laugh, knowing that not knowing what I was about to say would likely drive her crazy.

"No, go on," she said. "Go ahead, I'd love to hear it."

"No," I said simply, keeping my tone light.

"No?" she asked, and her lips rose at the corners.

"Nope," I said, popping the 'p'.

"Alright then, suit yourself," she said, and wandered back in the direction of the house.

I smiled and found a hammer and an old coffee can full of galvanized nails. It took maybe twenty minutes to pry up the spongy, broken board and put the new one down flush. I hammered it into place and took the can of nails and the hammer back where they belonged. I would need to get some stain but it should be alright for a day or two, even if it rained. Just would mean I'd need to sand it first, which could be a bitch, so here was to hoping the sky would stay clear at least through tomorrow.

I went in the back door and found Miri in the kitchen, her basket of herbs and whatnot on the edge of her counter while she was hard at work finishing up some sandwiches.

"Looks good, but what happened to 'meet me in your basement?'"

She smiled and said, "My stomach growled coming in the back door and I figured if I was hungry, then you were hungry."

"You ain't wrong." I slid onto one of the stools at the counter by her basket and peered into it.

"Almost done," she said, and I nodded.

"Hang up your coat and stay a while."

She'd taken hers off and had hung it off the coat tree by the back door. She was a country chick, for sure. One of those snap closure country western type plaid shirts in blue and white plaid, thin strips of accent purple through it clung to her upper body, the sleeves rolled back above her elbows, the shirt open to halfway down her stomach, displaying her white cotton tank underneath.

We'd woken after dark the night before, had a late dinner, and had relaxed by a fire in her big living room, which didn't have a TV. She cuddled under a blanket on one end of the green velvet couch and I'd sat on the other end facing her and we'd talked until it was so late it was early.

We'd slept better last night, had learned about each other, and made some decisions. I could respect her work ethic and how she held things down all by herself. Not just the bed and breakfast part of things, but also caring for her animals and helping the towns-people, not to mention her tea business with whatever shop bought it off of her.

She was a one-woman-show, a machine, and I didn't want to be a wrench in the works. I didn't know what I wanted to be, but a cog that made things run better, smoother, would be nice. I mean, I had nowhere else to be, even after I figured out what happened to Jack, and it almost felt like it would be shitting on a gift he'd given me from beyond the grave if I left after finding out the truth. I mean, he did lead me here, and I was betting that if he'd loved Miri, he'd want me to be the one to take care of things for him.

It wouldn't be hard, but damn. It was a lot of pressure, you know?

I pushed it to the back of my mind and tried not to think about it as I took off my own jacket and hung it beside hers. When I turned around, she was setting two plates at the breakfast nook. I slid into my spot as she went back across the kitchen.

"Where you going?" I asked and she turned and looked over her shoulder.

"Something to drink?" she asked.

"Aw, yeah huh?" I gave a nod and sucked air in past my teeth.

She came back with a pitcher of iced tea and I eyed it suspiciously. White folks up in these northern latitudes didn't sweeten their iced tea and it was bullshit. Miri laughed at me and poured two glasses.

"Just put it in your face," she commanded, and I closed one eye and peered at her out the other like, *Really?*

"It's proper sweet tea, I promise," she said.

I took a drink, and dragged my head back and made a face.

"It's close, but it's different. Like, not bad, just… different."

"I add honey to mine, and a touch of crystallized ginger during the brewing process."

"Ah."

We had made it through half of our sandwiches and chips when she asked, "So, have you decided what you're going to do yet? Like, how you're going to go about things?"

"Nobody but you knows I'm even related to Jack," I said and she gave a wry grin, her clear blue eyes sweeping over me appreciatively.

"And why would they?"

"Exactly. So, I figured I'd get a job doing labor down at the docks, see what I could come up with, and just keep my ear to the ground."

"Give it a few weeks and hope it just comes up?" she asked.

"Well, yeah and nah. Give it some time and see if it comes up but like, send you in to stir the pot."

"Oh, yeah? How so?"

"Ask a few questions around the right people. Bring Jack up and see if it busts something loose."

"Ah," she said, nodding, and sighed.

"I don't go into town much if I can avoid it. Not since he 'dumped' me." She put 'dumped' in quotations with her slim, delicate fingers.

"Embarrassing?" I asked softly.

"Yeah," she said and rolled her lips together.

"He would never have done that to you," I said, shaking my head. "All he could talk about was this beautiful woman he'd met and how he couldn't wait for me to meet his girl. Which is why I thought it was so weird when he just stopped… you know?"

She swallowed hard and closed her eyes, and leaned back in her seat, the rest of her food forgotten on her plate.

"I feel so damn guilty," she said.

"What, for believing the worst?" I asked.

"Yeah," she nodded.

"Babe, with the world we live in and how people treat each other like trash, it wasn't out of bounds," I told her.

"We were so stupid in love, we were still learning about each other, but I seriously thought that he may have fooled me," she said, and looked bleakly out the window.

"Oh, gosh, it's Ivan," she declared.

"Ivan?"

"Um, stay right there."

She got up and I peered out the window to see a seriously big fuckin' dude traipsing past in one of those big black duster coats. Like, dude was easily taller than my six-one and fuckin' wider through the shoulders. He had on a black hoodie under the coat, which not only bulked his already big ass up more, but he had the hood up, covering his head and hiding his face from me.

I got a vibe from him and it wasn't necessarily a good one. I got up as Miri reached the back door, but before I could tell her to wait, she had it open and was calling out around it, "Ivan, hello! Just to let you know, I have company."

He stepped up onto the porch and grunted and she stepped back into the kitchen holding the door wide for him to come through and I shit you not, my dude almost had to turn sideways to fit his shoulders through the opening.

"Ivan, this is Kavion. Kavion, this is Ivan."

We eyed each other up, and I threw him some chin.

"What's up, my dude?"

He didn't answer me, just turned back to my girl and stared in her direction. She cocked her head and asked softly, "The nightmares come back?"

"Da." He gave a hard nod and pulled his hood back off his face, uncovering short dark hair.

Miri looked sympathetic and said, "Come downstairs with us, I'll get you fixed up."

"Spasibo," he said in a heavy Russian accent. I had to guess it meant 'thank you.' At least I hoped it did.

She smiled at him and grabbed her basket of clippings and fresh stuff off her counter and led us to the door to her basement. She preceded us down the stairs and I followed behind her at the big man's insistence. The big-ass Russian preferred bringing up the rear, he could bring up the rear. I was cool.

It was dark as fuck down here and she stopped a slight ways into the deep gloom and asked softly, "Ivan, would you mind?"

I looked back at the dude who stood up slightly straighter and looked from Miri to me and back again. She smiled softly, understanding flickering through her eyes and across her fair face and she said, "It's okay. You can trust him, can't he, Kavion?"

"For sure," I said, and a moment later, the basement flared to life. As in, every candle, lantern, and the fireplace that was down here spontaneously combusted, but not like wildin' out, just flared up and then settled down into a normal light. I kept my mouth shut but heck yeah, I was impressed. That shit was dope.

"Thanks," Miri said softly, and went around behind a big, heavy table, shelves of jars and drawers behind her, five-gallon buckets lined up around the basement walls, with tight lids.

All sorts of shit was hanging off the rafters of the low ceiling – plants and herbs, all in various states of drying. It was way more than I figured the small space could hold but was way tidy and orderly. I was doubly impressed.

I wandered over by the wood burning stove and perched on a tall, three-legged stool there. Ivan just hung back by the stairs as Miri set to work pulling down jars and shit, and opening up a brown paper bag, bigger than a lunch sack, just smaller than your average grocery sack.

She stood it up on the work bench and asked, "How has it been for you falling asleep? Easier?"

He nodded once and she nodded back. "Staying asleep?"

He waffled his hand back and forth and she nodded again and

opened a book on her workbench, flipping through and running her fingertips down the page. She nodded and asked, "Have you been drinking it every night?"

"*Niet,*" he said, and she looked up.

"Just when it gets bad?"

"*Da.*"

"I see. You don't have to ration things, Ivan, I'm happy to help. You just come by and get what you need when you need it from me," she said gently.

He turned and let his dark blue eyes, so dark I'd thought they were black until the firelight hit them just right, roam, and stared at the row of pillar candles on the high windowsill, the white wax from them dripping down the walls.

Miri sighed and set to work, measuring this and taking scoops of that, adding it all to the bag and folding the top closed. She shook the contents up, added something new, and shook, repeating the process until she'd been through the whole list of ingredients. Then she busted out another bag like the first and did it all over again. She folded the tops over, once, twice, a third time, and took a single-hole punch to each bag top through the thick folds twice, looping some green twine through the holes and tying them closed neatly with a bow.

She took them around the bench to Ivan who brought out a wad of cash and looked nervously at the two bags. Miri put her hand gently over his big mitt with the wad of bills and pushed it away.

"On the house," she said gently and held the two bags out to him. He opened his mouth to protest and she raised her chin, "Ah, I can afford it, and it's not charity. You just pay me when you're in a better place, that's all."

He nodded, his jaw tightening, and he took the bags. He turned abruptly for the stairs and moved his way up them.

"Take care of yourself, Ivan," she called softly and he paused, midway up the steps and threw his hood up over his head. In a flash that should have been impossible for a dude of just his sheer size, he was gone.

"Wow," I said, and blinked at the empty space that was left in his wake.

"Yeah, all kinds find their way to Loving," she said softly.

"What is dude's deal?" I asked.

"Not sure, I didn't ask. He came to Loving a few years ago, asked for a room while the sale on his house finalized and went through. He had the money and it was the off-season. I heard him having trouble at night. He would wake up, screaming. I couldn't let him go on like that, not if I could fix it… so while he was here, I worked on perfecting a tea blend for him. Something calming with sleep aids to it. I've had to change the ratio over the years, but he finally trusts me enough to talk to me about it some. Insists on paying me for it – but I know his income is inconsistent."

"What does he do?" I asked.

"He's a blacksmith. Specializes in blades and the like."

"And the fire thing?" I asked.

"He's a witch, latent talent or ability. I don't think he's a practitioner, though. He doesn't strike me as the religious type."

"That's cool," I said, nodding and looked around us. "You got a lot of stuff down here."

"I do," she agreed, and put the things away she'd brought out to make Ivan's tea.

"What do you do with all of it?"

"I make teas for here at the bed and breakfast and for The Wick & Stone in town. Also, I make herbal remedies and teas for the townspeople that need them. Sometimes I also make soaps, lotions, and other body products."

"Sounds like you keep pretty busy," I said.

"Sometimes it's hard keeping on top of it all," she said, and not once did she stop moving around the workspace while we talked. "Between the B&B, the garden, and fulfilling orders for The Wick & Stone, it can get tough to find any 'me' time."

"Anything I can do to help?" I asked automatically, which was kind of laughable if you thought about it. I mean, it wasn't exactly my line of expertise, growing things or fixing people up with plant knowledge and a little bit of magic.

She smiled sweetly and shook her head saying, "Not for now."

I smiled back and said, "I get you. All you gotta do is tell me what to do. I take direction very well."

"Mm, by-product of your military life?" she asked.

"Some. I guess I've just always been good at it."

"I'll keep that in mind," she said, and winked.

I got up and wandered around looking at things, which was hard when all I wanted to do was make a beeline for her fine ass. I played it cool, touching this or that hanging from the ceiling while she listed off their names, her hands constantly moving as she ground something in a mortar and pestle to a fine powder. I came up behind her and it was the sweetest thing when she leaned back into me as I stepped up to her back.

"I think you need a short break from all this work," I murmured in her ear, and she chuckled lightly.

"Do you now?"

"Mm-hm," I kissed the side of her neck and she let her breath out in a rushing sigh that sounded like the breeze through the leaves and over grass, musical to the ear, and oh, so perfect.

I slid my hands around to her front, one delving below the waistband of her jeans. It was a tight fit, but I managed, even as I cupped one of her generous breasts through her clothes with the other, giving it a gentle squeeze.

"Oh, Goddess," she murmured and I knew I was on the right track. She sucked in a long breath through her teeth and her own hands went to her waistband to give me some more room.

"Don't want to distract you for too long, babe," I whispered, before taking her earlobe lightly between my teeth.

"Mm," was all she could manage, a throaty, sensual sound that made me go weak in the goddamn knees and my cock throb with anticipation.

I slid my hand around from off her breast and up her back, gripping her shoulder firmly, but gently, and pushing her over her workbench, the front of her body flat to the surface. She thrust her hips back, grinding into the front of my body with a slow roll of her pelvis and I smiled. She was picking up exactly what I was puttin' down and I helped myself to sliding her jeans and the panties beneath midway down those sexy legs of hers. I didn't think there was a single part of this woman's body that I wasn't in love with.

"Kavion," she gasped when I grasped her hips in my hands and pressed myself, still trapped in my clothes, against her.

"See how hard you make me?" I asked, dropping my voice low.

"Yes," she gasped, and writhed as much as she could with me pinning her between myself and the table.

"You want it?" I demanded.

"Yes!"

"How bad you want it?"

"Desperately," she breathed and I had to smile. *Well, in that case...*

I shoved my shorts, athletic leggings, and undershorts down enough to free myself and tease the head of my dick against her wetness. She was aroused, so much, and it just got me hotter, my blood heated, my need tying me up in knots.

"What are you waiting for?" she asked, voice strained, and I pushed against her back with the flat of my hand, pressing her to her table.

"Just stay there," I ordered, my voice strained, and taking her by the hips, I nudged my cock against her opening.

She gasped, shuddering in my grasp, thrusting her ass back towards me, pressing the rest of her body flatter against her work-bench, and I plunged myself deep into her silken wet heat. She had lips that gripped, tightening around me as she cried out and I stilled.

"You okay?"

"Yes! Don't stop!"

I laughed a little to myself at the desperation in her command and worked my way in and out of her. She was so tight and so responsive, it'd like to drive me crazy. I held onto her hips and pulled her back onto my dick even as I thrust forward, setting a punishing tempo.

Her moans were sweet, her body writhing against mine, so hot. I leaned over her and took one of her hands, pressed flat against the workbench's surface, and picked it up, dipping it below the table, and pressed her fingers into the little bud of nerve endings at the top of her pussy.

"Make yourself come for me, babe. I want you to come all over that dick."

The way she breathed, the way she writhed, and were it not for me pinning her to the bulky old table, how her legs wouldn't have held her up? It made me feel more like a man than anything – or anyone, I'd ever done.

I'd done some shit in the military, too. Jumped out of airplanes with over a hundred pounds of gear on my back, run miles with the same. Climbed the Stairway to Heaven out at Fort Benning, and that was some bullshit… None of it made me feel as manly as bringing this woman practically to her knees with pleasure did.

7

Miri...

"Kavion!" I gasped, my voice a mixture of pleading and panic. I didn't know if I was begging him to stop or begging him to get me there. This position was intense. The way he fit inside of me, how deep he went, it was almost painful but so worth it at the same time.

He practically ordered me to come, and it was just the right thing to say. So hot, so authoritative, so just what I needed to finish the slide down that razor's edge. The orgasm was powerful, cleaving me in two, and I was vaguely aware that I was practically screaming, crying out, shuddering and shaking as if electrocuted beneath the warm press of his body as he held me down to the table.

I shook beneath him, utterly spent, my passion cooling to embers as my breath sawed in and out of my chest. He lay over the top of me, making soothing sounds as I tried to remember how to speak. Of course, I would have to master that again only after I relearned how to breathe!

"You okay?" he asked, his breath hot and heavy against my

shoulder as he slid his hips back from mine, withdrawing from my body.

"Mm, yeah," I managed between breaths.

"I didn't hurt you, did I?" he asked.

"No."

"Good... good."

He cuddled me against my worktable until he was certain I could stand on my own.

"Where did that come from?" I asked.

"I don't know," he said honestly, and kissed the back of my neck. He stood slowly and I stood with him, leaning back against his chest, his arms around me. I held them to my body and closed my eyes, just breathing and drinking in this moment.

I could feel him withdraw emotionally, carefully closing himself behind his carefully-crafted walls, and that was okay.

Baby steps, I reminded myself. Things like love usually took time to build, but in an instantaneous-love scenario like this one, it was the trust that was absent, that needed to be built. I was okay with that. I understood it, probably more than anyone else would or even could without having been in my situation before.

Kavion certainly never had, and it struck me to ask...

"Does it bother you?"

He held me a little tighter but I wasn't sure if it was from my question or my somber tone.

"What?" he asked carefully.

"Making love to me knowing..."

He brought his lips to the side of my neck and buried his face in the crook between it and my shoulder and breathed me in. I closed my eyes and relished the feeling, afraid of his answer.

"Should it?" he asked softly.

"I know a lot of people who would be disturbed, or even angry..." I trailed off.

"I'm not that guy," he said. "I don't really get angry, and when I do..." It was his turn to trail off as I felt him shrug one shoulder.

"Why do you think that is?" I asked quietly and he sighed.

"Probably has something to do with the way I was raised," he said and shrugged again.

I tipped my head all the way back, resting it against his shoulder and looked up at him. He looked down at me, past his nose and looked like he was waiting for the other shoe to drop or something.

"I love you," I whispered and his face broke into a beautiful smile, made even lovelier by the concealed heartbreak in his eyes.

"Hold still," he said quietly. "I got you," and he bent at the waist and pulled my clothes back into place before he handled his own. I let him, and marveled at his gentle touch after the almost violent quickie we'd just had moments before.

None of the sex we'd had the night before last had been so… rough. Passionate, yes, but this had bordered on painful and I was a little confused by it. Not that it'd happened at all, but more that I was still trying to figure out if I liked it or not.

Which, by the way, I was leaning heavily towards *Yes, by a lot.*

"You're sure you're alright?" he asked, turning me around to face him, lightly holding me by my shoulders to do it. He massaged them through my shirt as he searched my face and I felt my lips crack into a smile.

"More than," I said. "I think you may have found a new guilty pleasure for me."

"Yeah?"

"Mm-hmm."

He smiled and bent, pulling up his pants and tucking himself away. I put my arms around his waist and pulled myself against him. He hugged me, holding me to him and swaying lightly to a music I couldn't hear, twisting slightly at his hips, rocking us soothingly.

"I don't know what came over me, what made me want to do you like that, and I'm not feeling particularly good about it, either," he said, miserably.

"Make it up to me later?" I asked.

"Yeah, how's that?"

"Take a bath with me, relax with me before bed."

He nodded slowly and said, "Sounds weird, but okay. If that's what you want."

I smiled and nodded faintly, "In the meantime, I need to get some work done down here. You know what you're going to do?"

"I honestly don't know. Seems a little late to go looking for work; I was going to hit it first thing in the morning."

I nodded, somber, and said, "Okay."

"I guess I could go read a book or something," he said and smiled a little.

"Go explore the house," I suggested. "Be careful if you decide to try and feed Shade or something. He can, and does, bite, and that beak of his packs a mighty pinch."

"I'll try to remember that," he murmured and lowered his face to mine. I let my eyes slip shut and just tried to concentrate on the feel of his mouth against mine, but I couldn't help it… my witch's intuition snaked out from the center of my being and twined around him. I let him kiss me and kissed him back, all while I took stock of some of his more severe damage.

Firstly, he appeared to harbor quite a bit of anxiety. I could tell he self-medicated with marijuana and though I didn't judge or begrudge him, I knew he would be urine-tested before being hired on for any dock work.

"I'm going to fix you some teas," I murmured against his lips.

"Oh, yeah?" he asked softly.

"Don't be mad, alright?" I said, and he went very still.

"Mad about what?"

"You can't smoke for a while; they drug test at the docks."

"Shit, I didn't think about that," he said. "Why would I be mad about that, though?"

"I thought you'd be mad about my reading you."

"Reading me?"

"Mm-hmm. I'm going to make you a tea to detox you and another to deal with the anxiety."

"Oh," he said, and sounded taken aback.

"I take it you've been self-medicating a while? In the case of anxiety, I make the recommendation of cannabis use to several of my… patients, for lack of a better word. I just understand that its use isn't always practical."

"Um, yeah, I either use that or hit the gym like crazy," he told me.

I nodded. "That explains the crazy-good physique," I murmured and put my hands on his waist, pulling myself on tip-toe. He smirked down at me and let me kiss him, for which I was grateful.

"Just do me a favor," he said against my lips.

"Anything," I whispered back, my breath warm, fanning back against my own lips with our close proximity.

"Next time you want to know something," he said gently, "all you gotta do is ask me. No need to pull any witchy-woo-woo stuff on me, 'k?"

"I didn't," I said defensively. "I don't always have control over what it shows me, sometimes I just have to go with it, but I promise to talk to you about it immediately. Just like I am now."

He nodded and puckered his lips some while he did it, finally he leaned down and gave me another kiss.

"I can live with that," he said, and I felt a flood of relief.

"Good," I said. "I'm glad."

"I'll see you when you're done down here?" he asked and I nodded. "Can I come check on you every now and again?" he asked and I had to smile.

"I'd like that," I said, and he nodded.

"Okay, cool."

He went upstairs and I turned back to my work table and the small disaster left behind by our intense quickie. I blew out my cheeks as I let out a breath and got to work cleaning it up and crafting the teas I'd promised to make him, as well as made a few other infusions I'd been meaning to get to.

By the time I was able to quit, he'd come back down and had quietly taken up the stool near the woodstove and its fire. He'd brought a book down from the library and was pretty engrossed in it while I tidied up from my work.

"What're you reading?" I asked.

"I think it's one of Jack's textbooks. It's about birds."

I went around to look and sure enough...

I nodded and said softly, "It was. I wonder how it got there."

"Dunno, I was looking through the shelves and this one fell off, I figured I was meant to pick it up, so I did. It's not bad, a little dry and boring, but it's a textbook about birds."

I smiled and laughed a little.

"Hungry?" I asked, changing the subject.

"Yeah, I could eat."

Guilt swirled in my breast as I eyed the textbook in Kavion's hands. Oaklyn, as well as being our fire and the heart of our sisterhood and little coven, had had an affinity with and for the dead, like I said. I knew a sign when I saw it, and I had to interpret it as Jackson Greene whispering to me, *don't forget about me...* Which, how could I, when my heart still ached, still bled for him?

God, I couldn't believe I'd fallen for it so easily, believed so casually that he would do something like that to me. I mean, it wasn't a blight on him when I really thought about it, but rather turned him into a casualty of how I thought of myself. That I could be so easy to leave... Of course, I had a bit of a track record in that arena.

I finished up in the workshop and followed Kavion upstairs, my hand in his and the text in his other. I stared at the cracked tome, one of Kavion's elegant fingers holding his place between the pages somewhere in the middle of the book, and felt myself blush at how unintentionally erotic the image was to me.

I needed to get my mind out of the gutter and help get him into a kind of shape that he could pass any physical tests, namely any drug tests, they might put him through. Two bags of loose leaf tea were clutched in my other hand, I had every intention of labeling a pair of jars for him and fixing him a cup of the detoxifying tea straight away.

He went to sit over at the nook in what was quickly becoming his usual seat as I moved around the kitchen.

"You know how to make a proper cup of tea?" I asked.

"Doc Miri in the house?" he asked, and I smiled.

"Yes, now come here."

He got up and wandered over and I poured one of the bags of tea into a quart Mason jar. I opened up the kitchen drawer and brought out my label printer.

"Two teaspoons in the bottom of this thing right here," I said, and jutted my chin at the gravity tea dispenser I'd set out.

He followed my instructions and I said, "You can either use the stove or the electric kettle, but get the water going," I said, and clipped the printed label off the machine, affixing it to the jar. 'Kavion's Detoxifying Blend'

"Okay," he said, and while he set about filling the electric kettle from the tap, I worked on labeling and sealing up a jar of his Calming Tea blend.

"You've gone awfully quiet," he said after several minutes of silence.

I pressed my lips together and nodded.

"Having a hard time processing everything. Feeling a bit overwhelmed and a lot guilty."

"About what?" he asked gently.

"About so easily believing of Jack that he'd ditch me via a text message." I flushed with embarrassment.

"How were you supposed to know?" he asked. "It's something I would have done when I was enlisted."

I frowned. "Really?"

He laughed a little sadly. "I guess I'm feeling a little guilty, too," he confessed.

"About what?" I asked softly.

"Not staying in touch, for one," he said. "That I didn't start asking questions sooner."

"There's nothing either of us really could have done," I said softly. "If he was killed, then it was already done."

"Good thing justice doesn't have any time limits," he said, but he sounded as down as I felt about it. Bitter, and God, was I bitter. Knowing that for the last, year plus that someone in this town - maybe even several 'someones'- knew and had likely seen what it did, and had kept quiet probably while looking me in the face as I had healed them… It made me sick just thinking about it.

"Okay, now what?" he asked when the kettle clicked off.

"Add water, let it steep no more than one to two minutes."

"Okay."

He poured the water, the bits of herbs and tea leaves floating to the top. I watched them swirl and slowly start to sink, the water turning a deep fawn color, the aromatics beginning to seep through the slight steam release of the lid.

"There's a bit of toasted dandelion root in there, so you're going to pee by like a lot. You need to stay hydrated, drink lots of water." I brought down a big, measured water bottle out of the cupboard with a twist-off lid.

"At least three of these a day," I said, expecting him to balk.

"Cool," was all he said, and he filled it at the tap.

"You're going to drink this mix twice a day," I said. "Morning, and at midday. Don't drink it before bed, or you'll be up and down peeing all night."

He laughed slightly and nodded. I picked up the tea maker and set it on the rim of a mug, the disc underneath depressing and the tea draining through the leaves and the fine wire mesh at the bottom, gravity doing its thing.

"That's a nifty gadget," he said.

I smiled and said, "A little bit of water from the tap just to loosen them up, swirl, and ditch the leaves in here." I showed him my kitchen's compost bin. "In fact, if you could put any food scraps you generate in here, it would be appreciated."

"No problem," he said.

"As for this one," I said. "Any time you start to feel anxious, make a cup of this," I said sliding the jar of calming tea at him. "At night, before bed, have a cup and add three drops of this, it's a valerian root decoction. It should help you sleep if you're having trouble." I set a stoppered brown vial next to the jar of calming tea that was already labeled. "No more than three drops, any more is apt to lay you out through the next day."

"As long as it won't lay me out forever, we're good." He smiled and winked as he said it, and I smiled back.

"That would be the nightshade," I said. "And only in high-enough doses – and it's really easy to overdose on, so don't go near it without supervision." I pointed a finger in his face and he grinned and latched onto it with his teeth gently, sucking it into his mouth.

My body went loose and I swayed slightly on my feet, getting a bit of a head-rush as butterflies took off in my stomach. I think I forgot to breathe.

He let go of my finger from his mouth and whispered in that husky, sexually charged tone of voice he got when he was turned on, "You got it."

The next thing I knew, we were in each other's arms, going at it all over again. Only this time, we managed to make it all the way upstairs to my bedroom.

8

𝒦avion...

The next few days were nice. I would let myself get lost in Miri for a time, but then something would always come up to remind me of what I was doing here in the first place. It was like my best friend's presence was all through the big house. Hints of him on this shelf, under that couch, or in that cupboard. I guessed something was up when I woke up one morning, Miri snug against my back, her arm over me, and sitting on the night stand was a squashed quarter.

When we were teens, we'd walk along the railroad tracks to get from school back to Jack's house. We'd put quarters along the tracks, just dumb kid stuff, and come back the next day to see 'em all stretched out and flattened. I'd had no idea he'd kept any of 'em. Of course, secretly, I had too. Made me think about him every time I saw one of those souvenir penny machines, you know? The ones you stuck a penny into, paid like a dollar worth of quarters, just to crank the arm and flatten the penny, pressing a design into the copper from wherever you were at.

First time I saw one, I did it. Had made a habit out of getting one from every machine I came across, even had a little vinyl album made just for 'em to put 'em all in. Just so the next time I saw Jack, I could tell him all the stupid shit I did, and where. Hell, a few times I'd woken up from some drunken bender back at the barracks and found one of those squished pennies in my pocket. Didn't even remember doing it. Was kind of nice knowing somewhat of where I'd been the night before.

Of course, there was no way I'd be able to show Jack that stupid little plastic book full of fucked-up coins. Not now, anyway.

It made my gut wrench just thinking about it. Wondering what happened to him, knowing how happy he must have been… I mean, Miri and this house. He couldn't have asked for more, living with a beautiful woman in this beautiful place. One who had her shit together like Miri. The girl was dope; the more I got to learn about her the more it killed me that the only reason I had a chance with someone like her was because of Jack, because he'd died.

"Bro, this should have been your life," I said quietly into the darkness off of Miri's front porch.

I leaned a shoulder heavily against one of the support pillars and a hip against the railing and blew on the cup of anxiety tea she'd blended for me. It was still too hot to drink, and I needed it, badly. I'd had another nightmare, had seen a few things in the military as a mechanic. Been on a few convoys and man… it was some rough shit. The dreams had been fucked up, though. Instead of the private that'd had half his face blown off by the IED we'd gone over, it was Jack I'd turned over in my arms. Add to that, instead of what the real life dude had said, which had been 'Am I gonna die', all Jack had to tell me was 'Take care of her.'

I was still fucked up about it, turning that mashed quarter over in my fingers as I waited to chug this tea and see if it really worked, let alone if it worked as well as some good-ass Kush.

"You alright?"

I jumped slightly at her voice. I hadn't even heard her come out here, but there she was, standing in her doorway in that emerald-green silk robe of hers that made her color pop like you wouldn't believe.

"Yeah," I lied, and she raised an eyebrow. Guess I should know better than to lie to an honest-to-god witch.

"What's going on?" she asked gently and came out to be with me. She gave me some space, leaning against the railing, her back against the pillar opposite mine. She hugged herself and I couldn't tell if it was because she was cold or if it was something else.

"Just had a bad dream, is all," I told her.

"Want to talk about it?" she asked softly.

I shook my head. I definitely didn't want to burden her with any of it. It was already burden enough that she'd been saddled with loving a trash person like me.

She let her light baby blues wander over me from head to toe and back again, her expression pinched and worried and finally nodded. She did this thing with me, where she asked if I wanted to talk and if the answer was 'No', she simply stood by or sat near me, not saying anything. Just occupying the same space with me in solidarity, or whatever.

"Think I'm gonna be good to start lookin' for work out there?" I asked, looking in the direction of town. We were up on the bluff and far enough back we couldn't see it from here, but I knew which way it was, could feel it out there in the night. It was just a different kind of energy to it; a buzzing, a different kind of alive than the woods out the opposite way. It was like I needed to head that direction, like there was something waiting for me, out in the dark, in the trees, overlooking the bay. Something important.

I kept it to myself, just thinking it was an overactive imagination or something.

"You should absolutely be good," she said, and I looked back her way, taking a sip of the tea blend she'd made me. I could taste a hint of lavender in there, along with some chamomile, but I didn't know what all else she had in it.

"You make it sound like I was good a while ago."

She shifted slightly and blushed, nodding. "Could have gone as soon as the day before yesterday," she murmured. "I guess I just wasn't ready to let you go quite yet."

"You scared?" I asked her, and watched grief flicker across her face, a deep well of sadness open up in her eyes.

"I don't know if I can do this twice," she said and refused to look at me. Instead, she cast those blue eyes of hers in the direction of town and I nodded.

"I know, love. I can't imagine this shit from your side of things."

She shook her head and said, "I feel like I've betrayed him twofold."

I shook my head. "You had no way of knowing."

"I should have thought better of him," she argued. I couldn't disagree with her there, I mean, it was Jack, of all people. Of course, I was missing a piece of the problem. Namely, her history before even Jack. Like, what could make a woman so skittish and mistrustful?

"I think both of us are still struggling," I said, staring down into the steaming liquid in my cup.

She sniffed, and I jerked my head back up. She was crying, silently, the tears streaming down her face. I set my cup on the railing and held out my arms. She stood a bit straighter, then her eyes closed, an expression almost like defeat crossing her features before she moved into the circle of my arms and let me hold her.

I didn't know what to make of it, but I had to agree with the sentiment, in that I knew Jack was the better man, that I was a trash person. But, Jack had led me here somehow, some way, of that I was sure. That, and he had entrusted me to take care of Miri, and I would. How could I not? I mean, I loved her with everything that I was, and it still weirded me out to admit that, but it was true.

I WENT into town the next morning. The sun was out, but it was cooler by the water. I parked a ways up from the docks and walked my way down. There was the old barrel and crate factory that was still in use, a ton of fishing boats –I didn't know the first thing about fishing, so that was pretty much out- and finally, there was a marine diesel mechanic.

I'd worked on my fair share of diesel engines, but didn't have too much experience with marine engines, which were a different animal. Still, I applied, and applied over at the barrel factory while I was at it.

I got a lot of side-eye from a lot of the dockworkers and even more from my prospective employers. I walked up out of there feelin' like a grilled cheese sandwich: toasted on the outside and gooey on the inside. I guessed keepin' up appearances and keepin' the lies straight would be a lot more effort than I had anticipated, but it'd be worth it, though.

I took a walk down the town's main street and just sort of spent time taking everything in. Miri and I decided I wouldn't hide the fact I was staying up at the Eilish House, but I wasn't making a thing out of it either unless I was directly asked. I was just a big-city boy looking to settle down somewhere small and quiet. At least it wasn't entirely off of the truth. I always liked the idea of small town livin', I just hadn't expected the small town I landed in to be so far north.

"Well, you're new, ain't 'cha?"

I turned in the direction of the voice to see a surly white boy standin' nearby. Of course, that was the second thing I noticed about him. The first was that he was wearing pigskin – as in, a cop's uniform.

"Yes, sir, I am," I said evenly. Mine and Jack's momma hadn't raised no fool, she expected me to act respectful. Especially when it came to anything in uniform. Her lessons had been reinforced in the military, and when I'd gotten out? Well, civilian life was different from when I'd gone in. Cops and black folk hadn't gotten along before but it was a whole different animal now, fueled by media outrage and shit-stirring. There was always that one cop, and when this one opened his mouth, I figured him to be it.

"Ain't gonna have any trouble from you now, are we?" he asked, hooking his thumbs in his patrol belt.

I shook my head as I said, "No, sir, not me."

"Good, good," he said, and nodded. "Name's Buchannan Daniels. Folks around town call me Bucky."

"Nice to meet you, Mr. Bucky," I said, holding out my hand and he laughed, striding forward to shake it.

"Mr. Bucky, now that's a new one, son!"

We were probably less than five years apart in age, so that made my eyebrows go up. I hid it by saying, "My momma always told me to respect the law."

"Sounds like you had a damn fine momma," he said, still chucking.

"She's alright," I said, thinking about my bio mom with the quip. I always thought of her first when someone mentioned my momma, but the truth was, Jack's momma was my momma more than the woman that'd given birth to me was, and Jack's momma was a damn fine woman. Guilt crept through me once again about not staying in touch better but was squashed by my next thought of my birth mom.

My actual momma? She kept track of me on social media. Tried to claim every one of my achievements as her own, but really it was just to hit me up for money from time to time. I wasn't any use to her for much else, and she wasn't any use to me at all as a result.

To say I had mommy issues was an understatement, but the vibe I was getting off of this guy? It wasn't like he was going to be taking Jack's place as my best friend, not any time soon; not at all.

"So, you just stickin' around post-festival?" he asked, and I nodded.

"It's a nice little town," I said.

"Yeah, we don't get too many outsiders that want to stick around."

"Well, I haven't been here real long. Figured I would find some work down at the docks and maybe stay for the summer and see if it suited me." I didn't elaborate much beyond that. Truth was, with Miri here, the mystery surrounding Jack notwithstanding this town was starting to suit me just fine.

"I see. Where you stayin' at?" he asked.

I didn't want to tell him, but there was no reason not to. I just didn't like the vibe comin' off of him. Like, *what the actual fuck, yo?* I felt like I was being straight grilled, right here on the sidewalk. Only thing missing was a pair of cuffs and being mashed up against his patrol car.

"Oh, up at the Eilish House," I answered, noting his nostrils flaring and his eyes widening some.

"Miriam Eilish is a nice girl," he said. "You wouldn't dream of giving her any trouble now, would you?"

"Wouldn't dream of it, brah," I said.

"Good to know." He tipped his hat and took a few steps towards me saying, "Welcome to Loving…" He leaned in close and said, "And I'm not your 'brah.'"

"Noted," I said coolly, and he wandered on by and up the street.

It was a weird exchange. The tension he held, the barely restrained hostility in his voice; Bucky-boy didn't take kindly to outsiders, it seemed. I had to think he really didn't take kindly to us black folk. I don't know, it just had that kind of feel and it was just one of those things. You knew, without a dude having to really say a word. It was a look, a tone of voice, the way they spoke full of derision. Usually it was because 'black', because 'other', but this might be something else. The way he tensed up, I had a feeling it had to do with Miri.

I would have to ask her tonight when I saw her.

Right now, my anxiety was acting squirrely and I couldn't smoke. I also couldn't get to the tea back at Miri's, so I did the next best thing when chemical intervention wasn't possible. I worked out. I fished a bandana out of my hoodie pocket and tied it up around my head to hold back my dreads from hitting me in the face. I started out with a brisk walk to warm up before breaking into a light trot.

I worked my way up to a solid pace, to a good sweat, my breath sawing in and out of my lungs evenly, my heart pounding in my chest, sending the blood rushing in my ears. Most of the people in this town seemed friendly enough, nodding at me with a smile, calling out a friendly 'hello', not at all what I was used to where I came from.

I slowed down and came to a stop in front of a shop with a stone façade. The shingle hanging out over the street above the door, had a candle in one of those old-fashioned holders with the loop on the back so you could carry it, a quill next to it, the copper, and stylized lettering proclaiming 'The Wick & Stone' proudly. A woman stood out front, an old-fashioned broom in her hands. It was the kind you'd expect the caricature of a witch to fly around on, peaked black hat, green skin, warts, and all.

She was dressed like Stevie Nicks, long flowing skirt and blouse with bell sleeves, a fringed shawl over her shoulders. She had the longest flowing white hair, and her blue eyes crinkled with laugh lines. Her smile was beautiful, creating deep brackets to either sides of her pale lips.

"Ah, you must be Kavion," she said, straightening.

"Yeah, how'd you know?" I asked.

"Small town," she said and tipped her head. "That, and Miri might have come to see me."

It clicked then, and I nodded slowly, trying to catch my breath. "You're her mentor," I said and the woman laughed.

"I don't teach Miri nearly as much as she teaches me," she said kindly. "Would you care to come inside for some tea?"

"Ah, nah, thank you but –"

"I think a cup of Miri's calming blend would do you wonders," she said with a knowing look.

"Yeah," I said, nodding. "Yeah, yeah, yeah; it would."

"I'm Gwen," she said kindly and put a hand out to usher me to the door. I went past her and dragged it open, standing by for her to pass through first.

"Such a gentleman," she said with a light, appreciative chuckle.

I smiled, and gave a shy nod. I mean, I tried, but I was still trash.

The inside of the shop was pretty unique. To the left, as you walked in the door, there was a long counter, one that was waist-high, with a line of leather covered pedestal bar stools, the single legs wrapped in copper accents. It reminded me of the old-fash-ioned lunch counters, or like the place might have been a soda fountain at one point. Like, some seriously old-school shit. We had an old-as-fuck pharmacy back home with the old setup. I kind of wondered how many other people my age would even know what it was without ever having seen one before.

There were a few two- and four-seat tables by the windows, but the rest of the shop, along the side and back walls, was nothing but bookshelves. There were more shelves out in the middle of the room, but they held all kinds of shit. Rocks, crystals, candles, scarves and cloths, these weird bowls and wands.

I slid into one of the seats at the counter. Gwen had gone behind it and had stood patiently, a hand out to indicate which one I should take. I sat, and she went to one of those old rolling wooden ladders on a track and pulled it along the wall of jars behind the counter. She rolled it along, climbed halfway up it, and pulled one of the squat glass canisters off the shelf.

"Miri told me the spell took you both on the night of the festi-val," she said, stepping back down.

"Ah, yeah." I nodded, and gritted my teeth. I didn't know this woman, and I was sucking it up here because Miri did. While I was keen on meeting new people, I wasn't keen on letting new people in on my business, or too close to me. That being said, I was curious, and so I'd see where this rabbit-hole went.

Gwen sighed and went over to the espresso machine taking up the end of the bar. Surprisingly, even though it was in here and they had coffee on the menu, it didn't smell like a coffee shop in here. It smelled earthy and herbal, like, well, a tea shop.

She scooped some of the herb blend that looked pretty much exactly like what I had in the Mason jar back home –I mean at Miri's place– into a teapot and used the tap on the espresso machine to fill it with steaming water. She dropped the lid on the little personal-sized teapot with an earthenware clatter and set it aside so it could steep for a couple of minutes.

"She loves you, so very much," she said, and looked as if her heart ached. She sighed and fixed me with cool, appraising blue eyes, the look unsettling, and said, "That girl has been through so much, too much, and I wanted to take your measure."

"O-kay," I drawled.

She smiled serenely and held out a hand, palm up.

"The hand you don't write with, if you please."

"You gonna read my palm?" I asked with a choked, incredulous laugh.

She arched one snowy brow and I gave my head a shake and smiled. I placed my left hand in hers, palm up and she searched my face carefully before casting her gaze to the lines on my palm.

She didn't say anything, perusing my hand like it was the morning paper. Finally she cleared her throat and let it go, reaching for a mug behind the counter and filling it with hot water. She swirled it around, poured it into the little stainless steel sink and set it in front of me. She didn't look happy, and my suspicions were raised, red flags going up in the back of my mind, a creeping sensation trailing down the back of my neck and spreading across my shoulders and down my back, causing me to itch.

"So, what did you see?" I asked as she filled the cup from the little tea pot, the fragrant aroma of lavender and lemon peel rising with the steam.

She pushed the mug across the counter on one of those cardboard coasters and said with a smile and a wink, "Oh, that part will cost you."

I laughed and shook my head, "I admire your hustle."

"Why thank you. Honestly, though, palm readings are typically twenty dollars."

"Fresh out of cash," I said, and blew on my tea.

She chuckled and said, "Well, at least the tea is on the house," before she winked one more time and went to wander away.

"I'll take that as you're satisfied with whatever you saw," I said dryly, and she looked back over her shoulder.

The look she gave me was cold as winter's ice when she said, "Very."

Shit.

I bit my lips together to keep from smiling and failed miserably at it. I tended to smile and laugh at inappropriate times and this was one of them. I lucked out that it seemed to serve me well in that Gwen smiled back, a tight-lipped little smile before going back out front to sweep.

This kind of sucked, though. I didn't really have anyone to talk to about this shit except for Miri, but I didn't want to hurt her more than she'd already been hurt. I'd done a lot of shit outside my comfort zone since getting here and this wasn't any different, so I nutted up and said, "I love her too, more than I've loved anything in my life. I mean, I didn't think I was even capable of this kind of feeling, you know?"

I wasn't trying to placate her mentor, but rather warn her.

She paused and drifted back over, leaning heavily on the counter in front of me.

"You have every right to feel everything that you feel right now," she said, meeting my eyes and I felt my own widen. "Angry, sad, frightened... hopeful, peaceful, and home. Every right," she repeated, and straightened. "There is no one here that would tell you otherwise. Not me, not Miri, and certainly not your dead friend." She arched an eyebrow and I knew dead to rights, she both knew something about it and was threatening me.

Fuck.

"My friend?" I asked quietly, not realizing I was holding my breath, hoping to get more.

"I believe his name was Jackson. Miri tended to call him Jack."

"Yeah, he wasn't my friend, though. He was my brother. Family."

Her face looked solemn, almost sad, and she shook her head.

"I'm sorry to hear that," she said. "I can feel things, though, and when his name is mentioned, or he's thought of, I get a sense of gratitude."

"Gratitude?"

She nodded.

"That you're here; that Miri isn't alone; that he will not be forgotten…"

I shook my head and took a big swallow of the almost-too-hot tea, choking it down and wishing it would do whatever it was meant to do because this was too fucking much for me.

"I ain't ever going to forget Jack," I said. I didn't need to add that I was gonna find out exactly what happened to him.

"As it should be," she said softly. She hesitated and said, "You need to let go of that guilt." She waved her hand over me, and it was like she gathered something out of thin air and tossed it aside. I frowned slightly, and she repeated the motion, and with every swipe of her arm I felt a little less wound-up. A little more together.

"I'm not sure I can, or that I ever will," and saying that, I tried to hold on to whatever she was trying to dispel. Something about this chick just wasn't sitting right.

"It's only serving to cloud your purpose here," she said.

"Which is?"

"To find Jack's killer. To set things right, and to love and protect Miri as she loves and protects you." She paused. "My suggestion is to focus on the latter."

"You two are good friends, yeah?" I asked.

"Indeed, we are," she said. "Miri is very important to me." Her look was way too pointed for me to be comfortable with.

"Thanks for the tea," I said softly, and she smiled.

"Of course."

Her hands stilled and she folded them, one on top of the other, atop the smooth, polished, and softly gleaming heartwood of the bar top.

"You should finish it before you leave," she chastised when I went to get up.

"No, thank you, Ma'am. Miri's gotta be expecting me by now."

"Ah, I see," she said and I gave a nod.

Between this bitch and Bucky, something fucked-up was going on in this town and I was seriously wondering how Jack had got wrapped up in it.

I also had to wonder how Miri could be blind to it.

9

Miri...

I was welcoming a new guest when Kavion came up the walk. I smiled and nodded politely and said, "Welcome back, Mr. Martin."

He nodded back and said, "Thank you, Ms. Eilish."

He was sweat-soaked and looked worn-down, and so I asked, "Did you enjoy your run?"

"I did, thanks," he said, and with a polite nod at the gentleman checking in, slipped past us and took the stairs two at a time.

I turned back to Mr. Hall and smiled. "Breakfast is between seven and nine in the morning; we don't provide lunch or dinner. If you want, there's a list of nearby restaurants and bistros in town. Some do deliver. I have you in the Thistle room, per your online booking. It's on the second floor, just off the top of the stairs. Shall I show you up?"

"That would be lovely, thank you," he said with a smile. He hefted his bag and I unlocked the cupboard under the stairs. I retrieved the key to the Thistle room from its hook and re-secured the cupboard's door.

I gave a slight jerk of my head and said, "Right this way."

Mr. Hall was a gentleman older than me, probably in his late forties, maybe in his early fifties. He'd driven up in a Mercedes SUV and had stepped out in a perfectly-tailored suit. His beard was close-trimmed, and he didn't have a hair out of place when it came to his boardroom haircut. He was handsome, quite dashing, but my heart one-hundred-percent belonged to Kavion so his looks, while nice, didn't affect me much.

I unlocked the door to Mr. Hall's room and stood aside so that he could enter.

"It has its own private bath?" he asked.

"It does. It's only one of a few rooms in the house that does. The bath is just through that door." I pointed to indicate.

"Ah, thank you."

"It's no problem. If you should need anything, just call or text this number." I handed him a plain white card with my cell phone number on it.

"Thank you, again."

"Of course." I handed him his key and stepped out of the doorway into the hall. He smiled, and with a respectful nod, closed himself away, and it was a real effort not to breathe a sigh of relief.

I quietly went up the stairs to the third floor and trailed down the hall to my room. When I let myself inside, Kavion, who was a bit of a fitness fiend, was just coming up from a sit-up. He stopped and eyed me as I shut my bedroom door and leaned heavily back on it.

"Anything, today?" I asked.

He shook his head and I sighed.

"It's only been a week, babe."

"I know, I know… got any big plans for your first weekend?"

He smiled and said, "I thought I'd get to know you more."

"While I would love nothing more than an entire weekend in bed, I had a thought," I said, chewing my bottom lip.

"What's that?" he asked.

"Jack took me out with him on one of his bird-watching trips, once," I said.

"And?"

"And I remember where, because there was a copious amount of this fungus I use in one of my remedies. I can't always grow everything myself. That which I cannot grow, I tend to forage."

"You want to go out that way and see if anything sticks out?" he asked.

"Does that sound stupid?" I asked, and then shook my head saying, "That sounds stupid." I put a hand to my forehead which suddenly felt hot, likely from my embarrassment. Kavion pushed himself up from the carpet and came to me.

"It doesn't sound stupid," he said pulling me into his arms. I looked up at him and he smiled down at me.

"Let's go get your magic mushrooms and see what comes up," he suggested and smiled kindly.

I nodded and let him pull me against him, even though he was all sweaty.

"Okay," I murmured.

"Ran into your friend in town today," he said, cautiously.

"Oh?" I asked, immediately thinking of Gwen.

"A couple of them, actually."

I frowned slightly and racked my brain, I didn't have many people I considered 'friends', Gwen being at the top of the list.

"All I can think of is Gwen," I said.

"Yeah, well, I was being sorta sarcastic. I ran into Bucky Daniels first."

The look must have shown on my face because he laughed.

"Yeah, dude is kind of a douche," he agreed.

"No 'kind of' about it. He is a douche, a grade 'A' bag of dicks."

Kavion laughed and pulled me tight against him. He kissed the top of my head and asked, "Wanna come take a shower with me?"

"Mm, I do," I said back.

He smoothed his hands up and down my arms and we just

stood there for what felt like a lifetime and just soaked each other in.

"Who else did you run into?" I asked.

"Gwen, outside her shop," he said, carefully.

I frowned and looked up at him.

"Why you say it like that?" I asked.

"No reason, just ran into her right after Bucky."

"Ah," I said nodding. "Any interaction with him is enough to color any after that," I mused and he captured the ball of his tongue ring, sticking it out from between his pressed lips and simply made a non-committal "Mm-hm."

"Okay, come on," he said gently, after a silence bordering on troubling stretched between us.

"You just want to see me naked," I teased.

"For sure, for sure," he said, turning me around and giving me a light smack on my ass.

"I have to bring my phone," I said.

"What for?"

"In case a guest needs something. They're supposed to call or text."

"Oh, smart," he said. "Also, a pain in my ass."

I giggled and put my robe over my arm and pulled down some towels from the top of my wardrobe. He picked up a bundle of his clothes and his shower cap. It still took some getting used to that he wore one, but he had a valid reason behind it. He said if he didn't, and his dreads got wet, they could start to smell bad. He had some sort of vinegar rinse he used in them from time to time to keep them clean, but as a general rule, didn't wash them as often as I washed my hair, which was every day to every other day or so.

I hadn't ever really thought too much about different grooming habits between different people, so Kavion's routine had been a little eye-opening, to say the least.

I still couldn't help but to stifle a giggle when he put on his shower cap. The only other person I had ever seen use one had been my grandmother.

"You ever gonna let that go?" he asked, giving me a sly, teasing side-eye.

"No," I said simply as he turned on the water and stepped into the old claw foot, whisking the shower curtain around on its oval ring above the tub.

It took me a little bit more to wriggle out of my clothes considering I had an extra layer or two on, but pretty soon, I was stepping in behind him. He turned me into the hot water coming from the showerhead and pressed tightly against me to keep me warm, which I appreciated beyond measure. I hated being cold.

The days may have been getting longer, the sun hanging around in the sky, but the temperatures were still hovering around the high fifties, low sixties. It was really only comfortable in the greenhouse, or in the house. Though, it was getting to be a good time to forage for some of the herbs and fungus that I needed, being that the weather was wet, creating ideal growing conditions.

There were some things that only Mother Nature could provide out in the wild that I couldn't adapt to greenhouse life, and I was alright with that. I loved being outdoors and in touch with the earth that nurtured us and allowed us to thrive.

It was part of the reason, I think, that made Jack and I such a good match for the spell in the first place. He had wanted so dearly to become a custodian of the earth, to protect her and love her, through the sciences used to better understand her. We balanced each other that way, had talked for hours and hours about his discoveries, his intentions to learn all he could about her finer ecosystems, to better understand them, to protect them, and to help her thrive.

I missed him with a terrible ache in the center of my being, one that made me feel terrible for Kavion, because though I loved him with all my heart and he was a very real second chance at happiness in Jack's absence, he would never take my Jack's place.

Kavion smoothed those long-fingered hands, slick with soap, over my skin, his touch gentle and sweet, bordering on the sensual simply because bathing with one another was such an intimate act, and it did wonders for keeping my mood elevated, preventing me from falling completely apart yet again.

He was so much stronger than I was, emotionally. Yet he was bold, unafraid of showing his sensitive side, at least with me. It was a cold comfort, but a comfort none-the-less, that I knew he ached as fiercely as I did over the loss of Jack. They had been friends for so long. Jack had been there for Kavion in ways that were difficult for me, with this sheltered life of privilege I had led, to understand.

"You're like a million miles away," he said gently, shaking me out of my thoughts.

"Sorry," I murmured, reaching for him, putting my hands over his lean hips, taking shelter against his much-taller, lean, muscular frame.

He let his hands go around my back and cradled me against his chest and asked, "Thinking about Jack?"

"And you," I confessed. "I feel like I am somehow being selfish, hurting over him like I do, when you-"

"Stop," he said with gentle correction. "We're both hurting, we both miss him. I was just thinking today, that even though I'm here for it, I can't imagine what you're going through."

"Me?" I asked, surprised.

"Yes, you. I mean, you loved my best friend, and here I blow into town and now you love me... How confusing it's all gotta be. How awkward it's gotta feel, you know."

"Sleeping with the both of you?" I asked, startled.

"Yeah."

"Does it bother you?" I asked.

"I mean, yeah, but naw..." he said, and I could tell he was afraid. Afraid of hurting me even more.

I gave him a little shake with my hands and said, "Talk to me."

He searched my face. Steam rising around us, the shower

making things sultry, our closeness inviting and still, I watched him struggle to trust, to make a decision. It hurt, vaguely, but I forced myself to understand that whatever his hold-up was, it wasn't me. It was likely a by-product of life experiences beyond me, damage sustained before I was even thought of. It made the bitter pill just slightly easier to swallow, and I was grateful in part to my witch's intuition for making it so.

He remained silent, but I could tell he so badly wanted to unburden himself. I finally cupped his face in my warm, wet palm and asked softly, "Who hurt you?"

It was the wrong thing to say.

Kavion's gaze immediately shuttered, his face closing down as he leaned, bodily, slightly back from me. Yet further proof that love and trust were two very different things and not mutually inclusive to one another.

I looked away and his rigid posture eased. He changed the subject by asking, "Who's the new guy in the house?"

"Guest, not guy," I said, and he gave me his smart-assed grin.

"Man, he's both."

"Okay, true, but let's try to stick with 'guest' and not slip up in front of said guest and be rude, okay?"

"Deal."

I tipped my head back and finished wetting my hair, saying, "I don't know anything beyond his name, the fact he drives an expensive car, and that he paid with a very high-end credit card. I just hope he isn't another land developer."

"Developer?"

"Yeah, they come around a bunch, looking to cash in on building the town up because of the magic, but part of the reason the magic has endured is the fact that we haven't let the town grow much. Letting the big box chains move in would ruin Loving's charm."

"It ruins every place eventually," he said, and I smiled.

"I can tell I'm preaching to the choir."

"For sho," he said and emptied the last of my shampoo bottle into his hand. I laughed a little and was glad the mood was lightening, but frustrated that I'd lost out on yet another chance to have a deeper, more meaningful conversation about who he was and where he came from.

There will be other chances... my mind whispered, but something else, be it a sixth sense or some sort of intuition, told me that there should be a little more urgency involved. I didn't know if it was really something I should heed or if it was just my own insecurities rising out of the ravaged ruin, the Jackson-sized hole left in my heart from his disappearance and passing.

I had to guess only time would tell, but I really wasn't looking forward to that. Something just felt -dangerous- yet I wasn't comfortable talking about it with Kavion. Not yet, not after my own history of just generally being disbelieved and blown off.

We each had our secrets, our hidden pasts and our hidden pain, our trust issues. I just prayed that we could both get past them, if not for ourselves, then for Jack, so we could figure out what had happened to him. I just hoped we could find a way to trust each other, because we certainly couldn't trust anyone else.

10

*K*avion...

"You okay?" she asked me.

"Yeah, yeah, yeah! I'm alright," I said, eyeing the steep bank and the thin trail cut into it, leading up into the woods.

"I'm really okay to go by myself," she said. "I do it all the time."

I shook my head. "I won't let you do that," I said. "Not without knowing what happened to Jack, and it's not that I'm scared or anything, just brings back some memories."

"Oh?" she asked carefully, her voice level, too controlled.

I instantly felt kind of bad about that, that I was so closed-off she felt like she couldn't talk to me. These memories weren't out-of-bounds, though, so I just kept it one hundred.

"Yeah, pitch of the trail reminds me of some of the hills and marches I went through during basic, just less paved, you know?"

"Oh," she said, and sounded relieved.

"What you do in there?" I asked.

She smiled and said, "Look for things I can't grow that I need for some of my poultices and teas. Just enjoy the trees, and watch for birds."

"I still don't know what Jack was doing all the way up here…" he said.

"He was doing his thesis on a specific kind of endangered woodpecker for one of his finals. Decided, after hearing about it, he needed to go on a bit of an adventure, get out of Louisiana. Said the humidity was awful, and he always wanted a break."

"Yeah, he couldn't stand a lot of the people back home," I agreed.

"He, um, called them ignorant," she said with a blush, refusing to look at me. "Said he was sick of them voting against their own self-interests and that coming this far north felt like he was finally reaching some civilization."

"Sounds like Jack," I agreed. "He was way too… I hate to say 'smart', because that isn't it; his ideas were just always like, the exact opposite of almost everyone around him."

"I think the word you're looking for is 'progressive,'" she said. "And he said that you just got him, in that regard." She was looking over at me and I paused. Her blue eyes were wide and clear as she stared into mine and I nodded.

"We just kind of clicked from the minute we met," I said. "Did all kinds of sports together, chased females… had a lot of the same interests." I laughed a little to myself. "Both of us couldn't wait to get out of that town. Just, when the time came, and we graduated, he had the backing of his parents to go to any college he wanted to. I didn't really have any of that, so my only option was the military, which I took gladly."

"He said you could have gotten a scholarship," she whispered, her eyes trained back out the car's window, and I nodded some.

"I was up for one, but it just didn't work out that way. Plus, I was kind of sick of school. Wanted to see other parts of the world… so I was happy to go military."

She turned her eyes back on me and I could see in them that she knew, that Jack had told her. I nodded and went outside of my comfort zone and didn't deny it. I just came out with it.

"The accusation of rape pretty much shot my chances of that scholarship to shit," I said.

"Jack said you didn't do anything," she said.

We'd discovered Jack had talked about me a lot, just that he'd always just called me his 'brother' and had never mentioned my name. It explained why she hadn't known me when I first showed up and why the fact Jack and I were related had been such a surprise. It did something to me, knowing that she hadn't even thought I'd been adopted. That she thought Jack's brother had been biological. It said something about Jack, too, and made the guilt twist and squeeze down harder. Made me commit even harder to finding out what happened, where his body was, bring him home to our mom. I refocused on the conversation at hand.

"I didn't," I said. "It was the quarterback's girlfriend, a cheerleader. He wanted the scholarship, but he wasn't as good a player as me so he put her up to it. It was pretty much a race thing, but I ain't bitter," I said.

"Bullshit," she called my ass out, and I laughed. "You have every right to be pissed-off, bitter, and angry as hell, and I believe you're all of those things," she said. "What you aren't is the type to dwell on them."

I nodded and had to smile. Her words felt good. Like, really good. Validating. I cracked a grin and tried to cover how I was really feeling like I always did with some humor. "That your witchy voodoo stuff tellin' you that?"

"One," she said dryly, "Witchcraft and Voudou are two very different religions."

"Vau-what?"

"You're from Louisiana, what you call 'voodoo' is probably really Vodou, which is a Haitian voudou. It's found more commonly throughout the south in states like Florida and Louisiana."

"How do you know that?" I asked.

"I took some comparative religion classes in college," she said with a bit of a sniff, opening up the passenger door on my car. She turned back to me and asked, "We ready?"

I nodded and said, "Let's do it," while I mulled that little slice of information over. I wondered what exactly she'd gone to college for as I hit the button on my key fob to lock up my car and trailed her across the leaf-strewn turnout to the trailhead.

She was serious about this hiking stuff, had the boots, backpack, and even a hiking stick that she said she'd cut from one of her honeysuckle vines and had finished by some craftsman in town. The thing was lighter than air, twisted beautifully, but sturdy. Like her. Beautiful, a little twisted up, and a lot stronger than she looked.

"What'd you go to college for?" I finally broke down and asked, seizing the opportunity to learn more about her. Seemed like as good a place as any to start.

"Business, with a focus in the hospitality industry," she answered. "In a small town like this, there isn't a whole lot of work to go around. My grandmother had always run it as a B&B the entire time I was growing up. I always envisioned taking over the business, so I decided to take classes that would help me to that end and just took a few extra in things I wanted to learn for the fun of it."

"Oh, so Eilish House is a family business, huh?"

She nodded and turned back to look at me as I strode over some tricky terrain. "My family is descended from some of the original townsfolk and one of the coven that put Jenny to rest and abolished the darkness in Cooper's Port," she said.

"Wow. So, like, you're legit," I said, and she nodded but didn't look happy about it.

I wondered what that was about, but we were working hard on getting up the hillside and to the top, where the trail leveled off. Momentarily losing our breath kind of killed the conversation.

We hit a spot where the trail leveled off and where there was a bunch of heavy rocks and boulders jutting out of the ground and we stopped to catch our breath. She slid her backpack off her shoulders and fished in it, handing over a bottle of water. I took a swish in my mouth, and held it without swallowing for a bit to quench my thirst.

She took back the bottle after sipping from hers, and I swallowed, looking up into the soaring trees.

"This is old growth," she said. "There's a particularly useful shelf fungus that grows here."

"What you be feeding that to people for?" I asked and made a face.

She laughed.

"I don't. It makes a good binding agent when dried and ground into a powder to use topically. Stops bleeding, fast."

"You get a lot of trauma patients?" I asked, grinning.

"No, but it's either me or Doctor Hollings, and if he's out fishing, sometimes the townsfolk are shit out of luck for things like stitches when it comes to kitchen accidents. Most of the time, though? It's a fish hook through a finger or the meat of someone's hand."

I tried not to gag at the thought, just something about the thought of someone showing up with a nasty-ass fish hook – ugh. It made me wanna shudder just thinking about it. She laughed at the expression on my face and we set off again, the trail flattening out and the going much easier from here.

"He wanted to be a game warden," she said and I nodded.

"He did, and he wanted to do it up here. Fell in love with the climate, et cetera," I said. I had to smile to myself, but before I could say, *'But naw, what really happened was he fell in love with YOU,'* she started speaking.

"I always took this place, this town, for granted, but it was like seeing it all brand-new through his eyes." She looked torn up, and I didn't really know how to comfort her, except to just keep my mouth shut and listen. I mean, she already knew I felt the same.

"Jack loved to hunt," I said, and hitched a laugh. "But more often than not, he'd get the damn deer in his sights and he'd be all ready to shoot, and before you knew it, his bow was getting lowered and he would just stare, you know? Like, he just liked to hunt for the sake of hunting, but if his family didn't need the meat, he wouldn't do it."

"I didn't know that about him," she said softly.

"Man, I hated going hunting with him. I mean, I was always like, what's the point if you ain't gonna shoot it? But I never did, either. I would get caught up watching him watch whatever he was looking at because it was more entertaining than anything. Watching him watch whatever fuckin' deer he was looking at like he was brand new or something."

"He would have made a good game warden," she said softly and I looked at her, and she was looking up into the leaves of the trees just like Jack would look at the turkey, or rabbit, or deer we was out after and the look in her eyes was the exact same. It was no wonder the town curse, magic, or whatever, put them together and it made me wonder – not for the first time – *What the hell was it thinking sticking her with the likes of me, after putting her with someone as pure as Jack?*

Of course, as soon as I thought it, as soon as I was even remotely down on myself, she reached out and took my hand. It was like she knew without knowing and it was always a little bit eerie, but like, not in a bad way. It was almost comforting, really.

I let my fingers slide between hers and gave her hand a squeeze. She smiled at me, and damn but my heart hitched in my chest every time she did it. Every. Time. Without fail. Even after living with her, sleeping in her bed every night, holding her close, being inside her, nothing about her didn't seem overwhelming or brand-new yet, and I was beginning to wonder if it ever would.

She froze in her step and I nearly crashed into her back. She ducked slightly and pointed, whispering excitedly, "Oh, look! There it is!"

"What?" I asked, slightly alarmed.

"The seaside blue-capped woodpecker! The bird Jack was studying."

I squinted and scanned the trees, and only caught sight of it because of a flash of sky blue. I stopped moving and studied the bird, which honestly didn't look like much. I mean, it was a woodpecker, alright. A deep brown body with a few lighter highlights made it blend nearly seamlessly with the bark of the tree it clung to. It had a light-blue cap on its head, a white underbelly, and when it flapped its wings, a matching blue stripe to its cap among its under feathers.

"Little bro knows how to accessorize," I said, and Miri had to stuff her hand against her mouth to keep from laughing so hard she startled it.

I grinned, and we watched the bird until it decided to haul ass out into the wood where we couldn't see it anymore.

Miri let out a heavy sigh and I couldn't tell if it was satisfaction or what. She looked up at me and I smiled down at her and she took further steps along the trail. I followed and did what she asked, which was keep an eye out for anything that could have been Jack's.

I mean, it was a long shot, but what did we have to lose?

11

*M*iri...

We were almost to the cliffs, north of town. The overlook was something special, a hell of a hike, but a beautiful view. Water as far as the eye could see, sunrise something special to behold, if you didn't mind making the crazy hike in the dark, which was super-dangerous for the inexperienced outdoorsman. It could sometimes be entirely too easy to lose sight of the trail and be legitimately lost out here.

Jack and I were experienced, but even so, we had come out here one summer during the day and had camped on the bluff. We had made love under the stars. We had greeted the dawn and made love all over again before we'd gone back down the trail and had made the drive home.

It was a strange sort of painful, emerging from the trees to that spectacular view without Jack being the one to hold my hand. I looked up at Kavion, who was almost a polar opposite to my Jack, and felt love, but also a deep aching void, the ragged edges of my heart where Jack had been still burning like cold fire in my breast.

"I didn't want to leave you, you know. Either of you."

"What the hell?" Kavion said, and I turned but there was no one there. Nothing. Just the light spring wind and the swaying branches of trees, the crash of ocean waves against the rocks below.

"Did you just hear…?" I asked, knowing full well he had.

"Yeah, that was Jack."

"Look around," I said.

We split up and started searching the overlook, one side to the other, moving dried leaves, scrapping our feet back and forth in a sweep, looking around trees for something, anything, that was his… that was Jack's.

"Anything?" Kavion asked after a while.

"You know I would have said something if there was," I snapped back and immediately regretted it. I stopped and put my hands to my face and let out a stressed-out moan.

"I'm sorry," I said. "I shouldn't have said that, or said it that way."

"It's okay," he said and came over to me. He put his arms around me and I cuddled in against his chest.

"I think he's here," I said, distressed. "I think he's stuck."

"I know he's here. I mean, I have to figure it wasn't an accident I ended up at your door."

"You think he put us together to find out what happened to him?"

"Most def," he said, "and if I know Jack, and I do know Jack, he did it so we wouldn't have to hurt alone."

"I hurt," I said, breaking down. "I hurt so damn much, and I know you hurt, and I'm trying to be strong, and I'm trying to be brave, but it hurts and I miss him, and I feel like I'm dying from the guilt!" I let it go, in this, mine and Jack's favorite place. I couldn't stop it, the floodgates opened and I let it go and just sobbed into Kavion's chest, both of us slipping to the leaf litter, holding each other tight while I wept.

"It's okay, love. I've got you," he whispered. "I've got you now."

I don't know how long we were like that. How long I held to him and let him be my rock as I let the storm of grief blow over and through me. He cradled me against his chest, a hand against my neck and cheek, pressing me to him like I was something precious, his thumb playing back and forth against my temple and the ridge of my cheekbone.

"You good?" he asked when I'd been quiet save for the odd sniffle now and again.

"I'm good," I said, but my voice sounded hollow, almost soulless, and I felt the same. I looked up into Kavion's eyes and though they mostly held hidden depths, I could see the echo of my feelings in his eyes. Both of us hurt so much. For Jack, for ourselves... *Damn it.*

"We should probably go back down, right?" he asked and I nodded.

"It'll be dusk by the time we finish doubling back down the trail, it's not a loop."

"Okay, come on, then."

He helped me to my feet, we took one last look around, and I despaired a little inside that we'd found not one trace of Jack. I was hoping for *something* for Blyn to touch, to read. *If she would even take my call...*

We made our way back down the trail, stopping here and there for me to gather something I missed on the way up. By the time we reached the bottom and the lot his car was in, it was deepest dusk, full dark creeping out from the tree line. In town, it would be sweeping out from the alleyways and the shadows between the buildings. Dusk didn't fall from the sky like we were taught to believe. It rose from the earth, instead.

I heaved a sigh. It would seem my thoughts were going dark right along with my emotions and the coming night. We slid down the steep start to the trail, spilling down onto the pine-needle-strewn blacktop, and to Bucky Daniels looking up from his notepad.

"Miri," he called. "You alright?"

"Of course, I'm alright! Why wouldn't I be?" I responded and just barely kept the acid off my tongue. Unfortunately, Bucky Daniels and I went way back. He'd carried a torch for me all through high school and I'd had as little interest in him then as I did now. That, however, didn't keep Bucky from trying.

"Mr. Martin," he called out in his authoritative-prick voice. "We meet again."

"'Sup?" Kavion asked, his tone guarded.

"What's up is you have an outstanding traffic warrant for failure to appear in Tennessee."

"What?" Kavion asked, caught off-guard.

"There's a warrant out for your arrest," Bucky stated caustically, as if Kavion were stupid rather than surprised.

I blinked and looked from Bucky to Kavion. His dark eyes closed and his shoulders dropped and he said, "Damn, I forgot all about that speeding ticket, I got it on the way up here, like a day or two after I left."

"Going to have to take you in," Bucky said, pulling out his handcuffs.

"Whoa, now!" I said, putting a hand out.

"Sorry, Miri," he said with a shit-eating grin. "Have to do my job, now."

I scowled at him and he stepped forward. I balled up my fists and stepped in front of Kavion, who put his hands gently to my shoulders and moved me aside.

"I ain't got no beef with you, man. I'll go, Miri can drive my car back to her place."

"Afraid not, gonna have to tow it," Bucky said.

"Come on, man, you obviously don't like me, but leave her out of it. Let her drive herself home." Kavion pulled his keys out of his pocket and pressed them into the palm of my hand.

"You are such an asshole, Bucky Daniels," I spat under my breath when he finally nodded and let Kavion hand over his keys.

"Don't take that tone with me, little girl," he said and I fought not to roll my eyes. "Turn around and put your hands behind your back," he ordered Kavion, who complied, just not fast enough for Bucky's taste.

He shoved Kavion around and up against the man's own car and I yelled, "Hey!"

"Stay out of this," Bucky warned, and I scowled and opened my mouth to speak but Kavion caught my eye, his own expression something almost cocky, yet with an undercurrent of warning. I held my tongue.

"When can I come get him?" I demanded.

"I'll let you know," Bucky called back to me, sarcastic flippancy in his tone, as he hauled Kavion by his hoodie toward the back of the patrol car.

"It'll be fine," Kavion called. "I'll make you my phone call, just stay by your phone!"

"Shut up, boy! I say what happens in my lockup," Bucky snapped.

I needed to get home, I needed to get online and look things up and figure out how to get him out- I needed to –

Bucky had gone around to the driver's side of his patrol car and gave me the wickedest grin over the roof, the red and blue strobing of his light bar turning it positively horrifying.

"I'll see you around, Miri," he called and I glared at him.

I immediately went around to the driver's side of Kavion's car and got in. It took me a while to figure out how to move his seat up so I could drive it and to adjust the mirrors, but soon I was rocketing towards home.

I couldn't even enjoy driving the muscle car, I was too frightened of what Bucky would say, what he would do to Kavion when he got him alone.

I pulled up at home, and went for the back steps, abandoning my backpack of wild finds on the kitchen counter. I took the stairs two at a time, all the way up to my room and the small desk with its MacBook waiting for me.

I searched the internet for the numbers and websites I would need, and finally broke down and called Mack at home.

"Hello?" he answered on the fourth ring, sounding absolutely miserable.

I winced and said, "Mack, I'm so sorry, it's Miri."

"Miri? What's the matter?"

"Bucky's gone and done something stupid again."

I told Mack what had happened and listened as he sucked in a breath. I practically heard his eyes rolling over the phone when he said, "Oh, God!"

He sighed and said, "Miri, it's gonna be fine. He's gonna end up locked up for tonight; Bucky's gotta reach out to Tennessee and ask if they want extradition, at which point Tennessee is gonna ask if Bucky's done lost his fuckin' mind. Best thing you can do is track down the ticket and pay it off if it's possible. It'll give Tennessee just one more reason to be like 'Fuck it, cut 'im loose.'"

"Thanks, Mack," I said, and let out a breath I hadn't even realized I'd been holding.

"No problem, Miri. That tea is helping loads, so thanks a million."

"Consider us more than even," I said and sighed.

"Not even close," he said.

"Get some rest," I ordered.

"Yes, Ma'am."

We ended our call and I slumped in my chair for a moment before pulling myself together. I was hoping that this ticket of his was in the glove box, and that Bucky wasn't being more of an asshole to Kavion than he usually was.

It was a slim hope.

12

*K*avion...

"I told you to get out of my town, didn't I?" he demanded, a smug look on what I could see of his face in the rearview mirror.

"Actually, nah. You said welcome to Loving and told me not to cause any trouble," I said.

"Yet here you are, in the back of my patrol car..."

"Not causing you trouble, though," I pointed out. I couldn't resist.

"Now if you weren't causing me trouble, why are you still here, boy?" he asked. I fought not to school his racist ass by pointing out that he'd caused all his own trouble by running my plates for no reason. I mean, I wasn't parked illegally, and I'm pretty sure there's nothing suspicious about a car parked at a trailhead with no occupants.

No, this had everything to do with the fact that I'd come out of those trees with Miri, who this clown seemed to have some kind of a hard-on for.

Too bad, so sad, brah. She picked me, I thought to myself, but kept my face neutral.

I was looking forward to Tennessee telling this nigga to get over himself when he called them up to see if they wanted me. He was just creating a whole lot of work for himself. He would have been better off just towing my car and leaving me to walk back to Miri's place, although I was pretty sure she'd have told him to get fucked and would have walked with me.

I went through the motions, let him lock me up, sat and waited. Sure enough, after letting me stew for a bunch of hours, they came back to let my black ass go.

"You're in luck," one of the cops said, coming back to unlock my cell, "Tennessee took a hard pass, just pay your fines and all is right with your world again."

"I kind of figured," I said.

"Friendly piece of advice," the officer said, low, and I nodded. "Stay off of Bucky Daniels' radar. Last guy who was on it disappeared."

I frowned and jerked my head back, and was just about to ask what the fuck that was supposed to mean when the man himself showed up in the doorway just the cock-of-the-walk, chest puffed out and tryin' to make himself look important.

"You're free to go, Mr. Martin."

"Thanks," I said, and kept the sarcasm to a minimum. "I'll see you fellas around."

"Will you now?" Bucky demanded.

"I'm expecting I got work on Monday morning," I said, grateful they didn't keep me in here the whole weekend.

"I expect you'll be putting in your two weeks' notice any day now," Bucky said.

As I passed him I didn't even look at him; my eyes were on the front of the police station and on Miri, who'd just come through the door.

"Nope," I said. "I kinda like it here, on a kind of its so welcoming and all. I think I'll stay."

I watched his face contort in rage and fought not to laugh. I'd poked the bear enough and was still playing his little underling's words back in my head. Miri practically wilted with relief when I pushed through the waist-high double swinging doors to go out to her.

"You okay?" she asked, her voice strained with stress and hopefulness.

"I'm good," I said, and she nodded.

I signed for my personal shit at the front desk and followed her out to the street.

"You sure you're okay?" she asked furtively, leading me up the block and unlocking the passenger door on her little white sedan.

"Just take me back to your place, let me get a shower, and I'll be all good," I said.

She nodded, but didn't look like she quite believed me. I got in the car and she handed me a travel mug.

"Figured you might need this," she said and I smiled and took a drink for her. The calming tea was still hot, but drinkable. I didn't think it was gonna work this time, though. I was already calm. That scary type of calm you get when you're so pissed-off you pull yourself up by the bootstraps and get down to business – get shit done. Past the point of being irrational, and right into the realm of cold calculation. Yeah, I was a cold piece, and I was gonna figure some shit out. I just needed to do it where I didn't hurt Miri any more than she'd already been.

The last thing my girl needed was to find out that people in her town, that she'd known all her life, had done something to Jack, had taken him away from her, knowing what it would do to her.

I recognized Bucky's type. Just about every small town on the planet had one of his kind. A bully. A selfish bastard who got off on terrorizing the rest of the townsfolk when he didn't get his way. Sometimes they were the town drunk, sometimes they were in a position of authority like a cop, or on the town council. Sometimes they were a hothead, angry; sometimes they were like Bucky, a combination of a hothead and a cold piece. Thing was, Bucky-boy hadn't met any piece colder 'n me when I was pushed to it, and he'd pushed me to it but good, trying to fuck with Miri.

The little friendly warning from his co-worker just sealed his fate, in that I was apt to kill the motherfucker given the chance, because he was bringing this down to him or me and it damn sure wasn't gonna be me. I wasn't about to go anywhere. Not with the beautiful woman at my side counting on me not to fuck her over.

I looked over to Miri and some of the ice in my veins thawed, but only for her. She looked uneasy, troubled, and as she shifted smoothly between gears, she looked like she couldn't get us back to her place fast enough.

I knew that big ol' house of hers was her sanctuary. Was her place to shut the world out and where she felt the safest. I also knew that Bucky had her shook and I wanted to know the whole truth of it, because if he put hands on her, at any point before or after I arrived, I was probably going to do some violence.

"You're sure you're alright?" she asked softly as she pulled the emergency brake in her driveway. I was staring out the window, lost in my thoughts and had forgot how quick the ride back to her place was from town.

I realized my car was parked neatly in front of one of the garage doors next to us and I nodded in answer to her question, "I'm cool."

"Really? Because it doesn't feel like it," she said, shifting nervously in her seat.

I kind of froze and looked over to her. Her eyes were a little wide and her face pale, her expression attempting neutral but screaming that she was uneasy. I reached out and she flinched and my hand froze.

"You ain't never gotta worry about me putting hands on you, love. I'm not that guy."

"No, I know," she said hurriedly, and she sounded like she meant it, but then she laughed nervously and said, "Just some old ghosts, I guess."

"Talk to me," I said, using her own words on her.

She gave me a funny little smile, her posture easing some and said, "Back in high school, our gym flooded right before my senior year's homecoming dance."

My gut had a sinking feeling as I nodded and kept my mouth shut, letting her speak.

"Ronnie Wilstad saved the day when he stepped up. His dad owns a small farm just outside town. Organic vegetables, mostly. He and Ronnie said the high school could use his barn for the dance, they just needed to come clean it out. We spent all weekend the weekend before the dance getting it ready. The night before the dance, we spent almost all night decorating. It was a labor of love, let me tell you."

We hadn't moved from the car, just sat in the quiet hush of the little sedan's interior, in our own little bubble as she spoke and I listened.

"The night of the dance, I was going stag with Blyn, Oaklyn, and Ash. We decided to go as a group. Safer that way. There were more girls than guys in our class, which wasn't very big to begin with, so, um, it made sense."

Her grip tightened on the steering wheel to white knuckles and I felt my chest squeeze down with it.

"Did he touch you?" I demanded.

"What? Who? Bucky?"

"Yeah."

She nodded, biting her lips together.

"Almost raped me, I guess Ash or Oaklyn saw it, or heard a warning, or something. They showed up with Blyn, and sort of outed us completely as witches, or a coven. I mean, people already suspected, but it sort of clinched it. You know how kids are..."

"I guess you guys had a rough senior year."

"We weren't necessarily *bullied* as much as shunned, mostly out of fear, I think."

"Fear about what Bucky'd do?"

She nodded, "He was the most popular guy in high school," she said with a bitter chuckle.

"Didn't do it for you, though," I said, and it wasn't a question, but she answered like it was, anyway.

"Something always felt, wrong, about him," she said. "Like, my magic knows what my eyes and my mind can't or isn't willing to comprehend. I can't exactly say what the wrongness is, but the older we get, the more me, and the rest of the town, are sort of starting to figure it out."

"He doesn't care about anybody but himself," I said.

"That's part of it, but I think it goes deeper than that."

"Psychopath?" I asked.

"Or sociopath…" she murmured.

"You're a healer, love. But whatever he's got going on, it ain't something you can heal."

"Right!" she declared like it'd suddenly clicked. "I think that's totally it. I can't fix whatever he's got broken, and it both scares me and bothers me."

"The fact you won't just bow down or fall all over his dumb ass probably like to drive him nuts," I said.

She rolled her eyes, "Oh, I know it does. Bucky Daniels doesn't like to hear the word 'no' and he lives to make anyone that dares say it to him pay for it."

"Fuck him," I said darkly and took off my seatbelt.

Miri startled a bit, like she forgot we were still sitting in her car, and quickly undid her own.

"Anyways," she said. "That's the ballad of Bucky Daniels."

"As I hear it, 'Miri told you no, now you is a butt-hurt little bitch about it.' Cool story, bro."

Miri laughed, and it was a genuine one.

"Come on, there's a hot shower with your name on it, inside."

"Got any vinegar?" I asked.

"White, red, apple, what? I'm a hedge witch. Of course, I have vinegar. What do you need it for?"

"I use a vinegar rinse for my hair."

"Oh, that's right. My bad." She looked like her interest had been piqued. "I bet you I could come up with something that smells a bit better. I mean, it would still have the vinegar notes but it wouldn't be as harsh. Let me think on it. For now you didn't answer my question. What variety do you prefer?"

"I got a whole recipe," I said.

"Oh, do tell! I know I can work a little magic now."

I smiled at her and had to laugh under my breath as I reached for the door handle. I knew that gleam in her eye. It looked like I would find her in her basement workshop playing with a little R&D, making improvements to the recipe I gave her. She was like that, putting a little magic into everything she cooked, everything she made, making people's lives better just a little at a time.

It bugged the shit out of me that anyone would give her a hard time.

I had a feeling eventually Bucky-boy and I would be having a come-to-Jesus meeting. I just needed to do a little askin' around, do a little digging, first. That deputy's words came back to haunt my ass the same way I figured Jack was hanging around, leading Miri and I along.

I'd heard him up on that bluff, the same as she had. I knew without a doubt my best friend put me together with his girl. What I didn't know was why? I didn't figure I would ever get an answer to that question, but I had the feeling it had a lot to do with the kind of man Jack was.

He wouldn't want anyone to suffer alone on account of him, so he made it so neither of us would be alone.

I stood under the hot shower spray thinking about it and let out a sigh.

"I got you, boy," I said to Jack, even though he wasn't here. "I got you, and I'll take care of your girl."

"She's your girl, now," I heard him say and I ripped open the shower curtain, but of course, there was no one there.

"Damn," I muttered, but I couldn't stop grinning. "Can't even let a nigga shower in peace."

13

*M*iri...

It had been one of the most nightmarish eighteen hours of my life, waiting, worrying, begging the powers that be that no harm should befall Kavion while he was in Bucky's custody, because let's face it... Bucky was capable of anything.

Even murder... a dark corner of my mind whispered, but it was so sudden, and so out of place, I couldn't quite convince myself that it was totally my mind that had conjured the thought. The intense feeling I wasn't alone swept over and through me, the hair raising on the back of my neck to the point I leaned forward over my bench to look.

"Who's there?" I called softly, and craned my neck, checking the stairs, but I was alone down here as far as I could tell.

"You'll never be alone, I'll always be with you."

I put my hands out as I reeled, pushing myself up off of my workbench. They came down on the wood, which was real and strong beneath my fingers. So startled was I, that I immediately threw up my shields, pulling my questing power back into my center. So busy was I with grounding myself, I missed the side of

110

my right hand nudging one of my apothecary jars filled with dried calendula. It was too close to the edge of the workbench and tipped to the stone floor. It shattered, crashing against the unyielding surface, the glass splintering like my heart was doing in my chest all over again.

"Miri!" I looked up to Kavion leaping down the stairs. His athletic shoes slapped against the stone floor and he made strides over some of the rush mats I had laid down as area rugs. They were easier to pick up and sweep if needed.

"What happened?" he demanded, pulling me into his arms.

"I thought I – I thought something, and I didn't know if it was my thought, because sometimes it isn't, you know? Sometimes, that's how spirits speak to you, whispering from your subconscious, and I don't know!" My breath was uneven, my chest heaving, and Kavion held my elbows, stooping to meet my eyes, steady, a rock in the latest tempest raging in my heart and my head.

"Slow down," he said. "You're upset, I think you're hyperventilating. You need a paper bag or something?"

I laughed at the absurd image that conjured and closed my eyes. Speaking to, or hearing spirits was way out of my wheelhouse. That was typically an ability of witches with an affinity for air. I was an earth witch all the way so it shouldn't be happening to me, right? I needed to talk to Gwen. She would know.

"Okay," Kavion said, when I had my shit a little more together. "You had a thought that wasn't your own. What was that thought?" he asked. "Let's start there."

"I was thinking Bucky was honestly capable of anything and then this trailing thought hit me, 'even murder', and my intuition kind of creeped up on me, telling me I wasn't alone. It was such a strong sense, I even called out asking if somebody was there."

"And did you hear something?"

"I heard Jack," I said.

"I did, too," he said and I looked up at him.

"When?"

"Upstairs, while I was in the shower."

"What did he say to you?" I asked.

He hesitated, but when he spoke, I could see the truth of it in his eyes.

"He said that you're my girl now, to take care of, to love and to hold onto..." He gave me a little squeeze and I got instantly emotional, which wasn't like me until – crap. *Nothing worse than a hedge witch the week before her period,* I thought.

I rested my forehead against the center of his chest and felt comfort, felt blessed. The man I'd fallen hopelessly in love with was gone, but he didn't go quietly. He'd brought his best friend into town and had set us up, reaching beyond the veil to make sure we were both taken care of. I knew it in the center of my piece-meal heart as sure as I knew the sun would rise tomorrow.

"What did he say to you?" Kavion asked me.

"That I would never be alone, that he'd always be here."

Kavion huffed a laugh. "Straight up sounds like something Jack would say."

"Right?" I asked.

"I don't know," he said. "Feels like he came back with us, from that cliff."

I nodded, I couldn't disagree. I mean, we'd been together for almost a month now, and it was only on the overlook that we first heard him. It took a lot of power for a spirit to manifest sound.

Oh how I wish you were still here, Oaklyn... I thought. I sighed and pushed back gently from Kavion.

"I feel like I need to do some homework."

"Okay, you, uh, wanna do that while I get this mess?"

I nodded. "Thank you, I appreciate it."

"It's no problem."

"I need to get my grandmother's book from upstairs and I need to feed Shade."

"Okay, I'll be here."

"Okay, I'll be right back."

I went upstairs as he plucked the broom leaning against the fireplace from its rest. The calendula was a total loss, but I was pretty sure I had some vacuum-sealed packs of it from my garden in one of the old wooden filing cabinets tucked under the basement stairs. I was a modern witch in many ways, and it was one of the best ways to keep dried herbs and spices fresh longer when I wasn't quite ready to use them.

I went over to Shade's cage first and lifted the latch, swinging open the enclosure's door. I reached in to check his water, and he stepped off one of his many perches to stand on my arm. I opened my mouth to gently chastise him, but he had tipped his head and was studying me a little intently with one of his beady eyes.

"Hungry, Shade?" I asked quietly instead.

"Hungry!" he parroted back, and I smiled.

"Okay, come on." I brought him out and he walked up to my shoulder without hesitation and settled there.

I went for the wall of books opposite the enclosure and pulled down the old copy of Fannie Farmer's Cookbook. It was my grandmother's favorite, and held the key to the built-in drawers beneath the book cases. I opened it to the back and the little cubby that had been cut into the pages, slipping out the old-fashioned skeleton key.

"Hungry," Shade said plaintively and I smiled again.

"I'll just be a moment, I promise," I said, as I slipped the key into the lock. I pulled the fabric-wrapped family grimoire from the drawer and slid it shut, putting the key back where it belonged and sliding the old cookbook back on the shelf among all the other spines.

"Okay, Shade," I said, hefting the much larger, much heavier tome with both hands. "To the kitchen."

We went to the kitchen where I fetched out the stainless steel bowl of scraps from the fridge and set it down. I whisked off the dishtowel and Shade lifted off my shoulder to the edge of the bowl to go to town.

"Behave yourself. I'll be downstairs, call me when you're done."

I picked up the family book and retreated back down the basement steps into the workshop. I would have kept the old book down there, but it could sometimes get cold and damp. It was much more climate-controlled upstairs and easier to reach should disaster strike. Not that the old book would burn, not with as many wards and spells placed upon it for protection as the generations before me had layered onto the thing.

I set it down on the workbench just as Kavion ditched the last of the broken glass and calendula into an old, semi-rusty bin I kept in the corner.

"Now that looks like a spell book," he declared.

"And how do you know what a spell book is supposed to look like?" I asked.

"Well, they're supposed to look like that, aren't they?"

I laughed and shook my head. "Some are big and gaudy like this; Samuel Eilish had a flare for the dramatics, I guess. Others, not so much. I know, Blyn's family grimoire is just a plain leather journal with a compass rose embossed on the cover. Oaklyn and Ash's family book is about half the size of this one. Our family has always pretty much been 'go big and stay home,'" I said with a sigh.

"What's that supposed to mean?" he asked.

"The Eilish family tree was moved here, but once we were? We put down deep roots. I don't think any one of us has ever left Loving for more than a vacation. Certainly, no one has relocated. Not like Blyn, or Ash."

"They left the small town for the big city, you was sayin'."

"Yeah, they did… Thing is, it's always temporary. The descendants of the original coven? They always come home."

"Always?" he asked.

I shrugged and sighed, "Unless they die young out there, yeah. It's like we hit retirement age and Loving just calls us home."

"Think that's part of the town's magic?" he asked.

"I don't doubt that it is," I answered, unwrapping and paging through the large old tome.

"What are you doing?"

"Looking for a certain spell, one of protection and warding. I don't usually bring out the big guns, but something tells me I need to for this."

"Couldn't hurt," he said, putting the broom and the bin back in their respective places. He drifted back over and slipped up onto one of the bar stools I had down here at the workbench.

"Sorry," he said suddenly, and held up his hands. "Am I cool to stay?"

"Of course you are," I said. "I may even need your help."

"Oh, okay." He sounded dubious about that last part and then perked back up a moment later, "Did you remember to feed Shade?"

"Yup, he's in the kitchen. He'll either call when he's ready to go back in his enclosure or he'll find his way down here."

"You just let him fly around the house?" he asked.

"Of course. It's his house, too. Plus, Shade can't fly. At least not very well or for very far. That's how he came to me, as a juvenile with a badly-broken wing. We did all we could but he wasn't good to go back into the wild, so he stayed with me."

"That's cool, I didn't realize."

I looked up from tracing my fingertips down one of the thick pages that felt almost like watercolor paper and said, "There's a lot we still don't know about each other. Hopefully we can get past our mutual barriers when it comes to trust. I want to open up more. I'm trying to open up more."

He pressed his lips together and nodded, but he had a hard time looking at me. My heart gave a fractured throbbing ache and I let things go. I didn't want to push, and by extension, push him away.

He cleared his throat. "Speaking of coming clean, one of the deputies at the jail said something interesting as I was being let go."

"Oh, yeah?" I asked, setting myself back on my heels and giving him my full attention.

"Said to stay off Bucky-boy's radar; that the last dude that was on it disappeared."

I straightened -stiffened is more like it- and felt a cold pit of dread open up in the bottom of my stomach.

"That's not ominous or anything," I said.

"Right?" he asked and I sighed.

"Okay, hold that thought. I'm going to get a few things together, here."

"No problem, you just tell me what to do and I'll do it. I'm good at taking orders."

I smiled in spite of the heavy mood and what felt like a dire situation.

"I don't disagree on that last part," I said and he gave me an almost shy, almost sheepish grin. It had to be one of the most adorable things I'd ever seen and it brought a titter of laughter out of me.

I gathered candles for the spell, white for purity and the destruction of negative energies, black for protection and to repel the bad, brown for structure and to support the spell, and turquoise for truth and opening lines of communication between the heart and spoken word. I know that last one seems odd, but for everything a place and everything in its place. Finally, I drew out a silver candle to represent the goddess, nurturing energy, and also in a bid that she watch over us.

I brought the five candles from the apothecary cabinet's drawers and took them to the workbench. I used chalk to draw out the five pointed star within the circle, and set each of the candles chosen at their respective points according to the book.

I used small, simple taper holders that Ivan had crafted for me in exchange for his teas one winter when times were lean, and waited to light them until I had the rest of the spell's needs met.

I anointed the candles with bergamot for protection, and

myrrh, a powerful purifier. I gathered several other herbs with similar properties and set a charcoal brazier at the center of my circle.

I worked quietly, Kavion observing, as I slid into that calm, meditative state where I performed magic best, the calm serenity my grandmother had insisted I learn to be a better healer and nurse, like she had been.

A lot of the men and women of my family had taken up the healing arts. Doctors, nurses, and even a veterinarian or two. I came from a long, proud line of hedge witches and I was proud to carry the tradition myself. I looked forward to imparting all that I had learned to my own daughter someday.

I know, I know, I didn't say 'son', but not because I didn't want one; rather because my family had a propensity for birthing girls. Sons were few and far between in my line.

I closed my eyes and set my palms flat on the bench and called my hidden power. Shade glided down into the basement and came to rest on the corner of the workbench, his talons clicking along the scarred surface of the wood as he came near. I felt my power-base expand, my connection to the earth deepen with the presence of my familiar, my friend.

Fire wasn't my element, so it took a bit more effort to get the candles and brazier to light than what it took Ivan. Fire was most definitely the smith's element, so it likely came to him as naturally as breathing.

I let these thoughts slip free as soon as they came to mind and homed my focus on the spell at hand before I spoke. Murmuring the incantation over and over, repeating everything times three. It wasn't a petty charm spell like the girls and I created for specific things all the time. No, this was heavy magic, circle magic.

Kavion remained silent, watching, listening, stoically, his face impassive. I threw herbs on the brazier and a satisfactory cloud of smoke billowed to the four corners of the basement, swirling up the stairs, cleansing every corner of the house, sweeping through it on eddies and currents of the building's energy, creeping along and reinforcing the ward lines that had been there since long before I was even born, adding my energy to the layers of magic of my family that had gone before.

The magic chased back the dark and brooding energies that could wish to gain purchase and corrupt. It held fast at every door and window, rejecting negativity and all who would bring negative influence to my door.

Finally, the tail end of the spell: "Let all who enter here have peace in their heart and truth on their lips. May all who enter here speak truth. So mote it be." I shoved that last bit of power meant to unlock into the wards around my house and felt them activate. I closed my eyes and breathed out a sigh of relief. No magic was definite, but my needs had been met.

The ritual candles, not much bigger than hearty birthday cake candles, went out, having reached their ends. The brazier gave one last belch of smoke and went out, too. I put my hands back to the table and smiled at Shade who cocked his head and echoed me, "So mote it be!"

"That's right, old friend," I said softly and scratched the crown of his feathered head with a fingertip, just the way he liked.

"That was," Kavion cleared his throat, "uh, wow."

I smiled and laughed slightly and said with a little shrug and a faint blush, "There's not much to really see."

"No, there's not, but feeling it is a whole different story."

I cocked my head curiously and asked, "Oh? How so? Describe it for me."

He shook his head, his dreadlocks wrapped up tight in some sort of cloth and he said, "I don't know if I really can, but it was like, you know, when all the hair on your body stands up, only more electric."

I nodded slowly and encouraged him with a simple, "Go on."

"Like I could feel whatever it was marching across my skin like ants." He gave a shrug and twisted his lips and I smiled. When I didn't say anything right away he gave a shrug and said, "That's it, though."

I smiled a touch wider and nodded. "Sounds like you may be a little more sensitive than the average person," I said gently.

"I don't know." He laughed a little nervously and said, "Is that a good or a bad thing?"

I shook my head, "Neither," I told him. "It simply is what it is. Neither good nor bad, just a thing, a talent you have. Just like having an edge athletically by running faster than the next guy. You're simply a little more in tune with your surroundings and can sense power a little more."

"Okay, that's cool… I guess." He didn't sound certain at all and I raised my eyebrows. He laughed and got up slowly from his seat.

"Hungry?" I asked him, and Shade shot back, "Hungry!"

"Oh, hush, you! I just fed you," I said and held out a hand to Kavion. He took it and drew me toward the stairs.

"I could eat," he said, then with a grin and a wink said, "I'm just not hungry for food."

I laughed and said, "Well, let me just put my book and Shade away and then you can suit yourself."

"Sounds like a plan, man."

14

*K*avion...

She lay back in her sheets and I started at her feet, kissing lightly all the way up her body, first one ankle, then the other, back and forth up each shin, each knee, fitting myself between her legs and using my lips, my breath, warm against her skin, to my advantage. She watched me, down the length of her body, between her perfect breasts as I worked my way to the apex of her thighs and the rich, copper-red curls there. Her gaze was transfixed, pupils dilated with desire, her lips parted in wonder. Her breathing was slow and even, her body shivering with every touch.

I was hard to the point of aching, but I didn't want to rush. We had all the time in the world and I wanted to suspend the crisis long enough to really love Miri tonight. We both were wound tight and needed to take these moments as the opportunity came up. We were running ourselves ragged, our thoughts caught in a hamster wheel, keeping us awake long into the night, our bodies wearing out from the constant mental load and emotional rollercoaster we were both trapped on.

Anybody who says stress doesn't affect your physical health is a liar or just plain deluded. So we were taking a time-out, relaxing the best way we both knew how. After all, smashing was a great way to shut off the brain for a little while. At least, it was for me.

I reached the delicate flesh between Miri's thighs and she let out a passionate gasp, her fingers winding in my dreads, her head tipping back to meet her pillows, all those wild red curls fanning out around her head in a halo of fire, her perfect tits thrust up toward the canopy on her bed.

God, she was wild. Wild and perfect, a beautiful creation of nature and magic packed into one powerhouse of a woman. She tasted as pure and sweet as the image of that body arching at my touch. The picture of all that sensual eroticism burned into my brain and I swore, I would always see her like this, as she was, right now. No matter how old we got, no matter how our skin wrinkled or things started to sag, she would always be this beautiful to me and I know for a fact there weren't no other female I had ever thought that way about.

Miri was it, she was the one, and I needed to work on my shit to guarantee she'd never ever want to be rid of me. I couldn't keep holding her at arm's length, I couldn't.

She gasped again as I worked her clit with the flat of my tongue, the ball of my tongue piercing working its intended magic as it went over it, my hands holding her silken thighs open. My cock throbbed painfully with the need to be inside her, but I wanted her totally wet and ready, so, orgasm by oral first.

I slipped a finger inside of her and her lush ass tried to rise off the bed. I wasn't having it, though. I put my free arm across her hips and pressed her back down into the bed as she moaned loudly, that moan turning into a cry as I found the right spot inside of her, teasing it to life. Her legs twitched against my shoulders and I smiled, sucking lightly on her clit, stroking her g-spot with my fingertip, working her up slow and steady until, panting, her pussy clenching, her body jerking, she came.

The wail she let out was a point of pride to me. I had her coming completely undone until she lay languid, whimpering in the nest of blankets on her bed.

I resumed my travels, planting kisses over her hips, back and forth on each rib, working my way up to pay lavish attention to first one breast, then the other. She whimpered and writhed beneath me and I held her safe and warm in the cradle of my arms but I couldn't be dissuaded from my current course of action, nor could I be persuaded to hurry my ass up.

Miri groaned with impatience and all I could do was chuckle against her breast. She gasped and gripped the blankets and sheets at her sides, but I simply lay flat against her, pinning her once more when her hips attempted to leave the bed.

"You are killing me!" she declared and I had to smile against her soft skin.

"You love it, though."

"Mm." She captured that lush bottom lip of hers between her teeth and I kissed my way further north.

I loved this, taking my time with her, showing her everything I had a difficult time saying. It was one thing when somebody said they loved you, but I'd heard that shit most of my life, and learned from an early age that it was mostly an empty thing. A lie.

My bio mom told me constantly that she loved me, but you didn't love a person and do the shit she did to me and my siblings. You just didn't.

So, as a result, I learned that actions spoke louder than words. Like Jack's mom, the woman who'd adopted my ass as a teen. Put up with my angry outbursts and my sullen rage. The woman who never left me behind, never let me down, was always there to pick my ass up right along with Jack. The woman who gave me my own bedroom, who let me pick my own clothes and bought me my first brand new shirt, the woman who called me regularly, sent me care packages when I was overseas, wrote me letters and told me she missed having her boys home when I ain't never come out of her –

she was my mom. She, aside from Jack, was the main reason I was here, and the main reason I'd met Miri. She was the reason I still had some fuckin' hope for humanity.

I couldn't ever express my gratitude to that woman. All I could do was try to pay it forward someday by adopting a kid, even if I already had kids of my own.

I smiled down at Miri, smoothing some of that wild red hair out of her face and kissed the tip of her nose. She laughed, and it was one of the purest, most uplifting sounds I'd ever heard.

"This is all done," I whispered, "I want to stay with you."

"Yeah?" she said, carefully searching my face.

"Yeah."

"I want you to stay with me," she murmured and touched the side of my face with light fingertips. I turned my head and planted a kiss on the inside of her wrist. Her eyes fluttered shut and a serene look painted her face, and I felt like I'd done good, felt proud of myself for telling her for real, how I was feeling. It was something small, but some ancient dude once said a journey of, like, a thousand miles began with but a single step. I'd just taken that step with this girl, and it felt phenomenal.

It felt even better when I rocked my hips against hers, hooked an arm beneath one of her knees and slid all the way inside her.

15

*M*iri...

"Oh, yes!"

I didn't even recognize my own voice, so breathy, so different. I shivered beneath him, though it certainly wasn't from cold. Kavion radiated heat and I swore it was enough to sustain me forever, just being close to him, drunk off his love.

His body fit mine like a key to a lock, and when he rotated his hips, I fell right open to him. The things I felt for this man, so soon after the loss of the man I had thought I would love forever, were so confusing. However, I couldn't deny they felt so right. In that, I felt Jack's presence. Knew that he blessed this union, that he wanted us to heal, and that he didn't want either of us to hurt or be sad.

He wanted us both to be happy and he made this happen. It was something I was torn about, yet forever grateful, because it did hurt less, not going through it alone.

Kavion shifted and I cried out as he went over that spot. The warm and sultry glow of impending orgasm started low, rising to flood the rest of my body like the light from the sun filling the sky after a long dark night.

He loved me long and slow, our breath twining and inter-locking as much, if not more than our bodies. He kissed every inch of my skin, front and back, made me come countless times, until both of us lay in the circle of the other's arms, panting and spent, too weak to even want to move.

I was cuddled close and snug against Kavion's body, listening to the throbbing echo of his heartbeat through his trim chest when his voice rumbled beneath my ear, "You ever give it any thought, what we're gonna do when we find the answer?"

I closed my eyes and breathed out slowly and finally shook my head. "It feels like we're never going to really know. I mean, where do we even go from here?"

"So you ain't thought about it?" he asked, and he sounded vaguely hurt.

"I... I've been too scared to let myself, I think."

"What're you afraid of?" he asked.

"That you'll die, or that you'll wake up once the mystery is solved like this was nothing but a dream and you'll want to leave."

He shifted under me and I looked up, sucking in a breath at how serious his expression was.

"I don't think either of those things are gonna happen, Miri."

I swallowed hard, pushed myself up so I could better look him in the eyes and said, "I didn't think anything was going to happen to Jack, either, but here we are."

I immediately and savagely cursed myself out for saying it, but I had done it to myself. The ward of the heavier spell I had cast was clearly working as the truth spilled from my lips.

To my surprise, Kavion's lips drew into a slight smile, if a sad one, and he said, "I'm not Jack. Jack was a soft touch; I'm a lot harder than that."

He heaved a big sigh. "Everything's gonna be okay." He pulled my forehead to his lips with a firm hand at the back of my neck and I let him, closing my eyes at the comforting touch of his warm soft kiss against my forehead. "I promise," he whispered and I sank back down onto his chest, comforted.

"I think we should go see Gwen tomorrow, if you're up for it," I murmured.

"Your mentor-lady?" he asked.

I smiled, "And friend."

"How come?"

"I think she might have a little more insight into things than I do, fortune-telling is her strong suit. She's also a hedge witch, but her element is more air. She might be able to think of something I haven't."

There was a silence as he mulled things over and finally he said, "That's cool, if you trust her."

"With my life," I said.

He nodded and held me closer, protectively, and I realized he was afraid for me as much as I feared for him.

THE NEXT MORNING, we were woken by Shade, perched on my headboard, cawing to get us up. It was a rude awakening and when I bolted upright in bed, the feathery miscreant cocked his head, blinked one beady eye and had the gall to say 'Hungry.'

I fixed the customary breakfast for my raven and went on to cook for our – I mean my guest and Kavion. Kavion was still posing as just a long-term guest for now. Though, I had to admit, under my roof we were pretty poor at disguising our infatuation with one another.

Lucky for us, Mr. Hall was gracious about it and didn't say a word. Of course, I had a feeling that was more because he wished for his privacy to be respected in return. He didn't have anything to worry about where that was concerned. I valued discretion when it came to my guests and I attempted not to pry.

I was in a relatively good mood this morning despite the rude awakening. What? It was hard not to be after a night of great sex, although that descriptor didn't really do what we did the night before any justice. Even though it was still a bit backwards, it wasn't just sex between me and Kavion.

It was love. True love, the undying kind, which served to dampen my mood if I weren't careful and thought about it too much.

I was still coming to terms that you could have more than one undying love in a lifetime and it still made me uneasy that I'd found another so soon after losing Jack.

"Are you feeling alright this morning, Ms. Eilish?"

I dropped the plate I had picked up to serve with and it crashed to my kitchen floor. I jumped, with a yip, and Mr. Hall rushed into the room.

"I am incredibly sorry!" he cried, and attempted to help me with the shards of pottery on the floor. I waved him off gently and shook my head.

"My fault," I declared. "I shouldn't have had my head so far into the clouds."

He chuckled and stood reluctantly as I used my dish towel to scrape everything into a neat pile.

"The question stands," he said.

I pasted on my best smile and said, "Everything will be just fine, thank you for asking."

It wasn't a lie, at least not the way I phrased it. I honestly believed everything would be just fine. The wards let the obfuscation past my lips and Mr. Hall only hesitated for a moment before nodding and standing. I finished sweeping up the broken, hand-thrown heavy pottery plate and told myself a trip to town was in order to get it replaced.

Meanwhile, I realized Mr. Hall still stood nearby.

"I'm sorry," I said. "Was there something you needed?"

"Indeed, I was told by the town pharmacist to come see you when I had my prescription filled."

"Oh?" I asked, intrigued.

"I, unfortunately, forgot my sleeping pills back in the city. I had my doctor send my prescription to the pharmacy and a most curious exchange ensued."

I chuckled lightly and said, "Let me guess, Philip hadn't filled one of its like in a while."

"Precisely what the pharmacist said. He had to check and make sure that the pills he had on the shelf weren't expired."

I nodded, "Sleep trouble, you said?"

"I did," he agreed, nodding, his hands buried in his slacks pockets.

I sent a thin, questing tendril of my power in his direction and came up against some interesting results.

He wasn't a witch, or any sort of magic-user. None the less, he was shielded very well. Personal shields, strong shields, his heart and his mind sealed behind some very heavy iron walls. Impenetrable to a normal person, but I wasn't normal. I never had been, and I was only trying to help.

Mr. Hall blinked, his body leaning ever so slightly away from me, which told me he may not be a magic-user but that he either had a strong intuition or was otherwise sensitive to otherworldly vibrations. I cocked my head slightly and met his eyes with mine, cool and assessing, and with a little bit of trust on his part, his shields relaxed.

It wasn't like I could read his mind. I wasn't terribly psychic; that was one of Blyn's powers. Rather, I had my own intuition about things and right now, it was telling me this man had seen and been through some terrible things. That the grey that frosted his hair had been there longer than it should have been and though he was handsome, he wasn't quite as old as he appeared... late thirties, perhaps early forties, not late forties, early fifties as I'd originally thought.

His body was in good health. Fit, and well-taken-care of. His mind, however -his mind was partially in shambles from some unknown personal demons. I didn't pry any further. I knew just what to do.

"I'll make you some tea," I murmured softly. "A cup before bed, you'll sleep like a baby."

He chuckled and hung his head, his smile soft with a slight edge of bitterness to it that he managed to mask quickly.

"You don't have any children, do you, Ms. Eilish?" he asked.

"No, I don't… not yet."

He smiled a bit more, genuinely, and fixed me with his blue eyes.

"Babies don't exactly sleep soundly," he said.

Though I wasn't psychic, I nevertheless garnered the strong impression there was more to that statement than he'd spoken aloud. That impression led me to believe that he meant to finish it *At least mine didn't.* There was a sorrow, just behind his eyes, and I nodded carefully.

"I'll have the tea blend ready before you finish breakfast," I told him.

"I was hoping you might join us this morning. I'm afraid Mr. Martin likes to talk and I am not one for small talk. Perhaps you could engage him?"

I smiled and nodded.

"Sure," I murmured.

He gave me a nod and stepped back before turning, his gaze lingering on me a moment more than was comfortable before he left the kitchen for the big dining room.

I hastily finished breakfast so that I could join the boys at the table, which wasn't something I typically did as a hostess. Still, it was just the three of us here, and it was at a guest's request, so why not? Sometimes change, even just a little one, was good for the soul.

"Hey," Kavion said and lifted his chin in my direction when I stepped out into the dining room. He took a seat at the big table at one of the place settings, across from Mr. Hall.

I smiled and said, "Good morning, Mr. Martin. How did you sleep?"

"Good! Good, thanks."

I nodded graciously and set a place at the head of the table saying, "I hope you don't mind, but Mr. Hall has asked me to join you two this morning."

"Nah! It's your house, innit?" he asked, raising his eyebrows with a glint of curiosity in his deep brown eyes.

"It is, but I like to give my guests their space."

"No need in the common areas, Ms. Eilish," Mr. Hall said and I could tell he was relaxing, relenting a bit in his stiff demeanor. "If we wish for privacy, that is what our rented rooms are for."

I gave a slight nod and went back to the kitchen to bring out the food. Kavion followed me in and I turned. His back firmly to Mr. Hall, he gave me a face that clearly read *"What the fuck is up with this dude?"* The look was so clearly Kavion, I heard his voice say that very thing in my head and I absolutely fought not to giggle or show any expression at all, seeing as Mr. Hall's eyes were locked on me from behind Kavion's back.

"Mr. Martin?" I asked.

"Just thought I'd give you a hand bringing things out," Kavion said with a wink.

"That's very sweet of you," I said. "But –"

"But nothing. I like to help out," he said.

Mr. Hall chuckled from the archway and said, "He is paying for the privilege, I believe."

I colored slightly and hung with the ruse that Kavion was paying me anything, which I wouldn't let him.

"Very well, if you could grab that plate of bacon and the pitcher of orange juice?"

I took up the stoneware dish of French toast and took it to the doorway, where Mr. Hall relieved me of them.

"I'll be right out with the oatmeal; don't feel you have to wait for me."

I turned and went for the cupboard and brought down another earthenware dish to put the oatmeal in. I used a rice cooker to make my oatmeal. It turned out fabulously and spared me from stirring a pot, allowing me to focus on other things.

I dished it out into the earthenware bowl and I heaped it, knowing Kavion liked his oatmeal before work, and brought it out to the table in one hand, the tray of milk, cinnamon, raisins, brown sugar, nuts and other assorted toppings in the other. Kavion met me at the open archway separating the kitchen from the rest of the house and took the heavy bowl of oats from me.

"Ah ha, yes!" he said with joyous anticipation.

"I should stop even cooking anything but oatmeal for you," I said, trying to keep my smile in check, which was always hard around him.

"Cool with me," he said with a shrug.

I lost and my suppressed smile became a grin.

I'd noticed that Kavion was quiet around new people, only becoming talkative around them when he was comfortable in their presence. I guess he'd cleared whatever invisible hurdle there had been when it came to Mr. Hall because he indeed tried to draw him into conversation.

I helped a bit, but like Kavion, I was becoming curious where this newcomer to town was concerned. Probably because of everything surrounding Jack and his disappearance.

A light rap at my back kitchen door, startled me out of my thoughts as Kavion asked a light question of Mr. Hall and we all stopped what we were doing.

"Excuse me," I murmured and rose from the table, setting my napkin aside. I reached the archway to my kitchen and called out, "Ivan! Come in!" but of course he wouldn't until I came to open the door. He was peculiar that way. Of course, I hadn't said it for his benefit, but for Kavion's.

A quick backward glance saw his shoulders ease out of their suddenly-stiff posture and he threw me a little bit of chin. I drifted through the archway and across the kitchen's stone tile to open the country back door. Ivan shifted from foot to foot, his big old gunny sack over one shoulder, clanking with whatever metal he'd salvaged for his craft.

"Out of tea already?" I asked quietly and he shook his big head.

"Niet," he pressed his lips together in a thin line and bowed his head and I smiled sympathetically. His English wasn't very good, and I was trying to bridge the gap, but Russian was a very complicated language. Especially when you threw in the Cyrillic script. Still, 'no' was easy, which is what he'd just said, and with his gunny sack clanking, I had to guess he was just trying to stock up while he was in town.

"Just stocking up while you're gathering steel, then?" I asked.

"Da."

"Not a problem, I have to make some of a similar sleep tea for another person, anyways. Your timing is uncanny." I held the door open wide and he turned slightly sideways to come through.

He loomed in my kitchen, snatching his hat from his head and crushing the brim slightly in his nervous state, his dark eyes flicking around the kitchen, checking corners, his chin coming up and nostrils flaring at the smells.

"Would you like to come have some breakfast?" I asked gently.

He looked like he wanted to, but when he heard Kavion say something, he rocked back on his heels and shook his head, his short hair dark, but shimmering in the muted daylight of my kitchen like one of Shade's wings.

"Go down to the basement," I said gently. "I'll bring you something and you can eat in private."

He nodded once, coloring slightly in embarrassment and said, *"Spasibo,* no –"

"But nothing," I said gently. "I insist. Go on, now."

He had said, *Thank you, but,* and I wasn't about to let him say 'no.' He lumbered down the basement steps and I went for a tray in the cupboard I kept them in and fixed him a generous plate of food and a heaping bowl of oatmeal.

"It's a client of mine; I'll be in the workshop downstairs if you need me," I told Kavion and our guest.

"Of course," Mr. Hall said graciously and Kavion gave a nod.

"I gotta get to work," Kavion said. "You straight?"

"As an arrow," I said with a smile and took up the tray to head down to the basement. "I'll be right up with that tea I promised you, Mr. Hall."

He smiled and said, "I look forward to it."

I went downstairs to a workshop already all aglow. Ivan had set his gunny sack aside by the bottom of the stair, hanging his hat on an exposed nail sticking out of the stair's support pillar above it. I usually used that nail to dry lavender when it was in season, but it was just as useful as a hat rack.

He had taken a seat at my work table using the stool that was quickly becoming Kavion's in my mind. He rested his big hands on the workbench and looked distinctly uncomfortable. I mean, more so than usual for Ivan, who was a loner by nature. I set the tray of food in front of him and he bowed his head.

"*Spasibo*," he muttered, which was 'thank you,' and I smiled.

"You're welcome." I hesitated and rested my hands on the workbench, standing at a ninety-degree angle from him. Finally I sighed and asked gently, "Why are you really here, Ivan?"

He had just stuck a spoonful of oatmeal in his mouth and his dark eyes regarded me as he chewed thoughtfully.

"I saw something," he said quietly. "In the fire."

I cocked my head and said, "I didn't know you had the sight."

He shook his head and said, "It does not happen, how do you say?"

"Often?"

"*Da.*"

"You saw something about me?" I asked.

"And your new man," he affirmed.

"Kavion?"

"The dark one, *da.*"

"Okay," I said, nodding once.

"He is good man," he said.

"Well, that's a relief," I said with a small smile.

"You are good together," he said.

"But?" I asked.

"But the *politseyskiy…*"

"*Politseyskiy…*" I murmured to myself and frowned, unfamiliar with the word. Hazarding a guess, I said, "Police? You mean Bucky?"

"*Da,* he is a bad man with bad –" He struggled and finally said, "*Etot chelovek plokhoy.*"

I shook my head and he frowned.

"The *politseyskiy* is just bad."

"All of them, or just him?"

"Just him. The others fear him, they will do what he says. They are men afraid. It does not make them bad, but it does."

I nodded. "I know that about him, and I figured that about them… That's most of this town, but thank you for the warning."

"He knows things," he said and I cocked my head. "About the light man; your first man."

"Did you see what happened to Jack? In the fire?"

"*Da.*"

It was as if all the air had been sucked from the room and I asked, breathlessly, "What happened?"

"Men from far away. They come to the town by boat, take things, bad things, and sail away… He saw, they killed him for it."

I swallowed hard and bit my lips together, unsure of what to do, or where to go from here. Usually, you would go to the police with that kind of information, but that was kind of hard here in Loving.

"I'm not sure what to do," I said dully.

"Do nothing. I would not like to see you get hurt."

I felt my shoulders droop and he took another careful bite of oatmeal, his eyes locked on mine. I nodded slowly and said, "I can't not do nothing…" I said and he frowned. I realized I'd used a triple negative and it might be a little beyond his English-speaking capabilities. I said, "I have to do something. I just don't know what," I said.

He nodded and looked sad. "I not see future," he said and heaved a big sigh.

"I see," I nodded. "Perhaps I'll go see Gwen, perhaps her fortune-telling abilities could give me guidance on what to do."

He nodded slowly and said, "The white-haired one."

"Yes."

He nodded slowly, hesitating before saying, *"Da."*

I smiled and moved around my workbench to the shelves of jars and bottles, "Since you're here, I'll make you up some more of your tea."

"Spasibo," he said with a nod and I looked back at him over my shoulder.

"You're a good friend, Ivan. Thank you for coming and telling me what you saw."

"Da," he said with a careful nod and continued eating.

It was probably one of the longest conversations I had ever had with Ivan, if not the longest. I set about making up his tea and some for Mr. Hall, too. I chose an old cookie tin to store Ivan's in, so he could just put it in his bag along with his metal finds from the junkyard outside of town. He was a frequent-flyer there, buying up chunks of leaf springs to craft some of his cutlery.

I had a full set of beautifully hand-crafted kitchen knives upstairs, which reminded me…

"Do you think you could sharpen my kitchen knives for me when you come back next?" I asked.

"How dull are they?" he asked in his thick accent and I smiled. His English, when it came to knives and metalsmithing was impeccable as was whatever came out of his forge.

"A couple are really getting there," I said. "But I think it could wait until your next visit."

"*Niet*," he said. "A dull blade is a dangerous blade. Bring them down. I will do them now."

The next thing I knew, he'd produced a sharpening stone and a vial of oil from one of his duster coat's deep pockets. I nodded and left my tea-mixing and jogged upstairs. Kavion was in the kitchen.

"Everything cool?" he asked, and though he seemed calm on the outside, I could see the anxiousness hiding just behind his eyes.

"Yeah, I'll tell you later, you'd better get going or you're going to be late."

"Okay," he said. "We gonna go see your girl when I get off work?" He seemed, I don't know, uneasy.

"Absolutely," I said with a nod.

He glanced back at the archway leading to the dining room and cleared his throat, "'K, bye."

"Bye for now," I said brightly, though I ached to add an 'I love you.'

I checked on Mr. Hall and he said he was fine, flicking the morning paper and looking over a pair of stylish reading glasses at me. I told him I would be right back, to holler if he needed anything, and went back down to give Ivan the knives.

*K*avion...

"You going to get that running today or what?"

I looked up and squinted, the light from the sun was behind the dude that had just spoken and he looked impatient when he moved to the side to block the light with his big head. I fought not to roll my eyes and said, "Start her up."

"Yeah?" Dude sounded surprised, but engines weren't no thing when it came to me. I got mad skills. I was behind on the curve where marine engines went, but I'd always had some kind of a knack for figuring out mechanical things and this had been no exception.

"Yeah, sometime today would be nice," I shot back, laughing. He went over and cranked the engine. She was slow starting, but after a second or two and a couple of tweaks, she finally rumbled to life.

"I'll be damned," the sailor said, and I hauled myself up and out of the engine compartment.

"What's the hurry?" I asked. "I thought this didn't need to be up and running 'til next week."

"Yeah, got a shipment going out early," he said and I frowned.

"A shipment? Shipment of what?"

"Never mind," he scowled. "Hard to remember you ain't been here all that long. You fit right in around here."

"Thanks," I said, wiping engine grease off my hands, but my suspicions were raised. I filed the awkwardness of his slip-up away. I didn't want to push my luck too hard, and getting this fixed meant I might be able to get off a little early and see Miri. Something about what he'd said didn't sit right with me, though.

This was a fishing town, more than anything else. Once, way back in the day, it'd been more about the timber and barrel-making, but it'd never been a port for sending out any kind of shipments of anything other than barrels and crates, and it hadn't performed that particular function in a long-ass time. At least, that's what Miri had told me. We would speak, late at night, about all kinds of things after making love or just to be closer as we drifted off. I got a lot about the town's history that way.

Something about the smell of this was off, and it wasn't the combo of rotting seaweed and diesel. No, this was the distinct odor of some bullshit, right here.

I went to work cleaning up and getting my ass off that vessel and onto the next project that needed doing. I was looking forward to getting off work, getting a hot shower. I was not looking forward to another run-in with Gwen, though she seemed like she was an important part of my woman's life. That was tough, because I didn't like the feeling I'd got off of her after our first run-in.

"Kavion." I looked up and over and the boss was standing up the dock. I threw chin and he called back, "Good work on the *Mayberry*," which was the name of the boat I'd just completed the work on ahead of schedule. "Go ahead and take the rest of the day, man. You've earned it."

The fuck? Boss-man wasn't like that, from what I knew, even though I'd only been at it here a few days. Whatever, though. I would take it. Even if it was suspicious as all get out the way a bunch of the guys were eyeing me from the other end of the dock.

I played dumb yokel and called back, "Ain't gotta tell me twice!" I gave the boss a happy grin I didn't feel and watched the tension ease outta the same guys that'd been watching the exchange so intently. Something was definitely up and it was something the lot of them didn't want me knowin' about.

I cleaned the rest of my shit up and put my tools away before I shot a text off to Miri to tell her I was on my way.

She, as always, met me at the back kitchen door. She never cared how greasy I was, never cared that I stank, she always was there – reaching for me, pulling herself close to my body, turning her beautiful face up to mine for a kiss- and I never thought I'd say it, but I wanted this to be my forever. It felt good to love and know I was loved in return. It wasn't a familiar feeling, but it was a good one, and I liked it. And, as I bowed my head to press my lips to hers, I found myself thanking Jack, silently, for bringing me here, which was always overshadowed by this extreme guilt and a resurgence of determination to find out what happened to him.

"You alright?" she murmured, and those gorgeous blue eyes of hers flickered open.

"Yeah, I'm good. Got some stuff to tell you."

"Oh?"

"Yeah, inside."

"Alright."

We went in and I took her hand, leading her upstairs so I could kill two birds with one stone and shower while I told her what's up.

She listened from the little seat at her vanity table and I had to peek out from behind the curtain to make sure she was still there, she'd gone so quiet.

"What are you thinking?" she asked finally, and I could see the pain behind her eyes. It struck me then, how small a town Loving was. So small-town that she likely knew these people, had helped them, or had them help her. So small-town, she was likely on a first-name basis with some of them, if not all of them.

Damn.

I told her the truth because that was really all you could do in this house since her spell thing went into effect.

"I think there's something shady as fuck going on down at the docks. I don't know that it's necessarily connected to Jack, but I wouldn't say that it isn't, either. What I do know after my time in jail, is that Bucky-boy definitely has something to do with it, and I wanna know what."

"That is why I want to talk to Gwen. It may require a greater working to uncover what's going on here, and if that's the case, I don't know what I am going to do."

"Why's that?"

"A greater working requires, at minimum, a circle of four, but for best results a full coven… neither of which I have access to."

"Shit."

"Hopefully Gwen has some ideas."

I shut off the tap and whisked back the curtain. Miri stood slowly from her seat and held out my towel to me.

"Thanks," I muttered, my own mind on the 'whole coven' thing.

"You don't have enough witches left around here to put a coven together?" I asked.

She shook her head.

"As far as I know, it's just me, Gwen, and Ivan, and I don't know that I could ask Ivan for his help. I get the impression he's uncomfortable with his latent talent on a good day and that he's downright afraid of it on a bad one."

"What makes you say that?" I asked, drying off. "He seemed alright to me lighting up your basement."

"That's a paltry thing. I'm sure he lights his forge much the same way. He did have some interesting things to say this morning, though."

"Oh, yeah? Like what?"

"He had an…" she trailed off, searching for the right word and finally settled on, "episode."

"What kind of episode?" I asked.

"The kind where he saw what happened to Jack, in his fire."

I rocked back on my heels as I wound the towel around my hips and tucked the corner.

"Shit."

"Considering he said men from far away came by boat to take bad things, Jack saw it, and they killed him for it… yeah, one big pile of shit. Especially considering what you just told me."

"Seems like the universe or the powers that be want this solved as bad as we do."

"Unfortunately, his message came with a warning about the police," she said and sighed.

"The police, or Bucky?" I asked.

"Bucky mostly, but his observation that the rest of the police force under Bucky are afraid of him to the point they'd look away on just about anything making them just as bad…" she trailed off and shrugged, and I nodded.

"Seems like all roads lead to Bucky-boy," I said.

"Well, not all roads." She chewed her bottom lip. "Ivan didn't say anything about Bucky being involved."

"No. Bucky's own man implicated him, though."

She let out a harsh sigh again and nodded, grimacing.

"You're right."

"Let's go get this thing with Gwen over with; it's a starting point."

She was stretching, fingers interlocked and arms raised above her head, standing on her toes in the cute little hiking boots she wore pretty much as every-day wear around her garden and such.

She frowned and let out a breath and asked, "Why'd you say it like that?"

I hesitated and said, "I ran into her several days back, like last week or the week before when I went out looking for work."

"That's right. Still, why did you say it like that?"

"Say it like what?" I asked, delaying the inevitable, knowing I'd been caught out.

"You didn't like her?" she asked, and I could hear the dismay in her voice.

"I mean, she didn't like do anything specifically to make me not like her…" I hedged. "It was right after I ran into Bucky the first time and I don't know." I gave a half-assed shrug and she cocked her head curiously. I failed to elaborate more on it. I mean, I didn't want to hurt her feelings and I couldn't exactly be sure that Gwen wasn't just being super-defensive of her friend.

Okay, that was a lie. She'd been a stone-cold bitch to me. Threatening without overtly making a threat. I didn't know what was up, I just knew I didn't like it, and I also knew I didn't want to start a fight with my girl so it was best I kept that shit to myself for now.

Miri waved me off slightly and said, "It was probably just your interaction with Bucky shading your interaction with Gwen."

"Yeah, maybe," I said noncommittally. I was dead ass that wasn't it, but again, I didn't want to start a fight with Miri. Sometimes it was just best to keep your mouth shut, you know?

"Let's go talk to Gwen," she murmured, and sounded as unhappy as I'd ever heard her. Worried. I guess I couldn't blame her. I mean, I could only imagine what it would have been like if I had a female on my arm who didn't like Jack.

No, you can't, because if they didn't like me, they wouldn't have been on your arm.

I heard the echo of his voice clearly inside my head and I had to agree with it. Still, I got dressed pretty quickly and followed Miri downstairs. If only for her, I was willing to give Gwen another chance. I mean, what if it was just the older woman was being protective or something? Yeah, maybe that was it…

The house was empty, and Miri did only the basic locking-up. She'd given each of her guests an after-hours key to the front door.

Still, it was unusual for her to do. Usually she didn't bother locking the place up at all, being out here on the edge of town and sort of in the sticks like it was.

"My car?" I asked and she smiled and nodded.

"We're going to The Wick and Stone, you know where it is?"

"Right on the main drag; that's where I ran into her, on my run."

"Ah, okay."

The drive was a silent one as she mulled things over. I didn't feel a need to fill the silence either, being that I was trying to think through shit just as much as she was. I found a parking spot right up against the curb in front of the shop and eased my way into it.

Shutting off the engine, we both sat for just a moment in total silence staring through the windows of the old stone building at the warm wood surrounding a crystal display.

"She's going to love you," Miri said softly, smiling.

"Yeah, how you know that?"

"Gwennie loves everybody."

I chuckled lightly and said, "Well that's good to know."

Her face lost that easy smile and she said, "It's going to break her heart knowing what this town is really like."

I reached out and twined my fingers with Miri's. She let out a heavy sigh and dashed a quick knuckle under each eye.

"It's not the whole town, love. Just a few," I said.

"I can't imagine everyone doesn't know," she said. "I feel like it's just me, you know?"

"You didn't," I pointed out. "And you're supposed to be some mystical all-knowing witch around these parts, aren't you? If you didn't know, I am betting there are a lot more who don't." I shook her hand back and forth to get her to look at me instead of out her window.

She turned and stared at me, her expression softening, her posture easing as her expression changed to something on the other side, but still on the edge of heartbreak.

"God and Goddess," she whispered, "I love your smile."

I felt it grow as love blossomed in her eyes and I raised the back of her hand to my lips. I kissed her there and she smiled, a little more bravely this time.

"I guess what I'm really afraid of," she said, "is that Gwennie will know, you know? About the smuggling, or whatever it is they're doing."

"And if she does?" I asked, and immediately answered the question before she could. "You'll feel betrayed?"

She nodded.

"To a certain extent, yeah."

"If she does," I hazarded, "it's a pretty likely thing that she legit thought you already knew and that's why it's never come up."

She nodded. "I'll know the truth," she said. "I don't think Gwen could lie to me. Even if she did, she's usually pretty bad at it."

"Only one way to find anything out," I told her gently and she nodded.

"Change is natural, change is good," she almost chanted.

"Still scary as fuck, though," I said even though I knew she'd intentionally left that part out.

"What is bravery but being afraid of something, yet doing it anyway?" she asked rhetorically.

"Yup. Look at you being all profound."

"Helps having a Muggle in the car," she said with light humor.

"Ha ha!" I mock-laughed. "You did not just go there."

"I did, and it's not really like you can deny it."

"You're right, I can't. Come on, let's go."

I reached for the handle on my door and checked for traffic before popping it open. I rolled my eyes when I saw a cop car rolling up on us and let out a gusty sigh.

Miri leaned down from her perch on the sidewalk and looked into the portal of the open door asking, "What's wrong?"

"Coming up on us," I said. She straightened and looked down the road.

"That's Bennett. Come on, you're fine."

I opened up my door and got out, jogging around the back of my Challenger and stepping up onto the curb beside Miri. Reflexively, she reached out for my hand, just as the patrol car glided by like a shark on the prowl. The cop inside looked our way, made eye contact with me briefly and gave me a nod, once down, once up.

I put on my plastic smile over gritted teeth and gripped Miri's hand lightly, turning for the open door of the bookshop.

Gwen stood waiting expectantly, her snow white hair crackling around her face like a cloud that held lightning at its core, but her smile was pure sunshine. Her blue eyes sparkled with genuine joy at seeing Miri.

"Come in, come in!" she cried. "I'll fix us some tea. Oh, Miri, how are you, my girl?" She hugged Miri fiercely, which forced her to momentarily let go of my hand, but as soon as she relinquished my girl, her hand was back in mine.

"Hey, what's up?" I said with a smile and a nod when her mentor turned to take me in.

"We meet again, Mr. Martin," she said warmly, but her eyes slid to Miri to take her in, like she was trying to trip me up, expecting I hadn't told Miri about our first meeting. I was suddenly glad I had.

"Ha, yeah," I answered.

"Welcome back," she said and smile lines fanned out from her blue eyes, equally deep lines bracketing her mouth as she smiled at me. Uniquely, instead of making her appear older and more wizened like it would other older ladies, on Gwen it made her look young. Of course, maybe that was just because she legit was young at heart. That, or she was a vampire. Seemed to me, whatever you were on the inside pretty much showed on the outside. Not always in the ways you'd think, but the signs were always there. Something about Gwen wasn't sitting right with me and I didn't know why, but for whatever reason it was, it had me firmly betting on vampire or something equally as dark and sinister.

If you were a good person, it showed, just like if you weren't, it showed too. You just didn't always see it with your eyes or the front of your brain. Instead, people called it things like vibes, or that their gut instinct was tellin' them something was off about a person. I always liked to think it was something else. Like our lizard brain or something. The one that told us fight or flight, a throwback to the days where it really was kill or be killed and you had to perceive if something was up or you'd get your dick shot off, like in the wild west.

I was cool. I would be keeping my family jewels right where they were. As much as I hated to say it, I had plenty of practice when it came to people. Call it how I was raised – or really the lack of how I was raised. At least, by my biological momma. With some of the guys she brought around and shit? I'd learned quick to observe and listen and keep my ass outta trouble.

Why was I thinking all of this? Because as much as I wanted to like Gwen, something was sending up a red flag about her and I couldn't quite put my finger on it. Maybe it was just the town in general, but I didn't think so. I couldn't tell you what it was, but I didn't like it. Unease was crawling down my spine and my instincts were telling me to shutter my expression and to try and not give too much away.

She smiled at me, an expression flickering across her face like she'd been caught, and sheepishly she apologized.

"I'm sorry," she said and I raised an eyebrow, freezing in place, mid-step, by the stool I was about to take.

"About what?" I asked, cautiously.

Miri was eyeing her mentor curiously, so whatever it was, she'd missed it, too.

"I couldn't help myself," Gwen said, biting her bottom lip. "I was prying, trying to read you. You're, um, very hard to get a look at," she said and had the grace to look embarrassed. "I had no idea you were sensitive to psychic-based energies."

I dropped onto the stool beside Miri's and said, "I didn't know that, either. My bad."

"What are you apologizing for?" Miri asked, laughing and I shrugged my shoulders, laughing, but uncomfortable, my senses still unnerved. That skin-crawling feeling you get when you've caught a spider on you and you've swatted it off, but the creepiness, the vaguely-violated heebie jeebies you get, knowing it was on you. That gross feeling you just can't shake after the encounter, remaining.

Gwen had turned and was making up some tea for the both of us, but I was jolted, and didn't want anything from this woman, but the way Miri had talked about her, the way my girl seemed to adore her... I didn't have the heart to say anything bad about the woman that might hurt mine. So, I did what any upstanding dude would do.

I kept that shit to myself.

*M*iri...

We talked -well, I talked- with Gwen, but Kavion had fallen uncharacteristically silent. He was beyond polite, he always was, but he was oddly formal with my mentor, stiff and stilted and I didn't know why. It was so unlike him, it made me uneasy. Gwen and I exchanged a look and I shrugged. She shot an apologetic look behind Kavion's back when he got up to go to the restroom, and when he was out of earshot she winced and said, "I may have probed a little harder than I should have. He has quite the walls."

I sighed and looked after where he'd gone and murmured, "He's had a very rough childhood, Gwen. A sad one. Even I don't know everything, but I know that it's a mark of his strength and Jack's kindness that he's even here."

I turned back to my mentor and best friend and she gave me a sympathetic look, saying, "Now I really feel awful, but Miri, are you sure he's trustworthy, with walls like that?"

"I trust the magic of the town, of our ancestors," I said, taken a bit aback. Gwen took a hurried sip of her tea, and lowering her cup with a clack against its saucer, nodded.

"No, of course, it's just… I worry about you."

"Worry about me?" I echoed, frowning.

"Of course!" she cried. "Jack's been murdered, and you're all alone in that big house –"

I laughed her off; I couldn't help it.

"I'm not alone," I reminded her. "Kavion's with me, and I've another guest. Plus, I've renewed the wards on the house, and Ivan has been by more frequently."

She made a face at the mention of Ivan's name. "Far be it from me to judge, but I'm not sure about him, either," she said, and I smiled and nodded.

"He's been through a lot, too."

Gwen smiled at me with affection, reaching out and giving my shoulder a squeeze, saying, "Miri, Miri, Miri… Out to heal the world one patient at a time."

"I try," I murmured softly, but I knew even some things were far outside my ability. Like solving crimes, for one, and healing broken hearts or aggressive cancers.

"Oh." Gwen whimpered in sympathy at my expression and I forced a smile.

"No, it's alright," I said, and she sighed.

"No, it's not, and it's alright that it's not. I'm just afraid today is not my day. It seems that no matter how I try, anything that can go wrong has gone wrong. It's just a black luck kind of day."

Kavion returned to his seat at last and took my hand in his, giving it a squeeze at my somber expression. Gwen smiled on us both and a bit of peace and happiness settled into her blue eyes.

I smiled back at her, and she changed the subject, sighing out musically, her breath light, as though satisfied the air had been cleared. She reached beneath the counter and extracted her silk-wrapped oracle deck. Setting it on the counter's glass top, she flipped back the covering and spread it out reverently to allow the deck room to breathe and do its work.

"Let's see if we can glean a little insight, shall we?" she asked.

It would seem the cards weren't cooperating any better than anything else for my friend today. Although I found some of her observations to be a little strange, I had to dismiss it. We all had our off days.

We chatted some more, Kavion's uncharacteristic silence getting to me, but I couldn't and wouldn't be rude in front of Gwen, and I wouldn't do the same to Kavion, so it would have to wait.

We were halfway back home when I finally couldn't endure the silence anymore and asked maybe a little too sharply, "What was that all about?"

"What was what?" he asked and I pursed my lips.

"You were totally unlike yourself in front of Gwen, how come?"

He was quiet, the look on his face thoughtful, and I could see it was a losing battle with whatever he was about to say. Finally he said, "I don't want to tell you."

"What? Why not?" I demanded, more than a little hurt and just a little bit outraged.

"'Cause you'll get mad," he said, matter-of-factly.

We pulled into my driveway, the car was parked and the engine cut, the sudden silence deafening.

"Well, it's a little late for that," I said, and got out of the car. He followed suit and looked at me over the roof.

"Come on, don't be like that," he said.

"Like what?" I scowled at him.

"I don't want to hurt your feelings," he said and shifted uncomfortably.

It was too late for that, too. I shook my head, hiking boots crunching across the gravel as I went for the gardens and greenhouses. I just wanted to be near my plants when I was upset and he was surely upsetting me by both not talking to me, not *communi-*

cating with me, and by being borderline rude to my best friend and mentor without explanation. He followed me, trailing behind a little forlorn.

"I don't like your friend," he said finally and I rounded and scowled harder. His approach to such a mammoth thing for me sucked ass.

"Why not?"

He shrugged. "I just don't. I don't trust her. Something is," he let out an explosive breath, "I don't know -off- about her. She's lying to you."

I made an incredulous noise.

He shrugged and said, "See, that's part of why I didn't want to tell you."

I felt for him in some ways, I mean, he was damned in either direction when you stopped to think about it, but still, this was turning into a Gordian knot of mixed emotions for me and I hated that. I didn't like my loyalties tested and I didn't want to believe anything bad about Gwen. I didn't. Kavion was wrong about her but the more I tried to figure out how to prove that the more upset I was becoming; upset because now I was stuck between a rock and a hard place.

Kavion leaned his perfect ass against one of the green house work tables, his hands stuffed in his pockets, his dark eyes roving over me. The plants shuddered in their pots and troughs at my discomfiture, my power raised and leaking out around my edges with my high emotions.

I tried to rein it in, but it was easier said than done. Finally, Kavion sighed and I realized with a bit of a start that he was holding it together remarkably well in the face of one of my more overt displays of power. Unease flickered in his dark eyes, unmistakable as a climbing vine nearby reached out to tangle with one of my curls, likely in a bid to comfort me.

God and Goddess, Gwen would have chastised me so hard for losing control like this. I couldn't help it, though. I loathed the powerlessness I felt in the pile of circumstance I was buried beneath.

Jack.

Bucky.

Loss.

Lies.

The overwhelming love I felt for the man in front of me... and the deep-seated feeling that he was right *about Gwen.*

Something about her card reading had been off. Even I had to recognize that, but at the same time, I could be reading too much into it.

"I hate this," I said, tears springing to my eyes.

"I know," Kavion said, and his expression crumbled into lines of empathy for my pain. It wasn't hard at all for me to remember that pain was shared. Jack had been his best friend, after all, and now, here he was, in love with that best friend's woman... likely not by chance. Not if the signs we were both receiving from Jack were any indication.

"I really want to hold you," he said suddenly, and it hit me in the center of my chest in all the worst ways that he felt like he needed to ask the question in his eyes, *Is it okay? Is it safe?*

"I really want you to hold me," I said, my voice cracking.

He came to me then and put his arms around me, gathering me close against his hard body, arms enfolding me, but sadly, not shutting any of it out. We were both far too embroiled in it.

"Why do you think Gwen is lying?" I asked, the foliage giving a shudder around us, as if wind passed through the leaves even though the air was still.

"Same reason you do," he said, kissing the top of my head. "Shit, we both know she ain't even try with any of that hoo-doo that y'all do."

I pressed my lips into a flat line and felt my shoulders relax under his touch as he leaned back to look me in the eyes.

"Seeing was never one of my better talents," I confessed.

"You sure?" he asked and cocked his head to the side, his dreads swinging attractively, two falling in front of his face.

"I'm sure," I murmured, brushing the hair from his eyes and holding it back as he bowed his head to touch his lips to mine. When you were this in love with another person, it was hard to focus sometimes. Harder still to keep your hands off of each other.

"Seems to me someone as powerful as you, who can make plants move just by how or what you're feeling – who can say a few words and wave your hands in the air and the people in your house have to tell you the truth? I think you can see just fine. You maybe just need to focus on doing it your way, with what works for you best."

I scraped my bottom lip between my teeth and closed my eyes, sending out a silent prayer to the Goddess, knowing that working magic frivolously held consequences and it wasn't something to be trifled with.

"I can always try," I said, and he nodded.

"That's my girl. Do you. See what you get."

I pushed away from him gently and the vines and leaning foliage retreated, settling back into their normal rhythm of photo-synthesis.

"My rune stones are in the library," I murmured, and he nodded and stood aside, gesturing for me to lead so he could follow. When it came to the magic, I guess I was the leader. I suppose he was when it came to any potential violence. It didn't seem fair when I thought about it like that, but then again, he'd been a soldier and had seen combat. We were worlds away from each other in that regard.

I fetched the little velvet bag of stones from the same drawer under the shelves that held the family grimoire. I motioned for him to follow me down to my basement workshop and went to the corner of the big room where the concrete floor had been busted out leaving a corner of raw earth. I knelt in front of it and dipped my fingers into the loose, sandy soil. Kavion leaned against the concrete and brick of the old foundation wall and crossed his arms.

"I really want you to be wrong," I said, and couldn't help the tremble in my voice.

"I know, love… but I'm not. I think you already know that, can feel it, too."

I sniffed and nodded, said my chant and cast the stones into the dirt.

I leaned forward and felt the bottom of my soul drop out… they indicated a great deception, a binding, and betrayal so deep there weren't any words yet invented to describe it. I'd held Gwen in my mind's eye when I'd cast the stones so there wasn't any misinterpreting the signs.

I cried.

I couldn't help myself. I wept and Kavion became my rock to weep the broken pieces of my heart against.

It wasn't fair. I didn't want it to be real… but it was.

IT WAS deepest night and I stood on the bluff, out on the beach and I didn't know how I had gotten there. The simple white country nightgown I wore whipped in the salty wind against my legs, my copper curls caught in the stiff wind, carried on the sea breeze and streaming into the dark. I turned full circle and listened to the crackling whisper of the tall sea grass as it shimmered and shook, the shafts bending under the cape's weather patterns.

A light beckoned inland and I cocked my head, listening, as a rhythmic clanging flittered out over the murmur of the flying sand. I walked, bare feet connecting with the earth, strength flowing up into my body which felt as light and insubstantial as the air whipping past it.

I strode with purpose across the dark planes of deepest night and loose sand, inexorably drawn to the light and warmth emanating from the garage-like portion of an old two-story house, my head cocking as I passed through the back fence, the weathered wood planks at waist height no barrier to me. I passed my hand through some of the tall sea grass infiltrating the back yard of the little house as I walked along the flagstone path, still warm from the sun's rays earlier in the day.

The clanging stopped the nearer I drew, and I stood at the threshold of the shop and raised my eyes to meet the big Russian's.

His mouth turned down at the corners and he nodded, once up and once down, and I could hear him clearly, in perfect communication though he didn't open his mouth to speak.

"Miri, what brings you to my door?"

I answered clearly, despite not opening my mouth myself.

"I don't know, exactly... I think... I think I'm asleep."

He nodded, *"Da, you're here but not here. I have seen it before."*

"How? When?"

"That does not matter," he answered. *"I see and hear your call. Tell your Gods I will answer."*

I frowned slightly, and woke, sitting up in the dark of my bed, gasping. Kavion sat up beside me demanding, alarmed, "What is it? What's a matter?"

I dragged my feet across the sheets and frowned at the feeling of grit, whipping back the blankets and ordering him, "Turn on the light."

He did, and we both frowned at the beach sand and silicate in our bed.

*K*avion...

It was raining outside, but that didn't stop her from flinging open the kitchen door and the window above the sink. It wasn't cold out, but it wasn't exactly warm, either. I think she just needed the fresh air. I know I did. I dropped onto one of the stools by her kitchen counter and smacked my palm lightly on the granite countertop, eyeing her nervously.

"So, you wanna tell me what just happened?" I asked.

She moved around the kitchen on her bare feet, her nightgown drifting alluringly around her legs, a shawl perched around her shoulders which vibrated with tension as she set about filling the electric kettle. She didn't speak immediately. Just went about making tea, face pinched with anxiety. It didn't surprise me when she reached for my calming blend.

I was vibrating, too, with pent-up energy borne of fear. She was afraid and wasn't talking to me, which in turn made me afraid - afraid for her, afraid for what just happened up there. One second we'd been sound asleep, the next she was sitting bolt upright practically screaming, and what the fuck was with the sand in the bed?

"I had a dream that wasn't a dream," she said.

"Okay," I said, freezing up and giving her some side-eye. "What about it?"

She licked her lips and rubbed them together, the water heating in the kettle the only sound for several moments.

"I dreamt I stood on the beach," she said.

"Okay," I said, when she didn't immediately pick up the story's thread.

She took a breath to continue and the floor outside the kitchen creaked. We both turned at the barefooted trudging across the old wood floors out there, and dude staying here stepped into the kitchen, hair mussed with sleep, rubbing a knuckle into his eye.

"You mind, bro?" I asked, not wanting the interruption.

"Sorry, I just had the strangest dream..." he said, and Miri and I exchanged a look.

"I'll make another cup," she said, and brought down a third mug.

That's how the three of us wound up at her little breakfast nook, the sound of pouring rain running down the drain spouts and rain chains around the outside of her covered porch the only sound between us as each of us waited for the other to start.

Dude took a breath first, and Miri perked up at my side. He looked at me, then to her, and let it out without saying anything and I frowned.

"You guys are straight about to kill me here," I said.

"Sorry, I just don't usually talk about this kind of shit."

"Bruh, believe me, I feel you, but – "

"What Kavion is trying to say is that something's happened," Miri said. "As in, a happening." She raised her eyebrows willing him to get it.

"As in..." he turned his head slightly, giving my woman a look that said he got it, but that he wanted or needed her to say it. She closed her eyes and exhaustion swept over her features and I instantly felt bad. The mental and emotional toll she was under was huge and it was starting to wear her thin, and by extension, me thin.

"For Christ's sake, talk to each other!"

The three of us jumped and exchanged looks.

"Jack?" Hall asked in disbelief and made to stand up.

"Isn't here," Miri said with a tired look. "I mean, he is, but he isn't."

"And I, for one, would really like to know how you just knew my homie's voice." I sat back in my seat as far as it would let me.

"Ah…"

"You're among friends," Miri told the man; I wasn't so sure who the fuck he was now.

"Nah, fuck that," I said. "You best start talkin', bruh. I'm gettin' tired of the lies and shit."

"You get what you give," he said, mistrust in his blue eyes.

Miri pressed her lips together, thinking for the moment.

"Alright, first things first. Mr. Hall, is that your real name?"

He looked from her to me and back again.

"Yeah, Holden Hall is my real name," he said.

"But?" I crossed my arms over my chest and he eyed me nervously.

"I'm an undercover agent with Customs and Border Protection."

Miri frowned, but I beat her to it.

"And just how do you know my brother?"

It was dude's turn to frown. "Brother?" he echoed.

"Jackson Greene," Miri clarified and the dude just kept staring at me, hard.

"Adopted," I said, and the lightbulb went off. Apparently the feds really weren't that bright.

"Ah. He was one of ours, too."

"Bullshit," I scowled.

"Jack was working on his thesis to become Fish and Wildlife," Miri said, confused, and I put my hand over hers where it rested flat on the table, her fingertips whiter than white with the pressure she had on them. She held my hand, grasping it firmly and something in this house had just gone down alright, and I was betting it had a lot to do with Jack.

"That was his cover," Holden Hall said.

"Bruh, you best get to talkin'," I repeated. I didn't add how I was fixin' to get violent if we didn't get some kind of a story and right quick.

It was a story, alright.

Turned out, Jack was with Customs and Border Protection and they were working internationally, trying to pin down a smuggling operation. Said smugglers were smuggling raw ingredients out of the U.S. and they were being refined into some crazy ass drug overseas, then the shit was being brought back inside the U.S. to be sold and distributed. Theirs was a joint operation with the DEA and FBI. A regular alphabet fuckin' soup of federal agencies in the mix.

"So how come it took you so long to come looking for Jack?" Miri asked in a whisper, trying to swallow everything dude was telling us and digest it.

"I'm not the first to come looking, actually. Jack was the first of three agents to disappear on this operation. The second and third was a set of partners that we sent in together."

There was something about the way he stared at Miri, just a little too hard, while she sat next to me, her hand clutching mine, turning a certain shade of green. She motioned at me and I got up out of her way, letting her out of the breakfast nook.

"And you came here, to Eilish House, to my house, because you thought I had something to do with it, didn't you?" she asked, pacing her kitchen.

"The thought had crossed my mind," he said quietly.

"And why are you all of a sudden being so free with your information now?" she asked.

"That's the part that I don't fully understand myself..." He trailed off and looked troubled and Miri went soft, like I knew she would.

"There's a reason why we love her," I heard whispered in my ear, and I glanced from dude to Miri, but they gave no indication they'd heard him that time. They were staring each other down cautiously, eyes bouncing over each other's features, gridlocked, trying to decide if the other were trustworthy or believable.

"Jack brought you here," I said. "Same as he did me."

"So it would seem," Hall said, but his eyes never left Miri's face.

"What did you dream?" she asked, her voice cracking as she visibly swallowed down the emotions that threatened to swamp her.

"Look, this is weird as –"

"Bruh, you're good, man. I've seen more than my fair share of weird since I got here, just tell us the story," I urged.

He rolled his lips, sucked his teeth, and took a slug of the tea sitting in front of him, then exhaled.

"Right, here goes…"

He dreamt he woke up, which okay, that's a little strange. He said he woke up in the dream and that Jack was standing there at the foot of the bed telling him not to freak out, that he was dead, and that no, it wasn't Miri but it was local guys. Hired thugs from down at the docks that were tasked with moving whatever raw ingredients from town out to sea, usually by a system of rope and pulley system off the clifftop from the trail Miri and I had taken.

He said he'd gotten caught up there, taking pictures and that they'd beat his ass and thrown him off the top. The ocean had pretty much taken care of the rest.

I stared at Miri, who stared at Hall, the heartbreak etched into every line of her face, her body tense and still, fists balled into the front of her nightgown as if it was her last ditch effort to hold herself together, from falling apart completely.

"How we know you're not blowing smoke up our asses?" I demanded.

"He can't, the wards are still working," Miri said, her voice tight.

"'K," I reasoned. "Still doesn't mean it's the truth, that it's what happened. Just because he dreamed it doesn't make it so," I said.

"I'm telling you, that's what he told me."

"Local guys? That was it?"

"He also said to tell Miri that he loved her, and that he never meant for it to be this way. He said he would have kissed her good-bye that morning, but he was distracted. Said that not only had he found some shit out about the smuggler's cliff top activities, but he'd found out some things about someone close to Miri. Said he knew it would break her heart and that he didn't want to do that to her. That he was trying to figure out how to make it easier on her... he never expected not to come back, but they somehow knew he was up there."

Miri dropped to her kitchen floor, sitting down, right there, like she was some kind of blow-up doll whose air pump had just been switched the fuck off. Deflating, wilting, tears trembling on her lashes and spilling over as she hugged herself and rocked forward over her lap, shuddering with silent, wracking sobs.

I went to her, kneeling on the cold stone floor and finally sitting down myself, pulling her into my lap to get her off the cold, cuddling her into my arms and holding on tight, telling dude over the top of her copper hair, "Alright, bruh. I believe you now."

19

*M*iri…

I'd prayed before going to bed the night before, I'd prayed to be the instrument of three times three, and it would appear that my prayers were being answered… *but of course, there was always a cost.* Always unintended consequences, though those unintended consequences this time, just so happened to be the truth… finally.

Of course, the truth usually hurt and this was no exception.

I let it out. I didn't hold it in. I couldn't bear to hold it in anymore. So I let the storm inside out to match the rain pouring from the sky, the crackling energy of nature fill my house, fill my spirit and galvanize me. When I sat up finally, both men in my kitchen silently bearing witness, it was with purpose.

"What is it you need to stop these people?"

"Unless you can raise the dead to testify…"

I raised my chin and said, "No, I can't raise the dead, but I might be able to raise the past. Call the echo of that night from the earth and the trees."

"You can do that?" Mr. –I mean Agent– Hall asked with a frown.

"It's no small feat, but it's been done before," I said.

"It would fall under magical-testimony laws." Hall sat back in his seat and chewed the corner of his lip, thoughtfully.

"You wouldn't even need me to testify really. If it's done correctly, you would see that night just as clearly as I would."

"This sounds heavy," Kavion said, meeting my eyes with a somber gaze.

"It is," I agreed. "I told you, I use magic as a last resort, not a first, but given the circumstances…"

"Yeah." He nodded and looked grim.

"So, when you want to do this?" Agent Hall asked.

"No time like the present," I murmured, thinking about my dream that wasn't a dream, but rather had to have been an astral projection. Something I had never done before, and likely would never do again.

"What do you need me to do?" Kavion asked.

I looked at him nervously and said, "Get the book."

IT HAD STOPPED RAINING, but it had been a cold and soggy climb to the clifftop. My hands and knees were coated in mud, and I wasn't the only one. Shade hunkered down on my shoulder, displeased with the field trip out into the cold and the wet, but it couldn't be helped. I needed him here as my familiar to act as a sort of magical battery pack. This was going to take all of my metaphorical juice and then some.

I stood in the center of the clearing, breath pluming the night air, my family grimoire heavy in my backpack, along with the things I would need. Shade, by comparison, was much lighter on my shoulder, the raven cocking his head and considering me. I smiled at him and brought my hand up. He stepped off my shoulder obediently, onto the proffered hand and I slipped my arm out of the strap on that side.

"Step up," I urged gently and he went back to my shoulder, his talons digging slightly into the denim of my jacket, the sheepskin collar brushing my cheek as I turned my head to look at him. "My beautiful boy," I murmured and he stretched out his neck as if to say *I am a beautiful boy, just look at me.*

It made me smile, but that smile didn't and couldn't last. The magic I was about to work required a lot and was super-dangerous for a solitary witch to do. I had modified the spell for a single person to accomplish, but ideally it took, at a minimum, a full circle.

I used the heel of my boot to rake out a circle in the dirt and loam of the forest clearing's floor. Set out the glassed in colored candles, already anointed with the proper oils, and set up the charcoal brazier Hall had carried up here for me. It was a larger model than the one I used in my basement on my worktable, almost one of those outdoor raised fire pits made commercially available. I waved Kavion forward and he took a hesitant step.

"I haven't consecrated the circle yet, its fine," I murmured. He stepped carefully over and between the lines and handed me the burlap bag of charcoal out of his big hiker's backpack we'd scared up out of the garage. I loaded the brazier and he handed me the other sack of herbs I'd mixed and blended. I gave him a nod and began to chant, handing him the family book, using the ribbon marking the pages to crack it. He stepped out of the circle and held the book open for me on his arms, turned so that I could see it, acting as a human book stand, and I loved him so much for it.

"Stay put," I ordered them both and Hall put up his hands in surrender, rooting himself to a spot at the edge of the clearing. I said the word of power and the candles and braziers sparked to life, the fire sweeping across the charcoal's surface, super-heating quickly, bringing the brazier to usefulness in a quarter of the time it would have taken naturally.

Shade cawed softly on my shoulder and I closed my eyes and cast herbs to flame, the smoke billowing, carried on the wind to the cliff's edge, creeping out from the center of the circle, filling the clearing low to the ground like mist, creeping along, raising old ghosts.

I reached out blindly with my power, drawing it from the earth, drawing it from Shade, using him as a conduit, tapping the ley lines deep below, the energy rushing down the lines that still bound me to Blyn and Ash, questing, asking for their help, burning with an emerald fire shadows that bound us from one another. A startling revelation that I had to shove away for now.

That emerald fire traveled down a third line, a third line I fully expected to terminate in the void, severed by the veil which Oaklyn had passed beyond, but it didn't. Unexpectedly, it travelled like the other two, but north, instead of south like Blyn's, and not nearly as far to the east as Ash's went. It stopped, just north of Loving, along the shore and ran smack into a great inferno of power that left me gasping, breathless at its magnitude.

An echoing wash of that power traveled back down the questing line and filled me, the color of fire and flame, alight with a very masculine energy, opposite the cool and soothing blue that came from Ash and the rush of white to fuel that fire further from Blyn. My sisters, unexpectedly answering the call in the predawn hours to aid me.

Tears sprang to my eyes at the joy and heartache traveling all those many miles to reach me, to assist me, but the reunion was short-lived. The power mingled with my green, earthy energy, filling me, overcharging me, burning me up from the inside out. I gasped and redoubled my efforts, pouring all of that power, backed with intent, into the earth, forcing the past and its hidden secrets up through the earth, the smoke from the braziers collecting, coalescing into vague shadowy figures as the players began to rise.

I focused on Jack and vaguely heard Hall whisper, "Oh, my God..." Kavion's admonition muffled as I was taken back, back, and further back, to that night, a dread filling me as a voice echoing with life and mercy, rich with growing things, the chittering of animal life and insect song intoned, "So mote it be," when I didn't back down.

The Goddess herself had spoken, and I was just along for the ride at this point, a helpless witness to the tableau about to play out before us.

I was ready to know. Come what may.

*K*avion...

"Oh, my God..." Hall muttered and I told him sharply, "Shut up!"

Miri's eyes had rolled back in her head to the point only white showed and it was creepy as fuck. Creepier still was, the smoke from the brazier she'd set up stopped acting like smoke. It went from billowing up and out like a campfire to being somehow suppressed, collecting in the bowl, filling it like a steady trickle of water up from the bottom, spilling over the sides like dry ice and rushing to the forest floor.

It stopped at the candles, at first, twisting and mounding, rising in the dark to swallow the pillars whole, expanding, growing, the little lights of the flames carried up, settling into the humanoid figures being created, at the center of their chests, the light fueled by the smoke, expanding as the humanoid shapes filled out, becoming solid, opaque; five players taking shape, gliding into position as they took on more distinct characteristics, like a chess board setting itself up mid-game, the pieces pausing, stopping, and filling out into people we knew.

Ropes and pulleys appeared in the frozen hands of some of the men from the dock. Gwen stood at the center of it all; one of those lights, we'd followed with our eyes to the edge of the clearing crouched in the underbrush, surprisingly close to where Hall stood, to the point he felt the need to move out of its way.

That one was hidden, practically invisible. Like, you wouldn't even know it was there if you weren't looking for it, and it was no surprise to me when it resolved into the form of my best friend, my brother in every way that counted - Jack.

Hall stood shoulder-to-shoulder with me, and we watched as the scene played out. Jack kneeling in the dark, shrouded in the underbrush, hidden from sight. Gwen talking to a taller man beside her that resolved into none other than Bucky Daniels, while the rest of the men worked around them, lowering a crate over the edge of the cliff, grunting in the dark with the weight of it.

"Be careful!" Gwen admonished them, and turned her attention back to Bucky who was scowling.

"I never agreed that Miri would love you or be infatuated with you, I merely agreed that she wouldn't be with anyone else," Gwen said.

Bucky scowled and said, "Well, she is with somebody else and I don't like it."

Gwen tsk'ed at him.

"I have no control over the wild magic of the town," she said.

"I told you I would help you if you helped me," he growled.

"I am well aware of what I did and did not agree to," she said, tartly.

"Well then why aren't you living up to your end of the bargain?" he demanded.

"I can't do everything for you, you spoiled boy!" she spat.

"And just what's that supposed to mean?" he demanded.

"Miriam Eilish isn't going to like you without any effort on your part to repair what damages have been done. You tried to rape her – "

"We were just kids, funnin' around!" he snarled and Gwen put up her hand.

"Be that as it may, I pay you a lot of money, on top of keeping my little pet earth witch under control. None of this would even exist without her." She swept an arm out to take in the operation underway. "Her magic keeps the earth fertile and thriving around these parts. She needs to be happy so we can continue to see the growth and keep production strong. You meddling is just going to dampen her spirits, and I can't have that."

A branch snapped and a soft curse; Gwen and Bucky's heads both snapped in the direction of Jack's hiding place, and I felt like it was about to go down – hating that despite how real all this looked, that I knew I couldn't do shit to stop it.

Gwen's arm flew out, and with it an almost visible arc of wind, rattling the trees and foliage, flattening it, allowing them a glimpse of Jack. She twisted her arm and raised her hand, palm up, and the wind lifted my bro and slammed him back high up, pinning him against a tree. Jack grunted and Gwen looked furious.

"It would seem you're going to get your wish, boy," she said and a seething hatred seeped into her voice. All of it directed at Jack.

What happened next was crazy.

They talked. Or rather, she interrogated my boy while he told her to pretty much go fuck herself and all of a sudden, with a motion of her hand, he started choking, his hands clawing at his throat, his chest, like he couldn't fuckin' breathe. All while this bitch stood there with a nasty little grin on her lips, a look of concentration in her ice blue eyes, which were staring at my bro. She was a stone-cold killer and I was warmed from the inside out with a rage like no other.

Jack crumpled to the base of the tree and I couldn't tell if he was just passed the fuck out or if he was already dead.

"Throw him over; go through his pockets first," she ordered and two of the men, their chests heaving from their exertions getting whatever had been in the crate lowered to the boats or whatever waiting below, came forward, one to either side of my brother. They went through his pockets, handing over his phone. Gwen closed her eyes and when she opened them, murmured the four-digit code to unlock it.

Meanwhile, one of the dudes swore and said, "He's some kind of a cop."

"Who cares?" Gwen demanded. "Throw him over. Between the rocks and the sea, there won't be anything left to find. Bucky and I will handle it." The men scowled but they each hauled him up between them, underneath his arms, without another word.

They dragged his limp body to the edge of the cliff and without hesitation, threw him over, and it killed me. I heard a choking sob and looked over in the direction of Miri, tears staining her fair cheeks, pouring from those wide-open eyes of hers, still a solid white, but I realized that despite how her lips moved, the low whispering chant of her voice, and how she kept this spell together so we could see, she was still there, still present, still living, and seeing this all right along with us and I'm telling you. That is the kind of strength that's indescribable and not only was my own heart burning with rage and pain for Jack, those flames rose higher for his woman, for our woman.

I didn't get to think about it, though because there was this 'chock' noise and a rattle, Hall giving a short shout of surprise before crashing to the ground, and when I turned, I dropped the book as my hands automatically went up at the gun pointed square at my chest by a very real, very solid Bucky Daniels, who looked freaked out by his double going through the motions from that night months ago, the night he had a hand in killing my brother.

"Well, this is unfortunate," Gwen said with a heavy sigh and I turned my head to where she emerged from the woods, the magic dropping, the smoke from the brazier returning to acting like smoke as Miri's eyes returned to their usual position, the sapphire depths filled with hatred and loathing as she turned them on her mentor.

Something told me school was out, and the student was about to become the master, but before Miri could lift a finger, the air was sucked out of my lungs, my own eyes going wide as I fell to my knees from the shock of it and I struggled to breathe.

*M*iri...

I felt them before I saw them. Moving through the trees out there in the dark, but I couldn't speak except to keep the spell alive, to bring it to its safe conclusion. If I let it go now, it could be beyond dangerous. I didn't want any unintended consequences from releasing that much wild magic so close to town with no true purpose behind it.

I heard Hall go down and wound the magic out and down, back down the threads, returning the help which I required to weave the spell in the first place. Returning order to the wild chaos of raw magic I had called upon this night.

"Well, this is unfortunate," I heard Gwen say, and the vision faded, dropping back to smoke, wafting away on the clifftop breeze, as my true sight returned, terrible sights returning with it. Hall face-down, unconscious on the forest floor. Bucky with his gun trained on Kavion in the dark, the light of the moon glinting off the hard black surface of the weapon, darker than any natural shadow, a harder edge against the white of Bucky's hand, against the deep shadows behind him.

It wasn't the gun that I should have been afraid of, though. Gwen, with a wicked gleam in her eye, did precisely what she'd done to Jack and I reached out a hand and screamed, "Don't!"

Kavion reached for his throat, clawing at his chest as she, a witch of the air, drew the very oxygen from his lungs and refused the life-binding agent reentry into his body. The command of her element was strong.

More men made their way out of the woods and went for Hall and I had to act fast. I did the only thing I could, used the only weapon I had at hand, and it was devastating to me, anathema to my entire being, to turn my magic into any other use than the one intended for it: to heal. I was a healer, taking my oath to 'harm none' seriously, unlike Gwen, apparently, and the only concession I could possibly make for what I did was to do my level best to remain non-lethal in turning my power into a weapon.

I flung out my arm and ivy whipped out of the dark, ensnaring at least one man by the ankle, dragging him back along the forest floor and into the trees. Shade cawed, flapping his wings in warning, buffeting the back of my head distracting me.

Gwen tightened her fist and Kavion sputtered and I threw out my hand, beseeching, "Please, stop!" I cried.

Gwen sighed and shook her head, "Miri, Miri, Miri..." she said, tutting my name. "Why couldn't you have just stayed complacent? All of this was going according to plan until you started digging. Until he came to town." She glared at Kavion and twisted her fist, and he bowed forward, fingers digging into the forest floor. She moved away from him in distaste and said to Bucky, "Don't let him go anywhere," before she released him.

I felt my insides sag with relief at the sound of Kavion sucking in a gout of air, beautiful, sweet, life-sustaining air, deep into his lungs. Coughing, but drawing it in.

Breathing, he's breathing, I assured myself, but the threat wasn't over yet.

"You used me," I said, hurt, and Gwen scoffed.

"Of course! How many times do I have to tell you, not everyone is your friend?" she demanded and I winced on the inside. She'd said the same about Blyn and Ash, when the accusations about Oaklyn had flown. About how I had to have known... but I hadn't, and I was beginning to realize...

"It was all a part of your big plan, wasn't it? Getting Blyn and Ash to leave, hiding Oaklyn's sickness from me... it was so you could be the big witch in town and run this little operation of yours, but why keep me here?"

"You're an earth witch," she said, like I was stupid. I just wanted her to incriminate herself further. Hall groaning, coming to; Kavion watching, his eyes meeting mine, a silent sort of knowing passing between us. He knew what I was doing. We were both working on a way to get out of this, we just hadn't worked it out completely yet.

There was at least one man down, but there were two more out there, I could feel their tread upon the earth and the plants eager to bind them, to stop them. I pushed my power into the ground and through the root systems below us and asked the flora to show me what exactly it was that Gwen was doing out here. Asked the trees to take my senses beyond the clearing to whatever it was she had going on.

The trees were my friends, knew my intentions were for the good of us all, and so they gladly swept that tiny bit of my power deep into the woods, down the less-steep back incline, a mile or two down from the cliff into the sweeping fields of poppy beyond Craig Wilstad's old barn.

Poppies... Opiates... of course. The specter-Gwen had said I'd been needed to help them grow and she had the right kind of magic to help them along, too, to keep the air warm, the climate ideal to grow them out of season. The old organic farm was off the beaten track, had been foreclosed upon, abandoned for several years, shutting down just after that fateful school dance where Bucky...

My eyes flicked to him and I glared. I would deal with him later.

Gwen stood by the clifftop and looked down. "It was perfect," she said. "You would be sad for a time, sure, but you had no reason to leave. We dealt with the next few that came to town much the same… You? You were harder, you just had to come during the festival." She shook her head at Kavion.

"Well, I suppose it doesn't matter now," she said. "Can't be helped."

She reached out and my mind was on fire, and I had to stop her. I threw out a hand as Kavion went back into choking, convulsive fits trying to breathe. A vine shot from the ground, wrapping around Gwen's hand and she laughed at me.

"You think I need silly hand gestures for this sort of thing? That stopping them will stop me?" Her face twisted into such a rage and I realized the depths of her ego in that moment. She pulled the air from Kavion's lungs with just a mere thought and I was so terribly afraid in that moment.

Afraid that my power was no match for hers, that I wouldn't be able to stop her, not without killing her and I didn't know if I could do it… not even to save the man I loved more than life itself.

I felt so incredibly weak in that moment, the defeat crossing my face and all Gwen did was laugh.

She laughed and laughed and I reached out, about to do something -anything- when that laugh abruptly stopped and turned into a scream. I opened my eyes, Kavion sagging and gasping once more as white-hot fire licked from the soles of Gwen's feet up her jeans-clad legs, her white hair lifting on eddies of current created by the heat which washed out through the clearing.

She lit up as if doused by gasoline, all of us standing or kneeling in open-mouthed horror at the sight. She whipped out an arm and the very air was pulled from my lungs, and I was suddenly drowning on dry land.

Shade cawed and launched himself at her, buffeting her with

his wings, scrabbling at her face with his talons in defense of his mistress, and Gwen, distracted by the pain and shock, threw up her arms and took a fateful step back.

"Shade!" I cried, and my raven tumbled back and away from Gwen, even as the cliff face crumbled beneath her heel, and with a shriek, she plunged.

Bucky gave a shout and I snapped back into myself, into my power and let the ground open up beneath the rest of the men out in the dark, quicksand swallowing them to their waists, even as Ivan stepped out of the shadows, his hands coated in the same blue-hot flames that'd engulfed Gwen.

Bucky's gun swung in his direction and I twisted my hand in the air, dragging it down; the forest floor beneath his feet turned to quicksand, swallowing him to his waist as well. He fired, his shot going wide and I felt punched in the gut, low and to the side, above my right hip, the pain of the impact somehow less than I expected, only rushing in a moment later as I crumpled to my knees.

"Miri!" Kavion shouted, and Ivan reared up, reaching out a hand and letting the fire claim Bucky, who screamed and screamed. Hall came to and scrambled away from the burning man, sticking from the ground.

"Miri!" I heard and it seemed far away, an echo of what it should have been. I was lifted and there was an awful pain followed by a gush of something wet. I looked up into Ivan's rugged face.

"Take care of them," I said, worried for Kavion and Hall.

"*Niet,* I take care of you." He pressed one of his big hands into my side and I cried out from the pain.

Ivan looked at Kavion, whose hand slid into mine. I gripped it and smiled. "I love you," I told him. He needed to know that.

"Just hold still," Jack urged and I flicked my gaze from Kavion, past Ivan, to where he stood near. I smiled sadly, tears tracking down my temples, knowing that if he were here and I could see him, it only meant one thing.

"I am sorry," Ivan said through gritted teeth, and fire erupted in my side and I screamed, just before I was swallowed whole by the dark.

*K*avion...

"Bruh, no! What did you do?" I cried and touched the side of Miri's face, her head limp and lolling on her shoulders, turning my way against the big Russian's chest.

"Stopped bleeding, but we must go," he said in his thick accent. "She needs hospital. Him too."

He thrust his chin at Hall who trudged in our direction, blood coating the side of his neck, soaking into his collar from the back of his head.

"I'm fine," he said, dazed, and I shook my head.

"Ain't none of us fine, we gots ta roll." I lifted Miri and Ivan let me take her. He went and gathered her raven, the bird croaking, flapping its wings, clearly injured itself.

"He is alive, that is good," Ivan said.

"Let's go, I'll call it in as soon as I got a signal," Hall said.

We crashed down the trail, trying to get to the highway, to cell service. As soon as he got a bar, Hall got on the line and even though the minutes stretched out and my body was having fits from nearly suffocating to death twice up there, I wasn't listening to it. Miri was limp, so much dead-weight in my arms, and she was getting heavy.

"Here." Ivan handed her bird off to Hall.

"What am I supposed to do with this?" he cried.

Ivan grunted and took Miri from me saying, "Do not let it die. He dies, she dies," as we made more progress down the trail.

"Bruh, you better take care of that fuckin' bird," I said, hating how helpless I felt. Not just in this moment but the whole time. Like, I was way in over my head here. This shit wasn't something I could fight with my fists, and I had no fucking magic of my own. It was bullshit, and I was angry. I was angry at my failing her, and I used that anger to fuel me. To take her from Ivan when he got tired, and to bring her fuckin' down off that cliff and to the ground. To load her into the big man's lap in the back seat of my car while Hall communicated with a dispatcher, telling him where to send the life-flight that was inbound.

I used that rage to drive at breakneck speeds, to stop at the edge of the open field outside town, to hustle my woman onto the helio, along with Hall, who they insisted on taking despite his protests, due to his head injury.

I couldn't go with her, though. They told me what hospital, in Boston. The best I could do was turn with Ivan, after Hall passed off her familiar, and drive there as fast as we could get there. Ivan had me stop at a twenty-four hour vet place with Shade to let him out. The big Russian swore to me he would find the hospital that he would meet me there and I made him make the pact on a soldier's honor. I left him there in the glow from the vet's office sign and drove at breakneck speed to the hospital, arriving to a still helicopter on the helipad outside.

I found Hall in the Emergency Department, holding gauze to the back of his head, wincing, and demanded, "Where they take her?"

"Surgery, all we can do is wait," he said as a nurse pried the hand holding pressure to his head back to look.

My anger, all that fuel, flamed out and I was left standing, shaking, dirty and spent, in the middle of the bustling emergency room, just as lost as I had been on the top of that fucking cliff. Useless. Worthless. Man, I was fuckin' trash... I had one job...

Protect Miri. My woman, my girl.

"I'm sorry, Jack. I couldn't even do that, bro..." I murmured into the controlled chaos.

"You say something?" Hall asked.

"Nah, bro. Nah..."

IVAN FOUND us in the waiting room outside surgery. Hall was glued to his phone, standing a ways away from where I sat, numb and waiting on pins and needles to hear something, anything, about Miri's progress.

The big man took a seat as far away from us as he could sit. As far away from everybody, including the nurses, and locked eyes on me. He gave me a nod and I gave him one back. He settled back in his seat and pulled the hood of his hoodie up from behind the collar of his duster and put it over his head, pulling the hood down low over his eyes, and I turned my gaze to my hands, still stained with Miri's blood in places, the knees of my basketball shorts and athletic leggings still stained with earth, pine needles trapped in the laces of my Nikes.

"My name is Blyn Courtney and I'm looking for my sister Miriam Eilish. Somebody told me she's been admitted and that she's on this floor?" I looked up.

The woman was standing at the nurses' station, both of her hands gloved in fine, chocolate-brown leather, gripping the strap of her expensive purse across her chest with worry. She was petite, her long hair dark, her eyes equally dark and large in her doll face. She looked stricken and I got up.

"Hey, yo, she's still in surgery. They haven't told us nothin' yet," I called out to her and the nurse checked her screen and nodded to her. She bypassed the nurses' station and walked up to me.

"And who are you?" she demanded.

"I'm Kavion, I guess you could say I'm her boyfriend. That's Agent Hall, and that's Ivan." I indicated the other two dudes with me and Blyn's gaze fell on Ivan. Her lips thinned down and she nodded, like she recognized him. He huddled in on himself a little bit more and nodded, affirming something for her that I didn't understand.

"You know Ivan, at least?"

"Yes and no," she said. "It's a magic thing."

"Shit." I swore and she frowned.

"What?"

"We forgot her family book."

"What?" she looked alarmed. "Where?"

"I'll have CSU look for it," Hall called out, and he spoke low into the phone again, taking a few more steps away from us.

"What happened?" Blyn asked and looked at me beseechingly. I opened my mouth to fill her in and she said, "You know what? I'm sorry, let's take a step back." She pulled her glove off of her right hand and held it out. "I'm Blyn, I grew up with Miri."

I shook it lightly and said "I'm Kavion, I met Miri through –" I stopped, her hand tensing in mine as her eyes flew wide. She ripped her hand from mine and staggered.

I reached out to help her and she cried sharply, "Don't touch me!"

I dropped my hands and nodded. "Air witch?" I asked.

She frowned, "How did you know?"

"You're the clairvoyant one. Miri told me about you. You know, you could have just asked."

"I'm sorry," she said, straightening. "And I'm sorry that happened to you tonight."

"S'okay," I said.

"It's not your fault, any of it. If anything, it's ours…"

"Mr. Martin?"

We looked over sharply to the man in the white lab coat and scrubs. Ivan stood up and Hall rushed off the phone.

"Yeah, that's me."

"Your girlfriend? Wife?"

"Yeah," I said, and tossed my head and my dreads out of my eyes.

"She's out of surgery and resting comfortably," he said.

"She going to be okay?" I asked.

"Yes, but…" he hesitated.

"But?"

"But she's unconscious and we don't know when she'll regain consciousness."

"What, like a coma?" Hall asked.

"Not exactly," the doctor said. "More like she just won't wake up, even though there's no reason why she shouldn't, at least not medically."

"Can we see her?" Blyn asked.

"Two at a time, please." We all four took a step forward and Ivan took a step back.

"You go," he said to me. "And you," he looked at Blyn. She nodded and without a backward glance followed the doctor.

"Thanks, man," I said and he gave me a nod.

We went into the room, Miri lying pale and fragile in the hospital bed. Blyn went and touched her hand and after a moment, the tension drained from her and she breathed out.

"She's in a place between worlds," she murmured. "All we can do is wait."

I pressed a knuckle against my lips and nodded, closing my eyes. The tears couldn't be forced back if I'd wanted to.

She put her gloved hand against my arm and gave it a reassuring squeeze.

"She's strong," she murmured. "She has to be okay."

I nodded but didn't say a word, just folded myself into the chair by her bedside, sliding my hand under hers, cradling it lightly in my palm.

"Not going anywhere, love. I'm right here," I said. "Just come back to me when you're ready."

*M*iri...

I sucked in a startled breath, my eyes flying open to the soft warm breeze and the light tinkling of chimes.

I stood in my bedroom, but things were different. Everything was lighter. The earthy tones of the gauzy draperies of the canopy on my bed were replaced with whites, creams, and golds. Even the nightgown I wore wasn't anything I owned. Light cream satin, slick and shiny, the front a deep cowl neck, plunging between my breasts nearly to my navel. The back non-existent, held up by thin straps. The satin smooth against my skin, plunging to the floor, covering the tops of my feet which rested on the warm bare hardwood.

That wasn't right, either. I had area rugs in my bedroom.

The windows were open, a hazy summer day outside, seed fluff drifting past the open portals, a light warm breeze rustling the curtains, identically gauzy and as insubstantial as the bed canopy.

Light musical tones from the wind chimes I had outside, downstairs, drifted through the windows, flitted about the room, soothing to the ear, and there was such a sense of peace to it all. A sense of peace I shouldn't have felt, but I couldn't readily remember why right now.

"Hey, baby…"

I startled at the voice and whirled. Jack stood behind me in the open doorway of the room leading out into the hall, shirtless, barefoot, in just a pair of off-white linen drawstring pants.

"Jack," I breathed and he smiled, somewhat sadly and opened his arms. I went to him without a second thought and held tightly to his body.

He hugged me back, lips against my hair and murmured, "I've missed this so much."

We clung together in the light musical enchantment of whatever place we were, which I knew in the front of my mind wasn't home, but felt so familiar to me I couldn't explain it.

"Where are we?" I whispered and he chuckled.

"The place in-between," he murmured. "Where magic dwells."

I closed my eyes and sighed out remembering the dark, the fire, and the pain. I didn't really want to know but couldn't resist asking, "Am I dead?"

"No, baby, no," he soothed. "Not yet," he said, voice full of regret, "but you have to choose and soon."

I felt my heart break all over again. I looked up at him and he smiled and brushed his fingertips against my face, as if memorizing the curve of my cheek, as if he already knew what my answer would be.

"Kiss me," I whispered and he lowered his mouth to mine, his goatee tickling my face, his lips soft and warm where they moved over my own. God, how I missed his silvered eyes. His touch, his kiss, the way his fingertips trailed over my form as we kissed and the way he rucked the fall of the skirt of the gown I wore, backing me up against the bed, even now.

Passion, love, spilling over and filling the void in my heart where he'd been ripped away so suddenly. Filling it with everything we hadn't said to one another just yet.

"I'm sorry..."

"It's okay..."

"It's not..."

"It is..."

"I should never have believed..."

"I forgive you..."

"I love you," he murmured aloud, breaking our kiss, hands beneath my ass, lifting me to the edge of the bed, stepping between my legs.

"I love you, too," I whispered against his lips, my fingers tangling in his short dark hair, his silvery blue eyes filling with yet more unspoken emotion as he returned his mouth to mine, freeing his cock from his pants and slipping inside me.

"Oh, Jack..." I breathed, my voice hoarse. He grunted in satisfaction and held me tight, and I returned the embrace, nails digging lightly into his back as he moved.

I couldn't help it. I couldn't help but compare. Jack was slightly smaller, in some ways a better fit for my body than Kavion, and the guilt struck sharp in the center of my breast, my heart twisting painfully.

Was this a betrayal? Would this hurt him? I didn't want to hurt him, I loved him so...

My heart squeezed down once again, knowing I had indeed made my choice. I wanted to live. I loved Kavion and Jack in equal measure, and Jack knew as well as I that this... this was a final good-bye. That this was the last time, for a long time, potentially an eternity.

I knew with sudden clarity that love springs eternal in the little town of Loving and our love had passed with the season and it had been beautiful. It had blossomed, and flowered into something so complete and it had been cut down too soon, but that love had passed and in its time it had been everything, but it was his brother's, his best friend's time now, and there wasn't any changing that.

"There ain't no coming back, baby," he murmured. "I'll miss you both, so much, and I'll try to come when the veil is thinnest, but for now, this is it," he whispered fervently in my ear and so I allowed this deeply intimate final good-bye, because how could I not?

"Jack," I whispered and gave myself over to the feel of his body against mine, inside mine, this final moment, this final time, knowing that this was as real as it could be even though my own body was far from this beautiful peace. This place between worlds.

I lay back so I could watch him, his beautiful eyes dark, hooded with passion, as he smoothed his hands over my thighs and drove himself deep. I arched beneath him, the dress staying put over my chest through sheer magic of its own. Jack laughing at me, joy spreading where pain once lived as I laughed too, as we somehow shared one another's thoughts here.

God and Goddess, how he loved me, and how I loved him, and yet fiercely, at the same time, missed his brother, Kavion. I knew my work wasn't done on the mortal plane. There were still so many who needed me. So much left undone. So many broken hearts and physical maladies to mend, so much pain in others I could ease… and I needed to do that.

It was my calling, and I wasn't done.

Still, for now I let it fall away for this one pure shining moment. I lost myself in the steady rhythm of my lover's hips as he slowly, torturously brought me high and higher, out of body, raising me up like an offering, the rich dark timbre of Kavion's voice reaching from the ceiling, calling me home…

"Not going anywhere, love. I'm right here," he said. "Just come back to me when you're ready."

"Just a little bit longer, baby. Stay with me just a few moments more…" Jack begged in counterpoint, and I was so torn but it felt so good, so unreal to be loved by two very different but equally good men. I felt incredibly blessed, incredibly rewarded for having them in my life.

Through the sweet pain of having to choose, having to leave

one over the other, Jack was there, kissing me softly, loving my body gently, and telling me, "It's okay, no guilt, no sorrow, Miri. I want you both to be happy, so much. I want you two to take care of each other. I love you so very much. You live for me. Both of you, for me, and tell my brother good-bye for now. I'll be waiting."

And I believed him, as I fell from on high, through time and space, through magic and promise, back to earth, back to my broken body lying in some hospital bed.

My eyes flew open and my hand gripped tight around Kavion's and I sucked in a sharp rusty breath and I lived.

For Jack.

For Kavion.

For my sisters.

For Ivan.

For myself…

Kavion...

She gasped, back arching off the bed a little, her hand tightening around mine as if she were drowning and had finally broken the surface, sucking in that first sweet breath of air, and I was painfully aware of how that felt. Her blue eyes were wide, fixed on nothing in particular at first before she turned, crying out from the pain in her side as she twisted to grasp my hand with her other, holding on tight with the both of hers.

"Miri? Miri? God and Goddess – Nurse!" Blyn cried and I leaned over my girl, smoothing some of those fiery red locks out of her face as I tried to get her to calm down. I don't know where she'd been or what she'd seen but her arms went around my neck, pulling me down to her and she clung to me for dear life as medical people filed into the room to check her out.

"Kavion," she sobbed into the side of my neck, and I couldn't help her, couldn't find out what it was because I was being pulled away from her, both me and her sisters – thrust out into the hall, the door to Miri's room shut firmly in our faces.

It'd been a few days. Ashlyn had blazed into Boston on her

motorcycle the day before, Blyn having stayed in touch with her every step of the way. She didn't seem the type to like anybody so I didn't take it personal that she didn't seem to like me.

"Well, this is bullshit," she said flatly and I nodded, raking some of my dreads out of my face, tying them half-up with a big, stretched-out hair tie.

I'd driven back to Miri's and gotten some clothes and things, had taken Ivan back to Loving with the promise I'd contact him with any news. Dude was hard to reach. He didn't have a phone or do the internet, so I followed through on that the only way I knew how. I shot a text to Hall who was still staying at Miri's place through the investigation or whatever. I asked him to let Ivan know and he shot back *10-4.*

I nodded and looked up, Blyn and Ashlyn staring at me.

"What?" I asked.

"What was that?" Ash demanded.

"Asked Agent Hall to let Ivan know Miri was awake."

Ash rolled her eyes and Blyn smiled faintly. "We could have done that," Blyn said gently.

"Oh, how?"

"Duh," Ash said. "Magic."

"Whatever Miri did up on that cliff top bound Ivan into our circle."

"No shit, and I don't know if I like it," Ash complained.

She had a reason to be bitchy about it, I guess. Her biological sister had been the one with cancer, the one to die.

We'd put some shit together while Miri had been unconscious, and a lot of roads led back to Gwen being a manipulative bitch. The worst kind of female there was. Conniving, back-stabbing, all with a fuckin' smile on her face. Some kind of evil, for real.

She'd done something to Miri without Miri knowing. Had blinded her to Oaklyn's illness, had conveniently planted the seeds of self-doubt into Miri, had singled her out, corralled her away from her circle mates, sowing dissent between the three of them left. Tellin' Miri one thing, Ash and Blyn another, breaking down their lines of communication.

I'd seen dudes do it to their women in the military. Classic abuser-type shit. Just, she'd been cold about it, clever, and had everyone fooled. Ash and Blyn were bitter as fuck for falling for it, for leaving Miri behind to pursue lives outside Loving, convinced their powers could be useful and do some good out there in the great wide world. All so Gwen could grow her poppies and have a pet earth witch nearby to keep the ground fertile and the operation running smoothly – all without her even knowing.

It was an intricate web of lies and my brother had gotten caught in it. He'd also been instrumental in unraveling the whole thing and I couldn't be prouder of him. Our mom, either, despite her pain.

Funeral arrangements were underway. She wanted me to bring Miri. I had a feeling it would be hella awkward, but I also had the feeling it was needed.

I just hoped Miri would still want me around after all of this.

I hung back when the door opened again and let her sisters go first. They had dibs; a rift and a pain that needed to heal as much as my woman did. I could respect that.

Still, I was encouraged by the desperate looks of longing Miri cast in my direction when her sisters weren't looking, and I was encouraged by it but still apprehensive, my own insecurities rising up.

Finally, she sent them away for the time being, asking for some time alone with me, and I pushed off the wall in the corner and went to the chair Blyn had been occupying to sit. She and Ash left the room reluctantly, but they respected Miri's wish and left us alone for the time being.

"Come here," she whispered and I smiled, putting down the railing on her bed, climbing up on it and tucking her into the curve of my body. She fit so nice, the weight of her arm at my waist, her head on my chest as she closed her eyes and listened to my heartbeat - everything.

"Where'd you go on me?" I asked her, knowing she'd been somewhere, even though I couldn't tell you how.

"I think, in a space between worlds," she murmured.

"Jack there?" I asked.

"Yeah, how did you know?" she asked.

"Just a guess," I said evenly, and she held to me tighter.

"I had to choose," she whispered and shuddered with emotion, but didn't break down, not yet. I held her close and felt the knot of anxiety in my chest loosen.

"How's that?" I asked.

"I could have stayed," she whispered. "But I chose you."

She could have stayed, which was just a nice way of saying she could have died, and I felt choked.

"I'm glad you're here," I said, not trusting my voice beyond those words and I held her tight and tighter, neither one of us wanting to say anything else, yet. This wasn't the time, this wasn't the place. I wanted to take her home for that.

Didn't stop me from kissing her forehead and staying right where I was until the hospital staff came back and kicked me out of her bed.

"TAKE IT EASY, love, take your time." I held my hands down to her. She'd gotten her legs swung out the passenger side of my car, her feet flat on the gravel of her drive, but the whole 'bending forward' to get her feet up under her to stand was still a challenge.

They'd let her go remarkably quick, she'd only had to stay one more night after she'd woken up, but medically, she was on the mend and didn't have any reason to stay. Her sisters had promised to stay in touch, and Ivan? Well, he stood on her back porch with

Hall, shifting his weight from foot to foot nervously, lookin' like he wanted to help somehow but I had it.

I had her and I wasn't about to let anyone else get too close. Not yet, at least.

"I'm okay, I'm okay!" she said sharply after standing, but the wince of pain on her face said otherwise. I knew she just didn't want me to worry, but that was too bad.

"You good?" I asked after the lines of pain had smoothed out.

"Yeah, I could use some of my pain-away tea," she said, and Ivan perked up, turning and disappearing into the kitchen door without a word.

My man, I thought to myself as I led her carefully to the back step.

She was hurting, but only because she refused to take any of the pills they prescribed her. She said she could wait to get home, for her own remedies. It'd like to drive me nuts though, seeing her like this.

Ivan was at the gas stove, the kettle heating rapidly, the flame beneath it running hotter than should have been possible, and I gave him a chin lift for his lookin' out for my girl. Hall closed the kitchen door behind us and Miri sighed, a tension leaving her at finally being home.

"Bed?" I asked her.

"Shade," she murmured and I nodded. We went to see her raven first. He looked a hot mess, feathers singed and patchy, but otherwise unhurt, according to the vet. I'd brought him home the same time I'd come back to get clothes for myself and Miri. Ivan had been lookin' out for him, coming by daily to feed him and change his cage lining.

"Oh, my beautiful boy, just look at you..." Miri crooned and Shade bobbed his head on his perch.

"Vet says he'll molt and be good as new, might have a bit of a bald patch, but he wasn't burned too bad, just singed really, and just his feathers."

"I was so worried," she murmured, and he cocked his head and cawed softly.

"Come on, love. Let's get you upstairs, huh?" I asked her and she nodded.

She didn't stop to look for her family book, trusting Hall and myself that we got it taken care of. It'd been collected by CSU and Hall had smuggled it out. I'd put it back in its drawer under lock and key for Miri. Hadn't even had a speck of dirt on it. Pages were fine, some of them oddly blank, but I figured that may have been because my ass wasn't a witch.

"I'll, uh, get your statement in the morning, Miri," Hall said, burying his hands in his pockets. "Welcome home."

She smiled at him and it was tired, her already porcelain skin a whiter shade of its usual pale, a tightness around her eyes and mouth that wasn't usually there. K, yeah, we were done. It was time for bed if I had to carry her there.

I gave a nod to Hall while Miri murmured her thanks and transferring her left hand to my left I stepped up beside and behind her, my arm around her, half ushering her gently to the foot of the stairs. She sighed out and looked up them, her expression a little lost and I said, "'K, yeah, I'm gonna pick you up, so you better hold onto me."

"No, no, I can make it," she insisted, and I laughed and picked her up carefully, one arm behind her back and the other beneath her knees.

She cried out in surprise but it didn't hold an edge of pain; still I paused as she put her arms around my shoulders, and I asked her, "You alright?"

"I'm okay," she said, relieved.

"Okay, here we go." I took the stairs slowly, moving carefully, watching her feet and making sure I didn't jostle her too hard. I was breathing hard, my arms trembling a little by the time we reached the third floor landing but I intended to take her all the way into her room.

Her sparkling laugh stopped me and she patted my shoulder.

"Okay, that's enough, down, down, down."

I set her on her feet carefully, her hand going to her injured side, holding it as I set her down. I worried I hurt her but she waved me off and took my hand, threading her fingers between mine. I let out the breath I'd been holding and gave a nod, and walked with her down the hall to the tower room door, which stood open.

She stopped just inside and looked around, a faint look of disappointment on her face, or regret. Whatever it was, it wasn't good and I worried.

"What's wrong? Something missing?"

"No," she murmured and pressed her lips together. "I need to tell you something, and I'm afraid to, because I don't want it to hurt you, but I can't keep it to myself anymore..."

I led her to the bed and made her sit, sitting beside her.

"What's going on?" I asked.

She told me, about her and Jack, and I didn't interrupt. It was a lot to take in, but at the same time, I had to admit, I didn't feel bad about it, about what she said or what she done, or whatever.

"I mean," I said, swallowing hard. "It's not like you cheated," I said. "Jack was kind of here first..."

She rolled her eyes to the ceiling, those baby blues of hers growing wet, glassy with unshed tears as she said, "I missed him. So much."

"I miss him too," I said, and put a hand on her back, rubbing it lightly, suddenly understanding why she'd been almost... distant. I couldn't be mad, though. I mean, it was good-bye, for like, for real... and she'd chosen me. I mean, she was here. How could I be mad about that?

"He told me to tell you he would try to come to us when the veil is thinnest."

"Is there such a thing?" I asked, curious.

She nodded. "Samhain, your Halloween..."

"Ah, yeah, that." I nodded. "For real, though. I'd like that," I said.

"So you're not mad?" she asked, and the brittle hope in her voice got to me. Nearly killed me.

I gripped the back of her head in my palm and brought my lips to her forehead, kissing it, her eyes drifting shut. "I'm not mad, love. I could never be mad about you and Jack," I told her, and it was true.

"Promise?" she asked and shit, she was so fragile, and this had been eating at her and was chewing her up from the inside out.

"I promise," I said with a smile, and twitched a thumb through the wetness leaking from her eye, wiping it away on the thigh of my jeans.

She closed her eyes, twin crystalline tracks magnifying her freckles as they slipped down her cheeks, and she whispered, "I don't deserve you, either of you."

"Gonna have to disagree with you there," I said, not understanding how she could be so down on herself.

I sighed and said, "Let me help you." She nodded and I slipped off the high bed and knelt at her feet, picking at the laces of her boots, slipping them and the socks off her feet.

The only evidence she'd been shot was one of those big, rectangle, fat Band-Aids on her stomach, low and off to one side, near her belly button. I swallowed hard, thinking about how the doctor had said she was lucky. Had the shot been angled toward the center of her body and not out the other way, how she could have been hit in the spine. As it was, she'd gotten lucky, the bullet had fragmented and hadn't gone out the other side. They'd had to go fish and get it all out. I was just amazed they'd been able to do it virtually through the entrance wound itself. All of it going down pretty much laparoscopically, the other little incision close enough that it all fit nice and neat under that one bandage no bigger than her palm.

I eased her out of her jeans and out of her blouse and bra. She sat in just a pair of panties while I eased a country white nightgown over her head. I was lowering it over her lap when Ivan cleared his throat in the doorway, a tray in his hands.

"Hold up, my guy," I told him, and helped Miri stand, folding back a triangle of blankets, letting her get into bed for real.

I threw chin at Ivan letting him know it was cool and he came in, setting the tray on the edge of the bedside table. I got out of his way and sat at the foot of the bed, by Miri's feet while she propped herself up against the headboard.

"Thank you, both of you," she murmured.

"*Niet*, is nothing," Ivan said, pouring a cup of the tea for her and asking, "Honey?"

"Yes, please," Miri murmured.

He gave a nod and passed the doctored cup on its matching saucer to my girl. She blew on it and took a sip, eyes closing as she sighed out, relieved at knowing relief was coming.

"So, tell me what happened," she said.

"Don't think Ivan's gonna be charged. Hall says it's 'justifiable homicide' by the book, with what Gwen was doing to you."

"What about Bucky?" she asked.

"Not dead," Ivan said and she blinked.

"Not dead?" she echoed.

"*Niet*," Ivan uttered and I nodded, drawing in my lips. I wished he had died, but honestly, with the amount of pain he was in back at the hospital's burn unit down south? Nah, he needed to suffer and he was gonna suffer some more when they threw his ass in prison. I told Miri about it. About the list of charges, how the Chief was up on some and how her guy Mack and like two other dudes were the only ones not facing charges, out of all of Loving's finest. She looked grim.

"Wow," she uttered and yeah, that about covered it.

"It is as it should be," Ivan said and Miri reached out a hand. He frowned, looking dubious, but took it.

"You saved our lives," she whispered. "I'm sorry you had to, but I'm grateful," she said. "Thank you."

Ivan pulled his hand from hers and gave a nod, his expression shutting down, shuttering, and Miri's face was empathetic.

"I must go," he said. "I am glad you are well."

She nodded in understanding and didn't protest, so I didn't either.

"I'll uh, see you out," I said, rising, and he waved me off.

"*Niet*, I know my way out."

"Okay, cool," I said, and with a final nod, he left, going out the door and tromping down the hall, his boot tread heavy on the stair. Miri sighed, a heavy thing, and looked worried for her friend. It was a feeling echoed in my own mind, but I didn't know how to help or anything.

"That okay?" I asked and she nodded, taking another drink of the tea in her hands.

"It will likely make me sleep," she warned. "So I can heal."

"That's cool," I said.

"Will you stay with me?" she asked timidly, and the shyness of her tone said she wasn't just asking about tonight.

"Always," I promised and raised the back of her hand to my lips. She gripped my hand, giving it a squeeze and I had to sigh inwardly. She was fragile, her world thoroughly rocked and in all the wrong ways.

"We'll get through it," I promised her, giving her hand a squeeze back.

She nodded, but she didn't look like she could believe me. I didn't take it personally. I knew what I was about and I would spend the rest of my life proving it if I had to.

I got you. I swore silently and she gave me a brave little smile, one I couldn't help but return.

2 5

*M*iri...

"You cool?" he asked from the driver's seat. I nodded vaguely and he gave my hand a final squeeze. Shade cawed softly, rustling his wings, excited that the car had stopped and ready to get out of it and maybe out of his big brass cage for a bit.

We were in Louisiana, parked outside Jack's house and I was suddenly nervous, more nervous than I'd ever been with either Jack or Kavion. I mean, I was about to see where they'd grown up, meet the woman who'd raised them, and attend my dead lover's funeral.

"Stay put, I'll get your door," he said and I nodded, eyes fixed on the front door of the ranch-style house with the struggling roses outside along the front.

I didn't think I was prepared for this. I especially didn't think I was prepared for the charade we'd both agreed needed to take place, here. Sleeping in separate rooms, keeping our love a secret. I understood it, and had readily agreed to it, but I don't think I'd realized how very hard it was going to be. Still, we didn't want to make waves, didn't, for one minute, want Linda, Jack's mom, to think we were dishonoring her son's memory.

She was fundamentally Christian. One of the good ones, sure, but still, it colored her perceptions and what I was, what had happened, the magic, all of it, we were afraid that it wouldn't resonate. That it wouldn't make sense and we just didn't think we were equipped to explain it satisfactorily.

The front door opened just as Kavion blocked my view to get my door for me. I was still a bit slow to move from my gunshot wound. Although all that outwardly remained of my injury was a flat, shiny, pink scar, no bigger than a dime, with another thin, slightly curved line nearby. I'd been amazed, but then again, I didn't give modern western medicine nearly the credit it was due, apparently. I was trying to rectify that, trying to be more under-standing, but that hadn't stopped me from slipping a grocery tote with an array of tea blends into the trunk with the rest of our bags to get us through our stay here.

He held down his hand, ever the gentleman despite his casual wear of jeans, tee, and sneakers, and I took it, levering myself care-fully out of my seat, the transition from sitting to standing still slightly uncomfortable though getting better every day.

"There you are! Oh, my God, it's so good to have you home!"

Jack and Kavion's mother was every bit the southern belle with her accent, though it remained to be seen if she was a steel magno-lia. I was betting yes, she was that too, when I got to look at her, when she finished fiercely hugging her adopted son. She was blonde and as tall as me, though thicker through the middle. In her fifties, maybe sixties, she had just a touch of iron at her temples, her hair pulled up and back, perfectly coiffed.

She wore mom jeans and a bright yellow blouse, casually untucked, the sleeves three-quarter sleeves and turned back just above the elbows. Her nails were natural, and weren't overly long, well taken care of, but they were hands used to housework and gardening.

I was taken aback slightly when she turned silvery blue eyes on me, and my fragile heart, which was on the mend, threatened to crack anew on me. She was every bit of Jack's mother. The eyes said it all.

She put her hands lightly on my cheeks, holding me at arm's length, her smile turning down slightly at the corners, her expression glad to see me, but so unhappy at the circumstances, and my own sorrow welled. I instantly liked her, no – loved her- for shaping the two men I loved into the men they were.

"You must be Miri, let me look at you. Aw, aren't you just lovely. Come here." She pulled me into a hug I hadn't experienced since before my gram died. A 'mom' hug, despite the fact my own mother was absent from my life.

"Welcome home, dear," she said, and I felt my smile grow brittle over her shoulder.

Jack's home. Kavion's home. Yes. My home? I didn't know about that… but I suppose she just wanted me to be at home, right?

"Thank you," I murmured and Shade threw up a ruckus from the back seat.

"Oh! I'm sorry, I have to get him," I said.

"My, my, of course!" Jack's mom said, mystified.

"Shade is Miri's… pet. She didn't have anybody to watch him, so we brought him with us," Kavion said. I set his big brass cage on the lid of Kavion's trunk and opened it up. Shade immediately hopped onto my wrist and climbed my arm to my shoulder.

"He's been cooped up, poor guy," I said.

He cocked his head at Kavion's mom and said, "Hungry."

"Oh! My, he talks?" she asked. I smiled and laughed slightly.

"He says a few things," I said.

She went to my side, opposite Shade, and wrapped both her arms around my one and said, "Come inside out of the heat."

"Oh, Kavion –"

"I already got it," he said smiling. "Right behind you, Momma."

Kavion was as good as his word, bringing our bags in while his mother sat me and Shade at the kitchen island to serve us up some iced tea.

~

HOURS LATER, Shade was back in his enclosure, sitting on Jack's old dresser. I sat on the edge of the bed, fingertips feeling over the texture of the handmade quilt on his old bed, eyes wandering the walls and other surfaces of his room.

Pictures of him and Kavion when they were just friends. At sporting events, standing with their dates before the school dance, at trophies and over sports pennants. The mishmash of childhood transitioning to manhood and my heart was heavy in the center of my chest.

Kavion was staying in his room, and with a lack of a guest room, Linda had asked if it would be alright with me or if it would be too much to ask, for me to stay in Jack's old room. I had thought I would be fine… I'd overestimated myself, I think.

I sat in the air-conditioned hush of the night-darkened house, the insect call of crickets faint through the closed bedroom window overlooking the backyard.

I stood up in my simple white country nightgown and gathered my velvet burnout kimono wrap off of the back of the desk chair where I'd put it in case I'd needed to leave the room for anything. God and Goddess, I needed to leave right now, the emotions were oppressive. I felt crushed in here, like I couldn't breathe and all I wanted was to be outside.

I took Shade with me, and worried just a bit that I might have been giving him a little bit too much free time outside his enclosure and that he would expect to be free range all of the time as a result, but so far, so good.

We crept through the house to the living room and its sliding glass door leading out to the back deck. I stepped lightly across the smooth, faux-wood planks, made from that newer plastic material that was supposed to be all-weather and last far beyond what a regular deck would.

I just wanted the grass, the earth beneath my feet, to listen to the crickets and life outside that oppressive room that would never have Jack in it again. I let Shade chill on the railing wrapping around the deck so I could pick up one of the lounge chairs and bring it down into the grass. He didn't like it, and glided the short distance to the ground, hopping along behind me.

It made me smile. He was such a comfort to me. More than just my familiar in such an unfamiliar place, he was my friend. Had saved my life. I would spend the rest of his life spoiling him rotten for it, too, at least as much as I could get away with it.

I took a seat, staring into the dark, listening to the frog- and insect-song and when I'd had my fill of connecting with the earth, the grass tickling my feet, I drew them up onto the lounger, wrapping myself more solidly in my kimono wrap with its light fringe. I leaned my head back and closed my eyes and just listened, Shade winging the short distance to the back of the chair above my head, rattling it some with his preening.

I relaxed, finally, felt free to breathe and to just be…

The sliding door opened behind me and I heard Kavion's voice, a gentle query on the night's soft breeze, "Hey, love?"

"I'm here," I called back quietly.

I listened to him pad down the few steps, the swish of the grass against his feet and looked up as he drew even with my chair.

He was heartbreakingly beautiful in the light cast from the back porch, his skin a deep ebony, traced in deep bronze by the light. Shirtless, barefoot like me, in a simple pair of solid gray lounge pants, the ink from his various Christian tattoos standing raised slightly against his skin. I smiled at him, and at the memory of how he'd said he'd gotten them at eighteen, not because he was particularly religious himself -in fact, he'd confessed he had no faith, professing to be more spiritual than any kind of religious. No, he'd gotten them because he knew they would please his mother and he'd always found the art of her religion to be kind of beautiful, so he'd figured 'Why not?' at the time.

I lifted a hand to take one of his, dangling at ease by his hip and he lowered himself into a crouch by my seat.

"What are you doing out here?" he asked. "Freaked me out, home girl. I went to Jack's room and you weren't there."

"Sorry, I thought I could do it, but I… I guess not," I murmured, and somehow felt as if I had let him down.

He cupped my cheek in the palm of his hand, warm where it rested against my skin and my heart ached for a different reason.

We'd yet to be intimate since that night on the cliff, and I was more than half-afraid it was because I'd told him, been honest about me and Jack in the world between realms. I covered his hand with mine and turned my cheek into his palm, his thumb smoothing along my skin.

"I kind of was worried about that," he confessed, and I sighed.

"It's different, you know? Actually being here. I thought I was ready, but now? Now, I don't know, I'm not so sure… you know?"

"Sit up," he murmured. "Let me get in here."

"What about your mom?" I asked, startled, looking over my shoulder at the house behind us.

"Ha, ha! Nah, she took one of her sleeping pills. She gonna sleep 'til morning. Ain't nothin' on the planet get her up when she's downed one of those."

"You're sure?" I asked, apprehensive.

"For sure, for sure," he said, straddling the lawn chair and lowering himself behind me. I either scooted forward or he was going to sit on me.

I laughed and moved out of his way and he settled back with a gusty satisfied sigh, pulling me back against his chest.

"Mm," I cuddled back into him, and let my legs drift out in front of me from their almost defensive raised position. For the first time since coming here, I felt like I was almost myself.

"Hey, quit it!" Kavion complained and ducked his head away from Shade.

I laughed softly again. My bird had an utter fascination with Kavion's dreads, picking them up and squishing them in his beak. I didn't think he was trying to eat them, exactly, but he definitely liked them.

"Shade, knock it off," I admonished, and he went, rather indifferently, back to preening.

Kavion and I sat quietly, him holding me close, my hands resting on his arms, holding him back. I closed my eyes and leaned back into him, my head resting back on his chest as we took in the night sounds and relaxed.

"Didn't think it was going to be this hard," he confessed.

"What?" I asked softly.

"Keeping my distance, pretending we're less than what we are. I'm not used to living my life being anything but one hundred, you know?"

"Is that why you avoided coming back here for so long?" I asked, and almost immediately regretted it.

"I think that's part of it," he said. "I didn't want to disappoint my mom – and by that I mean Linda."

"I know," I murmured. "She's been more of a mother to you than anyone else."

He nodded slowly and dipped his head, kissing the side of my neck. I closed my eyes, the wanting very real. I wanted him with a deep, fierce ache. Wanted his hands to smooth over my body, wanted his lips on my skin, wanted to wrap my fingers around the scorching length of him, to stroke him, to watch him come alive with passion and desire… but I couldn't do any of those things, not while we were here, under Jack's mother's roof.

His hands drifted down my body, stopping on the tops of my thighs, fingers curling, inching up the skirt of my nightgown.

"What are you doing?" I asked, breathless, the air stilled in my lungs.

He kissed the shell of my ear and nuzzled me behind it, murmuring, "I'm about to rock my woman's world."

"Kavion, we can't!" I hissed.

"Shh," he urged, dipping fingertips beneath the waistband of my panties, teasing along the seam of my sex.

I made a strangled noise of protest. Torn between how much I wanted this and how we probably shouldn't. He chuckled and put a hand over my mouth, pressing my head back into his shoulder, his fingertips playing with my pussy, teasing my clit. That strangled noise turned into a strangled moan from behind his hand.

I liked this, his insistence, his control, holding me at his mercy and stripping the decisions away, for the time being. Suspending me in his embrace, his legs winding around mine, prying them apart to give his hand better access, his middle finger sliding up inside me, the joint at the base of his index finger pressed to my clit. He rocked his hand, delicious friction, heat building faster than conjured flame.

I felt my eyes roll back in my head as I gave myself over completely to his attentions. *Lord and Lady, I missed this.* I missed his touch, his kiss, his desire wrapping me in warmth, his desire blanketing me in security. He gave selflessly, making me come against his hand, my body squirming and writhing against him, his erection hot where it pressed into my back.

He kept at me until I lay panting, quivering, and spent against his body, whimpering and still needy despite my momentary satiation. I felt empty, with this abominable aching desire for him to fill me.

I moved and he relinquished his hold on me so that I could stand, divest myself of my panties, and straddle him. He brought himself out of his lounge pants and I sank over the top of him gratefully, carefully, not wishing to upset us in the deck chair. They weren't exactly made for vigorous sex.

His arms went around me, his cock touching deep, filling me so perfectly, his girth almost too much, as it usually was. I crushed my mouth over his and his hands drifted down my body, settling at my hips, urging me to rock, to set things in motion that neither of us would want to take back.

I rolled my hips carefully, testing the deck furniture beneath us, gripping the back of the chair with my hands as our tongues explored each other's mouths, playing against each other, darting this way and that, dancing, sometimes sparring, the effect stoking our passions for each other high and higher.

He sucked in a breath through his teeth, staring up at me, his dark eyes liquid with relief at finally being able to join this way, in the purest expression of love two people could make. Natural power rose from the earth around us, the magic wild, and I welcomed it, the sensation an effervescent rush over our skins, through our blood, as we loved one another, healing invisible hurts.

"Miri." His voice was a confused whisper.

"Shh," I soothed, and kissed him again.

The magic of Loving and that long-ago spell had brought us together, but here and now, a different kind of magic took place. His hands went to my waist and he lifted me, my legs twining around his narrow hips as he laid me back in the grass, both of us touching the earth. He drove into me deep, and I moaned into his mouth. He tasted the sound, rolling it on his tongue like candy and drove another feral little sound from me.

I wrapped my arms around his shoulders as he brought us both to a fever pitch, safe and well-pleased to be cradled by the earth, my element calling to me, the life and growing things around and beneath me answering the rising magic's call.

"What is that?" he asked, voice filled with a sort of awe.

"Magic," I whispered.

"What for?" he asked.

"I have a guess – oh!" I arched as he drove over that sensitive spot inside me. "Healing," I gasped. "Binding."

"I'm all for it," he whispered fervently, and we were kissing again.

I closed my eyes, the magic wrapping round us like vines, holding us to one another, binding us heart, mind, body, and soul. Tears slicked down my temples as we giggled uncontrollably into one another's mouths. Happy tears, purest joy, as the broken pieces of my heart melded seamlessly, Kavion's light and love the binding agent needed to make me whole again.

"I love you so much," he murmured into the dark, for my ears only, and I smiled against his shoulder.

"I love you, too."

Then there were no more words. The magic and the tide of our romance sweeping us both into the ether, to a place only we could go, a world of pleasure of our own making.

So mote it be...

*K*avion...

"What in the world?" I blinked open my eyes, raising a hand to shade them from the sun. Miri sucked in sharp breath at my side, her head rising from my shoulder, pushing herself into a sitting position.

I pushed myself up and we blinked, bewildered. We had lain with each other outdoors, talking deep into the night and must have fallen asleep.

Busted. I thought, but when I looked back at my momma, she wasn't even looking at us.

"Oh, snap," I muttered in awe as Miri looked to the sky and smiled, raising a hand at one of the passing Commas butterflies, their orange wings sparking fire and cinders in the morning sun. I'd never seen so damn many.

Miri laughed and pushed to her feet and spun, her nightgown and wrap swinging out from her, her childlike glee at the sight infectious. I sat there, arms hooked around my knee and grinned, nodding.

"That's dope," I said, and she bit her bottom lip gently between her teeth.

"I've never seen anything like it," Mom said in an awed whisper. "It's a miracle." Miri blushed deep and I winked at her, but then it was time to face the music. "Just what in the world are you two doing out here, anyhow?"

"It's my fault," Miri said. "I couldn't sleep, Kavion found me out here and was keeping me company. We must have fallen asleep."

The grass swept and wavered in the morning breeze and I realized it was not only way longer, but it was the brightest green I'd ever seen it. Not a single patch of yellow.

"Hungry!" Shade cried from the porch railing and Miri went to him, offering her wrist.

"Liar, you've been out here feasting, I'm sure."

"Hungry!" the bird insisted.

"Well, I'm certain you two are, at the very least," Momma said, tsking at us. I got up and she cried, "Come on in the house before the neighbors see!"

Miri and I exchanged a guilty look and went inside. She disappeared in the direction of Jack's room and I slid onto one of the stools at the kitchen island while Momma went about fussing over breakfast. When the shower started up and Miri couldn't hear, the lecture started.

"Honest to God, Kavion what are you doing?" she whispered harshly. "The way you heard Jack talk about that one on the phone, she was gonna be the one."

"Nothing!" I swore, and hoped she'd believe it.

"Well, y'better not be, y'hear? The indecency of it!"

I couldn't disagree more, but there weren't any tellin' Momma that. Jack was her real son, and even though she not for one damn minute treated me any different, it was the reality of it. I tried changing the subject.

"When's Pops gettin' in?" I asked.

"Any minute now," she said with a tired sigh. He was an oil worker, and how I got out onto the rigs in the first place.

"They letting him have bereavement?" I asked, and she nodded.

"Of course they are, they have to. As far as they're concerned, he lost his only child. Dumb people, they don't know any better." She fixed me with a hard look and said, "Y'promise me there ain't no hanky-panky going on?"

I couldn't promise her that and I was scrambling for a loophole somewhere in my brain but the shower cut off and I raised my eyebrows, hoping it would be enough to save me. I don't think Mom had ever looked so disappointed in me though, and that cut deep.

"It's hard to explain," I said and she sighed out.

A thick silence, a tension you could cut with a knife, settled between us and Miri walked into it, faltering a step back in her cute little ankle-high boots when she ran into it like a physical thing. She shot me an alarmed look and I rose a shoulder and dropped it back down. She sighed and nodded, slipping up onto the stool next to mine. My moms did what she did best, and plastered on a smile and ignored the elephant in the room. Likely because she'd talk to my pops and send him after my ass, which was honestly always easier to deal with, so I hoped that was how this would go.

"My turn," I said and Miri smiled at me, brightly but stiff and gave a short nod, her denim-clad knee bouncing, the bohemian peasant blouse she wore dwarfing her slender frame. I loved her in things that hugged her curves but had to admit, this look suited her, too.

She cast a lingering look of sorrowful apology my way and I threw her some chin. It was okay. I'd walk through fire for her, and I had to believe that given time and a proper explanation even Mom would have to understand and believe. I just needed to convince my pops first.

I went in and showered quick, getting dressed in jeans and a plain white tee. Some classic Adidas on my feet and I was good to go for today. I went back out to Miri having Mom half-charmed already, moving around the kitchen with her in concert, her bag of teas on the counter.

"Hurting?" I asked her, worried.

"No, not at all," she said with a smile. "I thought we could both use a cup of special blend." She rose her eyebrows and I tossed my dreads back out of my eyes and said, "Aw, yeah, that would be great."

I really could use a cup of her calming blend.

"Would you like a cup?" she asked my mom innocently.

"Y'know, that might be nice, thank you kindly. Kavion, can you go pick up your Pop Pop?"

"Sure, yeah, what time?"

I had an hour yet before I had to leave so enough time for the tea.

"I thought I'd show Miri some pictures," Mom was saying, and I smiled. Miri smiled at me bravely, and I nodded.

"I think that'd be nice, Momma."

WHAT WASN'T nice was picking up Pops. He come out of the rig company's base of operations, a backpack slung over his shoulder, his coveralls stained and his expression haggard. I don't think I'd ever seen him look so... tired... or so old before. His shoulders hunched with his suffering.

He reached me where I stood and looked up at me, seemingly much shorter than his original five-foot-nine height and said, "Your mother called me... Jack's girl? Really?"

I hung my head, dreads swinging in front of my face and pressed my lips together even as a blush that ain't nobody could see but I damn sure could feel heated my face.

Pops knew, he always did. He sighed and held out his arms and ordered gruffly, "Bring it in here and let's go get a drink. I'm gonna need one before goin' home to face that woman."

I hugged him tight and he slapped me hard on the back saying, "I'm glad you're home, Son." His voice edged in a real pain I'd never heard out of him before, and I believed it from the soles of my kicks – he meant it. I mean, I heard it in his voice, that I was the only son he had left.

I knew right then and there that my pops wasn't mad at me. He just wanted to know the whole story and with being ravaged by unfamiliar emotions like he was, this hard, tough old bastard wanted a little something to numb the pain.

I wished ardently for one of Miri's miracle teas but would settle for the booze. I didn't think he'd be down to smoke any green with me. I'd, surprisingly, cut down on that by, like, a lot since Miri. It was nice, too. The tea left me way more clear-headed.

I opened my door and my pops went around to the passenger side and dropped his bag on the floorboard. He shrugged out of his coveralls, pushing them way down, stripping out of them before getting into my ride. If he were pissed at me, he'd have just gotten in.

I relaxed further and asked over the roof of my car, "Where'd you have in mind, Pops?"

"Where else you think?" he growled and it could only mean one place. The Fishin' Shack, a dive bar a couple miles from the house, out near the edge of one of the bayous. I nodded and got in the car. He followed suit, shoving his coveralls into the top of his backpack as I started it up with that familiar muscle car growl.

We didn't speak, the ride was about an hour back, and not a word was spoken. I knew he was way out of sorts, though. He would keep starin' out the passenger window and would reach over and pat my hand or my leg absently. Like he needed to touch me, to make sure I was for real.

"Now, don't take this the wrong way," he said about five minutes from the bar and I perked up a bit. He looked me in the eye, his own hazel ones filled with pain under his bushy salt-and-pepper eyebrows. They had way more salt in them than I remembered. His gravelly smoker's voice rumbled back to life in his big barrel chest when he said, "I always expected it was going to be you I buried first. On a kind of you goin' over there and on a kind of how this country is. I never even thought it might be Jack... It just never even crossed my mind."

I nodded, struck mute. I mean, he was right, though. Still didn't feel very good to hear it. We pulled into an empty gravel lot outside his favorite dive and I said, "You sure about this?"

"Yeah," he said door already open, heaving himself out the passenger seat. "I'm sure."

I followed him out and into the dimly lit interior of the bar.

The only people inside were the worn old bartender, who felt like he was just as old now as he'd been all my life with Pops coming here, and three old-timer regulars, Cajun by the way they spoke, low and with unfamiliar words, a pitcher of cheap beer and mostly empty glasses between them at a round table over near the jukebox.

"Marlon, a little early ain't it?" the bartender greeted.

"I bury one of my boys tomorrow, Jimmy, so, no. It's five o'clock somewhere and I aim to take advantage of it."

"Alright, then. The usual?"

"Nope, whiskey – neat. One for my boy here, too."

My pops slid onto the barstool and slapped a hand on the cracked green vinyl seat of the other one next to him.

"Ahhh, you sure?" I asked.

"Boy, I ain't drinkin' alone."

"Dad, it's like ten-thirty in the morning," I pointed out and he fixed me with a hard look. I looked at the bartender and said, "Whiskey, neat, please."

These racist fucks didn't pay me no mind because of who my dad was, but any other nigga come up in here, there would have been problems. You know what I mean? The only thing I got was some wary side-eye from the bartender as he poured our drinks, setting both of them in front of my pops.

My dad slid me one, and I sighed. I picked it up and we clicked glasses, taking a sip.

"To Jack," he said, and I nodded.

"To Jack," I echoed.

A short silence ensued before he sighed, and, jaw tight and working back and forth, he asked me, "She pretty?"

I sighed out and said, "Yeah, Pops. She's pretty." I pulled out my phone and scrolled through the pictures in it and stopped on a close-up one of Miri's smiling face. The light from her bedroom window perfectly reflected in her light blue eyes, her smile something else as she'd lain across my chest, laughing at something I'd said.

You couldn't tell we were nude, or even where she was, her hair foaming around her face in these wild copper curls. I slid the phone down the short distance of the clean but worn bar top to my pops and he picked it up, pulling his reading glasses out of his breast pocket from beside his pack of cigarettes.

"Eh, yeah, she's a knockout, alright." He handed me back my phone.

"So what happened, how did you two meet?" he asked.

I sighed and said, "That is a very long story and I'ma need you to keep an open mind."

"Why you say it like that?" he demanded.

"She's a witch," I said bluntly. "Like for reals, a witch. Spells and magic, the whole thing."

My pops downed the rest of what was in his glass and raised it to signal a refill.

"Start talking," he demanded, and so I did, starting at the very beginning and matching my dad pretty much drink for drink the whole way.

We got fuuuuuuucked up.

Still, when I was done talkin', he just sat there in stunned silence and finally said, "That's a lot to take in, my boy. You were right." He patted my shoulder and stared at me blearily. "Don't tell your mother."

I nodded, and speak of the proverbial devil, my pops' phone started ringing in his overstuffed breast pocket. He pulled it out from behind the pack of his cigarettes, an iPhone that was probably like five models out-of-date, and put it to his ear.

"Yell-oh," he said into it, and weaved back and forth a bit on his barstool. I heard my mom clear as day on the other end of the line demanding to know where we were.

"Drinkin'," my dad proclaimed. Her voice became irritated, her tone exasperated.

"He's been drinkin' too." A pause. "Fishin' Shack," he mumbled. "S'great idea! Come git us, have a drink." He pulled the phone away from his face and squinted at it, his glasses up on his head saying, "I think she hung up."

"She's got Miri with her, she can drive my car, it's cool," I said.

"You let her drive your car?" my dad asked.

"Yup," I said.

"You ain't never let no girl drive your car," he said.

"She ain't just any girl," I said.

He shook his head, "She's Jack's girl," and then with a hefty nod of acceptance he said, "She's your girl now."

Success. He was on board and would run interference with Mom.

He shook his head and said, "You just keep on keepin' it respectful in front of yer mother, get through tomorrow, and everything'll be okay."

I nodded. "I can do that."

Mom and Miri walked inside the bar's front door inside the next five minutes, Mom looking tired and frazzled, Miri looking worried. She came to me and put a hand on my arm and I rocked my head back, tossing my dreads out of my eyes and staring down my nose at her.

"You good to drive?" I asked her, and she smiled serenely at me.

"I'm good to drive your car," she murmured, and I nodded and fished my keys out my pocket.

"Good, 'cause I'm fucked up."

She laughed lightly and said, "I can see that."

*M*iri...

When we pulled back into the driveway was when I noticed the roses were no longer struggling. When we stepped out of the car, we were assaulted by their heavenly scent, thickly perfuming the air, the bushes wild and overgrown, climbing the trellises against the house, and a riot of colored blossoms that were bigger than my outstretched hand.

The problem with that was, these weren't a cabbage rose variety. This was likely a by-product of the magic we'd raised last night, like the butterflies that morning. We'd missed it pulling out of the garage head-first, Linda clucking and worrying over her husband and Kavion, calling them damned foolish.

She didn't pull back into the garage, just pulled up in front of us and said, awestruck, "What in the world?" as she got out of the car. Jack and Kavion's dad eyed me up and down, standing unsteadily out the passenger side of his wife's white SUV, his head swinging back and forth from the roses to Kavion and me.

"I didn't think to pack my hangover remedy, but I think I have enough teas with me that I can put together a bit of a blend to take the edge off tomorrow, but you'll have to drink it now," I murmured.

"Thanks," Kavion said, drawing out the 's' at the end and I smiled a bit sadly, knowing that the 'Love' was there, but that after whatever he and his dad had talked about? It was on ice.

"Come on, you," I murmured and went around to him, shutting the passenger door and putting his arm over my shoulder, acting as a steady guidance as he wove across the gravel to the front door of the house. Linda was ahead of us, giving his father an earful.

She was, indeed, a steel magnolia.

She was also unerringly polite, side-stepping anything having to do with Kavion and I being in any kind of relationship after my relationship with her late son, and she wouldn't dare mention the elephant in the room. She and I had pored over photo albums of both boys while she had regaled me with stories of being their mother, smiling fondly even through the challenges being the mom of two boys presented. Not once did she say anything about Kavion being anything resembling 'other.'

He was her son. Period. Whether anyone else realized it or not. She loved him precisely the same as she loved Jackson, and he may not have been a Greene by birth, but he was a Greene just the same. Just 'Greene' was pronounced 'Martin' in his case.

I helped him into his bedroom and he dropped onto the edge of the bed, bouncing, toeing off his shoes. He laid down and pressed the heels of his hands into his eye sockets groaning. I laughed softly and told him, "Rest for now, I'll be right back with some tea."

I turned to go and he caught my hand. I looked down into his so-very-serious brown eyes and he said, "I love you, you know that?"

"I do," I murmured.

He nodded and said, "I can't and don't ever just say that. Not to no females."

"I know," I told him, gripping his hand between mine. He became a bit maudlin, his eyes misting up, his voice choked as he swallowed hard around a lump in his throat. I smiled at him and moved a dreadlock off his forehead.

"Just wait here, I'll be back, I promise."

"For real?"

"Always."

"'K."

He let my hand go and I drifted through to the kitchen to put on some water to heat and to root through the bag of teas and herbs I'd brought with me. These two were going to have a hell of a hangover unless this witch stepped in to intervene. I wouldn't have, normally, but tomorrow was Jack's memorial service, and I was ever kind, and it was the merciful and kind thing to do.

"And what are you doing?" Linda asked, coming in from the living room, her husband in his recliner, football on the TV.

"Fixing up a remedy, to keep them from being hungover as bad tomorrow morning."

"Huh, they deserve a little headache for being such a pain," she said and I smiled.

"Normally I would agree with you and I would leave it, but tomorrow being what it is…"

She chuckled and smiled at me warmly. "You're a soft touch, just like my Jack was. Understanding to a fault."

"Maybe that's why the magic put us together," I said softly and she waved her hands at me.

"That's why God put you together."

We'd had a frank conversation earlier about deity and religion. While Linda didn't want to believe in witchcraft and paganism, she chose to view things a little differently, fitting it neatly inside her box. Magic wasn't magic but was rather God's work and a miracle.

The butterflies were a gift from her God; same with the roses, a sign from her God that Jackson was fine and in his loving embrace. She'd been prattling on about it to her husband the entire time she'd fussed over him, making him comfortable in his recliner.

If it kept the peace between us, I wasn't willing to quibble over semantics, even though her forced point of view was vaguely hurtful to me. I knew she didn't mean it to be and I also knew she was trying… trying very hard to cling to her faith in the face of wild and new, inexplicable things.

That was okay. It wasn't a battle worth having to me. Some things were more important, like her healing and having some type of closure where her son was concerned.

I fixed a mug of tea and took it to Kavion's father.

"Mr. Greene," I murmured gently and put a gentle spark of power behind the light touch I put to the back of his hand. He startled awake and I held out the mug.

"Oh, hey, what's this?" he asked, coughing, his smoker's cough rumbling in his chest worryingly.

"Some hot tea, to help your headache before it has a chance to start tomorrow."

"This one of your magic potions?" he asked with a chuckle.

"A concoction, sure, but nothing magic about it," I promised. "Just herbs and tea leaves from my garden back home."

"Eh, thank you kindly." He took the mug from me.

"You're very welcome," I murmured.

"Not used to hot tea down here," he muttered blowing on it, but he took a sip and a few would be all he needed. The more the better, but I didn't expect him to finish the whole cup.

"You're a sweet girl, Miriam Eilish," Linda said when I returned to the kitchen.

"Thank you Mrs. Greene," I murmured, fixing Kavion a cup.

"Pish, posh! I've told you, 'Linda' or 'Momma,' none of this 'Mrs. Greene.'"

"Yes, Ma'am," I said with a cheeky grin.

"Ooooh," she shook a finger at me and laughed. "You been hanging around Kavion too long, he's the same sort of way. Always clever, always finding some sort of a loophole." I smiled and kept the thought to myself: *Maybe that's why the magic put me together with him.*

I took his tea to him and he opened one eye, giving me some side-eye and said, "That was really dumb."

"What was?" I asked, sitting criss-cross-applesauce on the floor beside his bed. He reached out and took the steaming cup from me and pushed himself into a sitting position slowly.

"Matching my pops drink for drink like that. Man, I forgot how hardcore he could be."

"Well, lesson learnt, I hope. That should fix you right up, ease the coming hangover. Finish it up as much as you can and drink water."

"Hydration is key," he agreed, and blew on the fragrant steaming liquid in the plain white coffee mug.

"Your mom has some interesting takes on some of the, ah, more wild goings on around here of late," I murmured.

"Y' alright?" he asked.

I nodded carefully.

"A little homesick," I confessed.

"Yeah, me too," he said and I had to smile and laugh a little.

"You are home," I pointed out.

"Well, yeah," he said taking a subtle slurping sip and swallowing. "You're here and lately, home is wherever you are."

Emotion, strong and sure, hit me in the center of my being. The reaction was swift, sending chills from the crown of my head sweeping down my back in these pleasant little tingles.

I licked my lips and asked the question that'd been haunting me for days, ever since I'd woken up in the hospital, really.

"Where do we go from here, Kavion?" I stared at the ceiling, trying not to cry, a very real, very physical tearing sensation in the center of my chest at the thought of going home to Loving and facing everything, the town, its people all alone. Putting my life back together piece by piece all alone.

I knew it was a possibility, but it scared me, badly. I didn't want to imagine a life without Kavion in it.

"Hey, no, don't feel that way." He paused and I frowned and he sat up a little bit straighter.

"H-how do you know what I'm feeling?" I asked putting a hand to my chest.

"I don't know," he said, "Maybe something about whatever went down last night? Like, what even went down last night?"

"I don't know," I said softly, "but your mom seems to think it's a sign from God that her baby's okay, and I'm honestly okay with that."

He took another deeper drink of his tea, eyeing me over the rim of the cup. "Told you she was a little bit extra in that department."

"You did," I agreed.

"She sees the good in people, though. It's not like she'll start crying Satan or fire-and-brimstone. She ain't that kind of Christian. Worst I've ever heard her call anybody is 'godless', like it's some kind of an insult."

I nodded. "I gathered that about her," I murmured with a wry smile.

"She's hard," he said gently, "but she's never mean."

"No, she's not," I agreed. "I could see where Jack and where you get it."

"Yeah?"

"Yeah."

He chuckled and finished off his tea, sitting up enough to set it behind him on the shelf of a headboard. He patted the bed beside him and said, "Come up here. I wanna show you something."

I got up and he moved over. I sat down on the bed beside him and he held out the arm closest to me. I rolled my eyes and laid down with him, fully-clothed, my head on his shoulder as he plucked down an old picture off his wall beside the bed and held it up for both of us to see it clearly.

It was a young Kavion, and a young Jack, both standing next to the edge of a waterway, fishing poles leaning against their shoulders, holding up a decent sized fish between them.

"This was the day," he said with a gusty sigh.

"What day?" I asked softly.

"The day my whole life changed. The day Jack and I became friends."

I smiled and listened as Kavion poured his memories out, the important ones, the ones he'd never shared with me before no matter how often we'd talked. His real feelings, his most cherished moments and I could feel what he was feeling. The fondness, the heartache, the joys and the sorrows.

I cuddled into his side and shared with him, beginning to understand what the magic had been last night. The purest expression of love and devotion two souls could undertake.

He laughed with me, and even cried with me, and he shared so much with me as only a husband could share with his wife.

*K*avion...

The service Mom had for Jack was nice, even though it felt more than a little weird burying an empty casket. Miri insisted we wait, that we stay past everyone else at the grave-side and when we were the only two left, she told the cemetery workers to stand back, the pile of waiting earth moving at her will, filling in the grave with the call of her magic.

They'd traded dubious looks and two out of the three of them noped right the fuck out of there. The only one to stay behind had been a nigga our age who'd declared, "That was dope," with a shit-eating grin on his face. Likely because he was happy he didn't have to fill it in.

He went to start heaving a roll of sod, but my girl waived him off, throwing pocketfuls of seeds down on the rich, raw, brown dirt, and emerald sparks between her fingers and a low intent chant later, his grave was a carpet of green dotted with white flowers.

"That was nice, love," I murmured, touched, raising her hand in mine, touching the back of it to my lips.

"Can we go home to him, now?" she asked, her voice longing.

"Yeah, yeah I think it's time. You wanna leave tonight?" I asked.

"Depends, do you think your parents might take it badly?"

"Only one way to find out," I said.

We went back to the house, suffered through the wake and people and their condolences. It was harder on Miri, everyone coming up to her well-meaning, sure, but all the talk of what could have been wore on her. All that'd been taken from her so in her face with every face, was hard. I could feel her hurt, feel her strength as she silently and graciously endured.

"Hey, Pops. Y' got a minute?" I asked and my dad raised his eyes to mine from where he sat with some of his guys from the rig.

"Yeah, Son." He stepped out onto the back porch with me and shook out a cigarette from his pack, putting it between his lips.

"What's on yer mind?" he asked, setting aside his glass of Jack and Coke to light up.

"Miri's exhausted, homesick, and I think if it's alright with you and mom, we're gonna take off back up north tonight rather than tomorrow morning."

He nodded carefully, taking a drag off his cigarette and sighing out a plume of smoke. He looked up at me, his hazel eyes sparking and said, "You ain't need our permission. I get it. Yer mother, though, that's one you gotta run past her yourself."

I nodded, afraid he was gonna say that. I buried my hands in the pants pockets of my suit and felt the echo of a fractured and throbbing ache in the center of my chest and glanced through the sliding glass door to watch our Little League coach hug Miri.

"Mom's gonna have to live with this one," I murmured and my dad chuckled and nodded.

"Now you're gettin' it," he said with a smile. "When you comin' home?" he asked.

I shook my head. "When I'm with her, I am home, Pops."

"Figured you was gonna say that," he said, and he was staring at her too. "She's a good woman."

"You're just sayin' that 'cause she fixed your hangover," I said.

"Fixed it? I ain't have none!"

"Exactly."

We shared a bit of a laugh over that.

"So what're you gonna do for work up there?" he asked, and I thought about it.

"I dunno," I said. "Military experience ought to be good for something."

"You best come and visit," he said, and I nodded.

"I wouldn't do that to you guys," I said.

"Better not, you're the only son we got left."

Ouch.

I didn't have anything to say to that, so I didn't say anything at all. Just stood in silence with my pops while he finished his smoke, him keeping an eye on Mom, while my gaze followed Miri's every movement. Her blue eyes met mine through the glass and she smiled thinly. I didn't need no magic spell to pick up on her misery, but I felt it keenly all the same.

"Man, bro, it should be you standing here," I breathed, and my dad jumped slightly next to me.

"No," he said sharply. "I may not buy into all of Linda's bullshit, but I have to believe that God or whatever has some kind of a plan, and for whatever reason that plan includes you and not Jack. Jack's alright, Son. You got your whole life ahead of you yet to live. Do us all a favor, Son. Live it well."

He threw his cigarette butt in the coffee can he kept out here for 'em and went back in the house, leaving me to puzzle out just what he meant by that. Of course, I was pretty sure I was looking at her, shaking hands and hugging strangers, passing a little of herself with every healing touch she laid… because that was Miri. Her calling. Her life. Just like it was my calling, my life, to love and protect her, to be the man she needed me to be to support her in her mission.

We were a team now, and it felt good knowing neither one of us would ever be alone again.

Hours and hours later, it'd felt like we'd been at it for days instead. The last guest was being escorted out the door, and I loved my mom, but I knew Miri needed me and so my mom's fine sensibilities could take the hit. I pulled Miri in against my chest and held her, let her take a minute to recharge, acted as her emotional battery pack, because there were just some jobs that bird of hers couldn't do.

Speaking of… Shade had been pretty quiet.

"Shade alright?" I asked her, and she smiled and nodded, looking up at me.

"Tired. He was helping me all day."

"Ah. I knew it."

"Sometimes I just can't help myself," she murmured. "Um…" she chewed the corner of her bottom lip and looked at my dad.

I stiffened. "What's wrong?" I asked.

"Nothing yet, but he really needs to quit smoking or there will be."

"Shit, good luck convincing him of that one."

"One battle at time," she said tiredly.

"For real." I sucked in a deep breath and let it out in a gusty sigh asking, "You wanna go home?"

"You know I do," she murmured quietly, self-conscious, all too aware it would upset my mom. I smiled and let her take a step back before we were caught out.

"I was thinkin' about leaving a little sooner than tonight, maybe in the next hour or two?"

She looked so hopeful and that clinched it. I nodded, and she nodded, and we were on the same page.

We helped clean up. We changed into comfortable travel

clothes. I loaded up the car, and we got the fuck out of Dodge just as the sun started to set.

Shade was quiet in the back seat and Miri kept checking on him. He seemed okay, though, and he was eating when she offered him the odd treat, so it was likely that he was just tired, like she said.

We both were. Mentally. Emotionally. Just fuckin' dead ass.

Still, I put some distance between me and back home, a good four hours' worth, before I pulled off at a cheap roadside motel so we could crash for the rest of the night. I helped Miri sneak Shade and his cage into our room and she covered it, so he could have some peace. Meanwhile, I pulled her into my arms.

Finally.

"Mm." She made a sound like she was savoring something good when I kissed her, her hands immediately going beneath my shirt to play along my skin.

It sent goosebumps all over, just having her hands on me. I stripped my shirt off over my head so she could have free rein and she raised her arms for me to slip her blouse off over her head. She stepped into me, putting her body against mine as I returned my mouth to hers.

Just having her body up against mine like that had me all amped, like *It's about to go down.* I don't remember unhooking her bra, or her undoing my belt. I don't really remember at what point we found ourselves in the bed, but that wasn't all that important. What was important was the feel of her body against mine, her hot, delicate mouth moving across my skin as I lay there, aching for her to touch me where it really counted most.

She did not disappoint, her mouth wrapping around the head of my cock, her hand cradling my balls as she worked her way up to taking as much of me in as she could tolerate, her other hand wrapping around my shaft as I threw an arm over my eyes and groaned in pleasure.

Everything about Miri was gentle and sensual. Her touch light, driving me crazy; her mouth careful, making me want more. It was aggravating in all the best ways, just how she naturally held me on that edge of wanting more without tipping the scales that last little bit. It was enough to drive a brother insane and I gripped the sheets in my fist, the other clenching in the air by my head where my arm rested over my eyes.

She felt so good, so real, and so fine where her feather-light touch got me going and I was practically to the point I was ready to beg when her mouth left me, her hands disappearing. The bed shifted and I put my arm down, looking at her, radiant in the dim glow of the hotel lamp light. She swung a leg over my hips and settled over me, rubbing her pussy lips against my shaft, hot and slick, wet and ready.

I wanted to penetrate her so bad, but she was delighting in teasing me and truthfully, as much as it drove me nuts, I was enjoying it too, knowing I wouldn't be held hostage forever, knowing she wanted and needed me, too.

She bent over me, her lips gentle, soft, and so alive against my own. My hands drifted over her body, pausing at the change in texture over her fresh, new, scar. One that wouldn't be there if it hadn't been for me. If I'd been less of a pussy, had been able to protect her, but instead she'd protected me and I couldn't tell you how much that bothered me.

She paused above me and whispered against my mouth, "Make it up to me... touch me."

I had to smile at that, my hands cupping her breasts, my hips arching to urge her to move again and I don't know how long we drove each other crazy, desperate to climax, to fit my body into hers, but holding off. It was amazing, for real, just burying myself in her calming essence, intimate beyond words as we pretty much worshiped each other, until finally I couldn't take it anymore.

I wrapped my arms around her and sat up, laying her down, her voice high and light with her joyous laughter and I swore I would do anything to hear that musical sound at least once every day.

I put myself at her opening and she gasped, arching, wet and ready. Her hands on my shoulders, her fingers flexed and nails dug lightly into my skin urging me to take her and I couldn't deny her any more than I could deny myself at this point.

I slipped inside her, her walls hot and slick, pressing against me, taking me deep and the feel of her beneath me, wrapped around me, was irresistible.

"Kavion…" her voice was breathy, begging, and I loved that sound, too. I loved everything about her, her soft skin, her deep blue eyes gazing at me longingly, her hands on my body, her lips that gripped and pulled me in deeper, as deep as I could go and it still didn't feel like enough.

Man, I loved her.

I loved her with everything that I was and everything I wanted to be. I loved her so deeply, so completely, I couldn't imagine a life without her in it.

I was grateful. So very grateful that I didn't have to, either…

She was my life now, my wife in every way that counted and I was committed. She was my forever and fuck anyone that tried to get between us. They ever did and it would be their funeral.

"I got you, love," I whispered as I made love to her. "I got you."

*M*iri...

It was good to be home. I had unfinished business on more than one front, so it would seem. I returned to a very thick white envelope just inside my front door and I wasn't sure what to make of it. It was from some lawyers, and so I set it on my kitchen counter and went about setting my home to rights, unpacking our bags, putting Shade in his large enclosure, and then and only then did I confront whatever was inside, with a cup of calming tea at my elbow, and Kavion beside me, of course.

"Staring at it isn't going to make it give up its secrets, love," he said in a lightly chiding tone.

"No, I know that, I just don't know what it could be and the unknown is scary, you know?"

"You want me to open it?" he asked.

"No," I murmured and flicked a nail under the flap and ran it along the sealed seam. I pulled the fat sheaf of papers out and opened them, my eyes skimming the pages and a frown creasing my brow.

"It's the deed to The Wick & Stone," I said frowning.

"What?" Kavion sat back on his stool.

"Yeah, Gwen left me the shop in her will…"

"That don't make any sense," he said and I shook my head.

"No, it doesn't…"

"What're you going to do with it?" he asked.

"I honestly don't know," I murmured.

He nodded and slipped off his stool, taking me gently by the hips and turning me so we were facing each other.

"What do you want to do with it?" he asked.

I hesitated, feeling that he wanted me to really think about what he was asking.

"I want to keep it," I said surprising even myself. "I want things to change. I want it to be just you and me for a while and I can't do that with guests coming and going but I need some kind of an income… so I guess I need to go to this lawyer's office and check things out. I mean, I don't know how Gwen's extracurriculars might affect the shop, you know?"

He nodded carefully and asked, "Can we just get back to the part where you said you just want it to be you and me for a while?"

I felt my face break into a very real, very genuine smile and nodded.

"You for real?" he asked cautiously.

"We're for real," I whispered, hooking my pinky finger with his and giving his hand a bit of a shake. "I love you, Kavion Martin, and I don't want to imagine a life without you in it."

"That's dope," he said with a smile that was bright enough to rival the sun. His mouth headed for mine slowly. I don't think I'd ever seen him so giddy before and I was so unrealistically happy that I could make him feel that way.

It wasn't especially late in the day when we'd arrived home, but we went to bed anyway. Exhausted from the road and the emotional good-byes that weren't really good-bye so much as they were 'Until we meet again'.

I smiled, happy, whole, and healing. I think all of us needed time to heal, but when we all were? Well, we'd be good as new.

*M*iri...

I shook the long-reach match and lowered myself back flat to the floor. The entire house was awash in candlelight, waiting for my man to come home from work. The weather outside was less than ideal, rain pattering ceaselessly from the overcast sky which flickered with blue fire and rumbled like a sleeping giant in a fitful sleep.

I smiled at the crunch of gravel out back and the heavy tread of his boots on the back step. Tonight was special, All Hallows Eve, and the weather perfect for magic despite being terrible for all the would-be trick-or-treaters out there.

It didn't matter, my porch light was out. *Nobody home.*

I had dressed for the occasion in light silk and little else. Kavion came through the archway into the library, lifting off his Smokey-the-Bear uniform hat, already shrugging out of his Loving Police-issued rain slicker, letting it drop to the floor, his gun belt following with a loud thud as he came to me, pulling me up tight against his body, his mouth covering mine.

I captured some of his rough dreadlocks in my hands and held them back from our faces as his hands pressed to my lower back, drawing me in, his voice when he broke the kiss holding a far off sort of echo.

"I've missed you two."

I smiled and bit my bottom lip and said gently, "We missed you, too."

"Feels strange," Jack murmured through Kavion's lips.

"You both alright?" I asked gently.

"Never better," and it was both of their voices, a strange sort of dualism. I laughed and smiled and held on tight as they carried me upstairs.

One thing was for certain, the love we shared was a love that transcended all things that were technically supposed to be possible. Kavion and I, Jack and I? We were proof that love springs eternal in Loving and I don't think any of us could complain. Even if we only got Jack this one night a year, even if the boys had only one body to share. It was worth every moment.

THE END

ABOUT THE AUTHOR

Timber Philips hails from a land filled with beauty and steeped in magic; the Pacific Northwest. She swears you can see fairies and goblins, magic and promise around every tree and in every drop of water and she shares that magic whenever she can. She loves welcoming everyone to her worlds of romance rooted in fable and fantasy.

Stalker Information:
www.timberphilips.com